Wild Borders

USA Today Bestselling Author

CHEYENNE MCCRAY

ELLORA'S CAVE
ROMANTICA PUBLISHING

What the critics are saying...

ॐ

5 Stars "Ms. McCray is truly a talented writer [...] There are plot twists that come out of left field and will keep you guessing. This book has a lot to offer any reader, there's action, adventure, and most importantly love." ~ *Just Erotic Romance Reviews*

4 Stars! "This great love story has a lot to offer: a plus-sized heroine, a hunky hero who shows amazing sensitivity, strong secondary characters and an intriguing, well-researched plot." ~ *Romantic Times*

"Red alert! Red alert! This book may cause hot flashes! WILD BORDERS is such an erotically charged story brimming with sexual tension that when Lani finally gives in to her lustful feelings for Rick, it was enough to cause this reviewer to go stand outside in the freezing cold." ~ *Romance Reviews Today*

"A beautifully crafted novel [...] WILD BORDERS sizzles with sensuality and is the kind of romance that will make your heart melt." ~ *Sizzling Romances*

An Ellora's Cave Romantica Publication

www.ellorascave.com

Wild Borders

ISBN 9781419951756
ALL RIGHTS RESERVED.
Wild Borders Copyright © 2003 Cheyenne McCray
Cover art by Darrell King.

This book printed in the U.S.A. by Jasmine–Jade Enterprises, LLC.

Electronic book Publication December 2003
Trade paperback Publication November 2007

Also by Cheyenne McCray

Blackstar: Future Knight
Castaways
Ellora's Cavemen: Seasons of Seduction II *(anthology)*
Ellora's Cavemen: Tales from the Temple III *(anthology)*
Erotic Invitation
Erotic Stranger
Erotic Weekend
Hearts Are Wild *(anthology)*
Kalina's Discovery
Lord Kir of Oz *with Mackenzie McKade*
Seraphine Chronicles 1: Forbidden
Seraphine Chronicles 2: Bewitched
Seraphine Chronicles 3: Spellbound
Seraphine Chronicles 4: Untamed
Stranger in My Stocking
Taboo: Taking Instruction
Taboo: Taking It Personal
Taboo: Taking On the Law
Taboo: Taking the Job
Things That Go Bump in the Night 3 *(anthology)*
Vampire Dreams *with Annie Windsor*
Wild 1: Wildfire
Wild 2: Wildcat
Wild 3: Wildcard
Wonderland 1: King of Hearts
Wonderland 2: King of Spades
Wonderland 3: King of Diamonds
Wonderland 4: King of Clubs

About the Author

ಬಿ

USA Today Bestselling Author Cheyenne McCray has a passion for sensual romance and a happily-ever-after, but always with a twist. Among other accolades, Chey has been presented with the prestigious Romantic Times BOOKreviews Reviewers' Choice Award for "Best Erotic Romance of the Year". Chey is the award-winning novelist of eighteen books and nine novellas.

Chey has been writing ever since she can remember, back to her kindergarten days when she penned her first poem. She always knew one day she would write novels, hoping her readers would get lost in the worlds she created, as she did when she was lost in a good book. Cheyenne enjoys spending time with her husband and three sons, traveling, and of course writing, writing, writing.

Cheyenne welcomes comments from readers. You can find her website and email address on her author bio page at www.ellorascave.com.

Tell Us What You Think

We appreciate hearing reader opinions about our books. You can email us at Comments@EllorasCave.com.

WILD BORDERS

&

Dedication

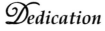

To:

Mom and Dad
I love you

Thank you to all the border patrol agents,
ranchers, and residents of southeastern Arizona
who aided me in my research for Wild Borders

Author's Note

When I began researching for Wild Borders, I was given the utmost courtesy by members of the U.S. Border Patrol. I enjoyed going on a "ride-along" with a Special Operations Supervisor, as well as the interviews with the Supervisor and Border Patrol Agents.

The ranchers and residents of Cochise County in Southeastern Arizona were especially accommodating, giving me their views and opinions on the climate of living in a border community and how the situation affected them.

Changes have taken place since I originally researched and wrote Wild Borders. Although I have attempted to accommodate some of these changes, I have kept most as it was originally written to stay true to my plotline.

I have taken liberties with buildings and locations throughout the towns of Douglas and Bisbee. However the histories of both Bisbee and Tombstone are well-known and what I included in this book should be fairly accurate.

In this same corner of Arizona, I grew up on a ranch much like the JL Star. I hope you enjoy your visit to this little part of the world that I'm originally from, and a place that I still love to revisit from time to time.

Chey McCray

Prologue
ஒ

"Now that the divorce is final, it's time you started dating again, Lani." Calinda picked up a shrimp roll with her chopsticks. Her blue eyes sparkled and she gave an impish grin. "You need a *real* man."

"Mmmm-hmm." Theresa snatched a pork bun from the carousel at the center of the table. "You've got that right, girl. James was nothing but a loser. You're well rid of the jerk, and it's time you started living."

Lani Simms tucked a strand of honey-blonde hair behind her ear and forced a smile. She had agreed to having lunch with her two friends, a sort of bon voyage party, but she couldn't agree with their matchmaking efforts over the past couple of months. Theresa Cortez had been Lani's editor at San Francisco's *City by the Bay* magazine for the last five years, and was her closest friend. Calinda Foxe owned the travel agency that the newspaper used for all of the staff's travel arrangements.

Theresa had introduced Lani and Calinda ages ago, and the three enjoyed eating *dim sum* once a week at their favorite Chinese restaurant on Grant Street. The place was filled with tantalizing smells and it was impossible to not want to try a little bit of everything from the *dim sum* cart.

"Like I've told you before, I don't need a man." Lani studied the plates of food on the carousel and decided on another potsticker. "I've sworn off men. Who needs them, anyway?" She poured a generous amount of soy sauce over the dumpling and cut it with her fork before using her chopsticks to eat it.

"Save one of those egg rolls for me," Calinda said to

Theresa. "I know you'll swipe 'em all if I don't keep an eye on you."

Theresa snorted and tossed her black hair over her shoulder. "You snooze, you lose."

With a laugh, Calinda snagged the last egg roll off the carousel. "Lani, how can you swear off men when you've only had one, and the biggest ass of the century, no less?"

Lani sighed. "He was enough of an ass to turn me off for a lifetime."

"Well, I think you should keep your options open." Calinda tilted her head and studied Lani. "Who knows, maybe you'll meet someone on this trip out to Arizona."

"Oh, sure." Lani rolled her eyes. "That's all I need—a three week relationship with some cowboy."

"This trip will be good for you." Theresa pointed a chopstick at her. "It'll be an awesome series of articles and it'll give you a chance to put some distance between you and the jerk."

Steam warmed Lani's hand as she poured tea from the teapot into the small porcelain cup. She usually enjoyed the relaxing scent of green tea, but talking about James automatically made her tense. She picked up the Chinese teacup and frowned into the tealeaves.

Calinda cut her egg roll with her knife. "So, tell me about this rancher you'll be staying with."

Grateful for the change in topic, Lani shrugged. "Not much to tell. My friend Trace MacLeod—er, Lawless—arranged for me to board with Charles and Sadie Turner who own a small ranch about twenty-five miles from the U.S.—Mexico border."

"Why not a hotel?" Calinda asked.

"After Lani told me about her friend and this rancher couple," Theresa said, "I figured it would be perfect for the feature if she actually stayed on a ranch. The Turners belong to the Cattleman's Association and know all the ranchers in the area." She turned to Lani, "And like Trace said, they have contacts with the U.S. Border Patrol, so you're bound to get some inside information."

Lani sipped her tea and sighed. "All the same, I still feel a little uncomfortable imposing on them."

"Nonsense." Theresa dabbed the corners of her mouth with her napkin. "People in that part of the country are known for their hospitality."

Calinda nodded. "You'll have a great time and come home with a terrific feature."

"I hope you're right about this," Lani said.

Theresa reached for the teapot and poured herself a cup. "Of course we are. After all, I'm your editor and I know everything that's good for you."

Lani stared heavenward. "Yeah, right."

"Oh, and I've already lined up an interview for you with the mayor of Douglas, Eduardo Montaño," Theresa said.

Lani looked back at her friend. "Isn't he expected to win a seat in the U.S. Congress in this fall's election?"

"Sure is." Theresa nodded and sipped her tea. "And a fine looking man. He has such charisma and sex appeal. And what a bod."

"I don't know about that." Lani shrugged. "He doesn't do anything for me."

Theresa brushed her heavy fall of thick black hair over her shoulder. "I wouldn't kick that man out of bed."

"Is that all you think about?" Lani replied with a teasing look to her friend.

Calinda leaned forward. "I think Lani just needs to get laid by a real man."

"Calinda!" Heat flushed over Lani and she was sure she was as crimson as the tablecloth.

"Mmmm—hmmm." Theresa chuckled. "It always cracks me up how bright red Lani turns when she's embarrassed. But

I have to agree with Calinda."

"Oh, my." Calinda's gaze followed something across the room. "Talk about a fine hunk of cowboy ass."

Lani tossed a look over her shoulder, and her jaw almost hit the table. Calinda wasn't kidding. Well over six feet with broad shoulders and a trim waist and an ass you could just bite. He was wearing boots, a Stetson and Wranglers, and looked a little out of place in the Chinese restaurant, but *damn*.

He was helping a petite brunette sit down and then took the seat opposite her. Just as Lani tried to tear her gaze away, the man removed his Stetson and set it on the chair beside him—and then he looked up, right at Lani.

For that moment, that fraction of time, the world seemed to stop revolving. Heat flushed Lani and her nipples tightened beneath her blouse. He gave a sexy smile and Lani turned back to the table so fast her head spun.

Only to see her two friends grinning at her like a pair of idiots.

"You're ready," Theresa said with a nod. "I'd bet if that man didn't have a date he'd be more than willing to teach you all about roping and wrangling."

"Shush." Lani's cheeks were still warm. The cowboy's presence was so tangible, it was like he was right next to her.

Calinda laughed. "I think we found Lani's weakness. Cowboys."

"Check please," Lani said as the waiter paused at their table. She turned back to her friends. "I'm not interested in having casual sex, or finding myself a cowboy, so let's just change the subject." Lani accepted the tray with the luncheon bill and three fortune cookies. "Okay, ladies, time for the ritual. You go first, Theresa."

"Give me a good one." Theresa took hers, closed her eyes, brought the fortune cookie to her lips and kissed it. She cracked the cookie, then opened her eyes to read the slip of paper inside, "Success in conspiracy is yours."

"That sounds just like you," Lani said with a laugh.

Calinda giggled and then repeated the tradition. "It is wise to use a light touch in matters of the heart."

After Lani performed the ritual, she broke her cookie open and rolled her eyes. "Oh, pleeeeeeease."

"What?" Theresa demanded, and Calinda leaned close to Lani, trying to read the fortune over her shoulder.

With a grimace, Lani read, "Love comes in a tall, dark and handsome package."

Theresa and Calinda exchanged looks and burst out laughing.

"See? It's in the stars," Calinda said between fits of giggles. "You're destined to find love."

"No thanks." Lani shook her head and sighed. "Not this girl."

* * * * *

The day after her lunch with Calinda and Theresa, Lani spent a busy, tiring afternoon shopping for her business trip. On her way home, the wail of a saxophone floated on the evening breeze, a haunting sound that touched Lani's soul as nothing else could. Old Louie was playing for coins outside Da Vinci's Bakery as usual, and as usual, his sad, sad music made her feel even more alone.

She couldn't help but think of the night she had left James. December, over six months ago.

"You disgust me," James had said with a sneer as he tossed his coat over the back of the ivory divan. "I see my friends with their 110-pound wives. And then I see you." His handsome face contorted with distaste, ice-gray eyes calculating and cruel.

Lani's face burned as if he had slapped her and her knuckles whitened from the death grip she had on her satin evening bag.

James R. Kavanaugh III, the lawyers' lawyer. He should have been a surgeon, so well he could slice with words instead of blades.

17

No other remark could have twisted inside her like a rusted knife, shredding the already damaged remains of her self-esteem. Lani was tall and large-boned, and she was comfortable at being a size 14. But it wasn't good enough for James. After their marriage, he had begun verbally and emotionally abusing her, insisting that she become rail thin. Gradually, over the years, she had started to see herself through his eyes, the abuse taking its toll.

"You were the fattest woman at the Christmas party tonight," James continued, moving across the Persian carpet to the wet bar. "I'm sure I was the laughingstock of the entire firm."

Flames ignited in Lani's stomach, and her chest tightened. Her jaw ached from clenching her teeth to hold back the words he wanted to hear. Not this time.

Ice clinked against crystal, and then James poured himself a scotch. "Well?" he asked.

Lani knew he was waiting for her to cry so that he could continue his tirade. Like her mother had accepted her father's constant berating, Lani was letting the same thing happen to her in hopes of saving her marriage, of wanting to keep from being a failure.

No. Never again, *she promised herself.* Never again.

James'ss eyes narrowed. "Lani, I want — "

"I don't care what you want."

She flinched as he slammed the glass onto the marble counter of the wet bar. Scotch splashed on his expensively tailored shirt. "Excuse me?"

Lani fought to shove the hurt down deep inside, fought to keep her voice from trembling. And for once, she managed not to burst into tears. Never had she been so furious. Never had her thoughts been so clear.

San Francisco city lights glittered outside the picture window as her gaze swept over the sterile living room of their home. The abstract paintings, the cold black and white furnishings, the spotless décor where not a speck of dust dare remain. No, it wasn't a home, and it never had been.

It was a prison.

"What did you just say?" James'ss voice was ruthless, tinged with his fury. "Answer me."

Lani faced him, raising her chin to keep her stare level with his. "Why don't you find yourself a wife who fits your precious parameters?"

"Lani!" A mixture of surprise and rage flickered across James's sculpted features. "You had best be careful what you ask for."

Waves of anger washed over Lani. Hot, satisfying anger. She was asking for exactly what she wanted. Exactly what she would have. As James strode across the floor, she loathed everything about him, from his perfect hair to his perfect stride. He stopped only a foot away and reached for her.

Lani dodged him, the heavy musk of his aftershave causing her stomach to churn.

She turned her back on James, feeling his icy stare stabbing between her shoulder blades. Trying to stop her. Trying to bend her once again, and make her crawl. But she was through with crawling.

Lani's steps actually quickened as she walked to the front door. The click of her heels on the Italian tile foyer thrilled her. The sound felt angry, true, and free.

"Where are you going?" James demanded. "Get back here! I'm not finished with you."

She snatched her coat from the expensive coat tree beside the door. With one hand on the door handle, Lani paused and faced him. "Well, I'm finished with you. We're over, James."

"What?" he shouted, spittle flying from his mouth. "Don't you dare walk out that door. You'll regret it!"

The two-carat marquis diamond of her wedding ring glinted, the sparkle as cold as James's eyes. Lani slipped the wide band from her finger and looked up at her husband, the man who had spent the last five years trying to destroy her emotionally. She gave a grim smile and tossed the ring to him.

His jaw dropped in shock as he caught the diamond. "Lani!"

"Goodbye, James."

And she walked out.

On five years of marriage. Five years of verbal and emotional abuse, and fear of what would happen when she dared to take the lawyer to court.

All her dreams, turned to ashes.

She could almost imagine the dirty remains of their so-called love rolling out with the San Francisco fog.

Lani shivered as she brought herself back to the present, forcing the memory to the back of her mind. Sometimes it made her feel stronger, proud of herself.

Other times, the memory just made her feel empty.

She hugged her jacket tight as she walked toward her apartment. It was the middle of summer, but thanks to the cool San Francisco climate, she was freezing her tail off. She was carrying shopping bags filled with lightweight clothing she had bought at Macy's and Nordstrom's for the upcoming business venture. From what she had read and been told, it would be hot in southeastern Arizona. She was looking forward to seeing new horizons, and thrilled to be leaving her jacket behind.

At the same time, her stomach clenched at the thought of flying. God, how she hated to fly. At least it was a commercial airliner, not a little commuter plane. She would never get on one of those things again. Ever.

Cars honked along Market Street, and sirens screamed in the distance, but the sounds were almost drowned out by Old Louie's forlorn tune. Lani stopped to pull a dollar out of her purse and a handful of coins, and tossed them into the open saxophone case. Old Louie nodded and smiled around the mouthpiece, and kept on playing.

Lani's footsteps echoed as she jogged up the narrow steps to her apartment above the Italian bakery. Smells of fresh baked bread and cookies filled the air, and it took an incredible amount of willpower not to succumb to the temptation of ducking into the shop and purchasing a *canoli* or two.

As she reached the top of the stairs the delicious smells

faded, replaced by the odors of must and age. When she stepped into the hall she unlocked the door to her apartment, and hurried inside.

After she locked the door behind her, she flipped on the light and took a deep breath. She dropped her packages and wandered into her small living room, trying to calm her tense nerves. Her apartment was her haven—warm and inviting—and she loved it. She had wanted to be surrounded by color and chose to decorate her place in hues that would remind her that she was free of James.

The furnishings were eighteenth century antiques, upholstered in a deep cranberry. A tasteful area rug covered the floor with a pattern of flowers done in cranberry, pinks, forest and sage-green. Impressionist oil paintings decorated her walls, all done in vibrant tones. If she wasn't away from home so often, she would have filled the house with plants and pets. She wanted to be surrounded by living things, but the best she could do for now were silk flower arrangements and foliage.

Despite Lani's relief at being divorced from her ex-husband, a wave of loneliness washed over her as she stood in the tiny living room. She would never get used to that feeling.

Hollow. Empty. Alone.

And that was exactly what she had been for the past five years, regardless of her marriage to James. He had come into her life before everything had spiraled out of control. Then, in her vulnerable state, he had convinced her that she needed him. That he would help fill the void in her life. Instead, she discovered that the man she married was a stranger. A stranger bent on dominating her.

Automatically, Lani moved to the brick fireplace mantle and picked up the silver framed picture of her family. Her mother's soft smile, her sister Naya's gamin grin. Lani's own innocent expression, her brown eyes alight with happiness and love.

Then there was their father behind them, the military

general with a heart as impenetrable as an army tank. He hadn't known how to love and his words had always been hard and cutting. Lani realized now that she had grown up with emotional abuse almost as bad as what she'd gone through with James. She just hadn't known any different or any better.

It made her heart ache even more to know that she didn't miss her father as much as she missed her mother and sister. She didn't miss the cold and cutting words, but he was her father and she had loved him despite it all.

But more than anything, Lani missed her soft spoken mother and her mischievous sister.

Lani caressed the cool metal of the frame and squeezed her eyes shut. *I am not going to cry. Tears can't change anything.* Her chin trembled in defiance of her resolution, and she bit her lip to hold back the tears.

Taking another deep breath, she opened her eyes gave a smile. She would be on her way to Arizona tomorrow.

And just maybe she wouldn't be coming back. Tucson might be a nice place to move to—far from all the memories that weighted her here.

Chapter One

🔊

Rick McAllister dragged his hand over his stubbled face as he settled into the plastic airport seat while waiting to board the plane he'd be taking to Tucson. He was ready to get out of dreary San Francisco, back to Arizona, and home to his son.

And then catch those damn *coyotes*, the people-smugglers who'd managed to elude him for far too long. Especially the bastard known as *El Torero*.

It was dark outside, a slow drizzle rolling down the large panes of glass, and he was looking forward to Arizona sunshine. He pulled his black Stetson low so that he could observe people around him without being obvious. In his line of work as an Intelligence Agent with the U.S. Border Patrol, people-watching was a necessary skill. But now he was doing it to pass the time before his plane was scheduled to depart.

Hair at Rick's nape prickled—he had the distinct feeling *he* was being watched. He casually looked to his left to see a young woman staring at the screen of a notebook computer. Something in his gut told him she'd been studying him a fraction of a second earlier.

And damned if it wasn't the same woman he'd seen a couple of days ago at the Chinese restaurant when his sister had taken him there for lunch.

Rick pushed up the brim of his Stetson and raked his gaze over the woman. She sure was pretty, her shoulder-length hair the golden color of an Arizona sunrise. She had the type of shapely figure he preferred, nicely rounded and sexy as hell. From a gap in her pink silk blouse he could see a bit of lace covering her generous breasts, and her nipples pushed up against the soft material. His gaze traveled down to those long legs beneath the skirt that hit a couple of inches above her knees. Yeah, she sure had terrific legs and he'd bet she had a great ass—

He broke off his appraisal as the woman glanced up and her gaze met his. She had gorgeous eyes, warm and deep brown. Just like yesterday, the connection between Rick and the woman, for that fraction of time, was tangible. Like she'd lassoed him with that one look. She immediately blushed a pretty shade of pink and looked back at her computer.

Rick couldn't help but grin. Damn, she was cute. She might be worth getting to know.

Well, hell. Wasn't it just last night he'd told his sister Callie that he didn't want a relationship? In the five years since Lorraine's death, he hadn't met a single woman he was interested in pursuing. Not one. He'd gone on dates, but few and far between, and often just in the line of work. Yet there he was, fascinated with a stranger in an airport a thousand miles from home.

"Flight 1216 with non-stop service to Tucson is now boarding everyone with an A card," announced a voice over the intercom. This particular airline had "cattle call" boarding with no assigned seats.

Rick stood, and he noticed the woman had slipped her laptop into a bag and was already walking toward the gate, giving him a nice view.

Yeah, she definitely had sexy legs, and she had a great ass, too.

Several passengers crowded in front of Rick, so he had to wait a while longer for his turn to board. When he finally made it onto the plane, he worked his way back and noticed the pretty blonde in a window seat, staring outside, and no one was sitting in the middle seat next to her.

He took off his Stetson and set it in the overhead compartment. With his big frame, he normally disliked sitting in the middle, but this time it would be just fine. Careful not to bump the woman, he eased into the seat next to her, extended the seatbelt, and buckled it.

A flight attendant helped an elderly lady put her bag into the overhead compartment, and then the lady sat next to Rick. He nodded to her and said, "Ma'am."

The woman's pale blue eyes held a hint of amusement. "You're too polite to be a Californian."

"Just spent a week in Frisco with my sister and her twins." He smiled at the memory, wishing he'd been able to spend more time with his niece and nephew. If he hadn't had to go to that briefing in San Diego beforehand, he could've taken his son Trevor to Callie's with him. He sure missed the kid and looked forward to getting home.

"I'm visiting my grandchildren in Tucson." The lady shook her head and sighed. "Hellions, all. Love them, but a weekend is about as much as I can handle. Now *those* kids could use some lessons in manners."

She punctuated her statement with a jab of her fist in the air, then began digging through an enormous purse. "In here somewhere, I have pictures their father sent ..."

Rick held back a grin and glanced at the woman in pink on his other side. Her forehead was pressed to the pane, and she was apparently lost in her thoughts. She sure smelled good. Real good. Like honeysuckle and soap, clean and fresh.

The windowpane felt cool against Lani's forehead as she stared into the darkness. She couldn't help thinking about her lunch with Theresa and Calinda a couple of days ago and seeing that same cowboy just now in the airport. She wouldn't dare tell her friends or they'd razz her for not introducing herself to him.

And wait until she told Trace MacLeod—make that Trace Lawless now—whose idea it was for Lani to make this trip in the first place. Trace had come back to Arizona from England six months ago. After falling in love with a sexy cowboy named Jess Lawless, Trace married him and moved to Texas.

Lani sighed and turned her thoughts back to that gorgeous hunk of man in boots she'd seen in the restaurant and then again in the airport. She'd been so embarrassed to find him studying her from beneath his black cowboy hat. What incredible blue eyes he had—and that sexy grin could melt a woman's soul. Thank goodness he hadn't noticed her watching him a minute before. As a journalist she'd become a people-watcher, and lord, was that man something to watch.

Lani groaned. What was wrong with her? She had no interest in men after being married to the biggest asshole of the century. After seeing what her father had put her mother through when she was growing up, Lani should have known better. She should never have let James'ss lies make her believe in happily-ever-afters.

But as far as that cowboy, what harm was there in looking? Kind of like window shopping with no intention of sampling or buying the merchandise.

She was finally free, finally divorced from James.

"Good riddance, jerk," she grumbled, her breath fogging the pane.

"Beg pardon?"

Lani jumped at the sound of the husky voice, so close that a shiver sprinted down her spine. As she whirled in the cramped seat, her elbow rammed hard flesh. Heat crept up her neck when she saw the cowboy's blue eyes wince.

"I'm so sorry!" Her gaze swept over the tanned face, strong chin, and the chestnut hair that had been hidden under the cowboy hat earlier. "Did I hurt you?"

The man grabbed his side and grimaced as if in mortal pain. "I'm not sure I'll live."

He winked.

That familiar flush spread throughout Lani, the telltale blush that would redden her face from the roots of her hair to the tips of her toes. She offered a half-smile and turned back to the window.

Lights flashed on the wing and reflected on the wet asphalt, a steady rhythm in time with her throbbing pulse. She watched as a man guided the plane onto the runway. Her heart rate rocketed, her palms slick with sweat. The scar on her leg ached and she rubbed it through her skirt.

"I apologize if I embarrassed you," the man beside her said, his voice low and disturbingly close.

A thrill rippled in her belly as she forced herself to face the man. "Not at all."

"Rick McAllister." White teeth flashed against tan skin as he smiled and offered his hand.

Lani caught his earthy scent of sun-warmed flesh and apples, and she fought the desire to dry her moist palm on her skirt before his calloused hand engulfed hers. His grasp sent tingles from her mons to her breasts, and she quickly pulled away.

"And your name, Ma'am?" he said in that slow and sexy voice that made her nipples even tighter.

"Oh." She swallowed, feeling flustered and on edge. "I'm Lani. Lani Stanton."

"Lainee," Rick drawled, a slight, almost imperceptible country twang to his voice, and she shivered. "A pretty name for a pretty lady."

Just the way he was looking at her, the way he said her name, made her want to squirm in her seat.

Good lord. If just talking to this man was making her feel like this, what would it feel like to really be with him?

Nope. Not going there. She'd had it with men, and that was that.

The plane started to taxi down the runway, throwing Lani into her worst fear. All she could do was close her eyes tight, pray, and try to shove the heart-wrenching memories from her mind. Every muscle in her body tensed, and she gripped the armrests, as if the mere act would guide the plane into the air and keep it there.

At least until it was time to land.

"You all right?"

Lani heard his voice, but refused to open her eyes. Not until they were safely at cruising altitude.

Rick McAllister's hand closed around hers, and he gave her fingers a comforting squeeze. The stranger's touch startled her, but not enough to make her look at him or speak a word. It surprised her how his warm grasp calmed her nerves, if only for a few minutes.

As the craft lifted, her chest tightened, and her breath rasped out in shallow huffs. The rumble of the plane, the roar of the engines, the smell of burning fuel, the pause in the air conditioning, the way the pressure clamped down on her head…she hated it all.

Ten morbid thoughts later, she felt the plane level out, and in a rush, she released the breath she'd been holding. "I knew I should have driven," she muttered.

The man chuckled. "All the way to Tucson from San Francisco?"

Lani opened one eye and peeked at him. "Yes."

"Don't you know flying is safer than driving?" He smiled, and she opened her other eye.

She sighed and allowed her muscles to relax. "Yeah. Right."

"If it makes you feel better, I'm a pilot."

"It doesn't." Feeling was coming back into Lani's limbs, and she brushed a wisp of hair behind her ear. "You can let go of my hand now."

"Sure." A spark of mischief lit his blue eyes. But he didn't move.

"What'll you two have to drink?" the flight attendant asked before Lani had a chance to tell Rick exactly what she would do if he didn't release her.

"I'll have orange juice," he said and turned to Lani. "What'll you have, darlin'?"

She'd darlin' him in a minute.

Lani asked the attendant for a diet soda. After the woman had taken their drink orders and moved to the next row, Rick said, "That stuff'll kill you."

"When I get my drink, it's going in your lap if you don't release my hand, cowboy." She gave him a dangerous smile. One that could leave no doubt she intended to follow through with her threat.

"I give up." He raised his hands in mock self-defense, coming within a breath of hitting the woman on the other side of him. He was truly too big for the seat, his broad shoulders and chest spanning the width.

"Pardon, Ma'am," he said to the elderly woman, who patted his knee and then returned to showing a stack of photographs to the man across the aisle.

Lani reached up to open the air vent, and punched the button for the reading light. Yes, the cowboy was definitely too handsome for his own good.

While she dug in her laptop bag, she felt the intensity of Rick's presence, but avoided looking at him. Where was it? Ah, there. She withdrew the spiral-bound notebook and slipped on her gold-rimmed reading glasses.

Theresa had loved the idea of the immigration feature. It would be the most comprehensive feature Lani had written, and she intended to make it the best series of articles any reporter had done on the subject of illegal immigration along the Mexican border.

Lani was looking forward to the experience with desperate enthusiasm. What better way to distance herself from James and all the bad memories?

"What're you working on?" Rick asked as she began jotting down questions for her feature.

"I'm a journalist." She shifted her attention from her notepad to the cowboy. "I'm writing a few notes for a feature I'm doing."

"For a newspaper?" He looked genuinely interested, and Lani found herself warming to his friendliness.

"I write for *City by the Bay*." She rustled in her bag, pulled out a copy and handed it to him. "It's a San Francisco-based magazine that primarily carries local interest stories, but occasionally runs features on national topics."

Rick's fingers brushed hers as he took the magazine. Lani caught her breath at the tingle that skittered within her at the innocent contact. Her eyes cut to his, to see if he'd noticed, but he seemed intent on flipping through the magazine.

"That's the current issue." She pulled off her glasses and slid them back into their case. "I wrote a feature on single-parenting. My pseudonym is Lane E. Stanton."

He cocked an eyebrow and his gaze met hers. "You're a single parent?"

"My editor assigned the story." Her smile faltered. "I don't have any children. But I wish I did."

Before Rick could ask her anything more personal, she said, "So, what do you do?"

"Law enforcement," he replied with a shrug.

Surprised, Lani blinked. "And here I thought you were a cowboy."

He smiled. "Grew up on a ranch, but following in my folks' footsteps never appealed to me. As a kid I always wanted to be the good guy tracking down the bad guys."

"I'll just bet." Her mouth quirked as she imagined him on a white horse, tracking down desperados.

Lightning flashed outside the plane and her heart dropped. She turned away from Rick to glance out the window. Another flash illuminated the swirling mass of a thunderstorm.

The plane bucked and dropped, then leveled out, shooting her stomach straight to her toes. She gasped and clutched the armrests, her heart pounding so loud she thought it would jump out of her chest and the cowboy next to her could lasso it.

When Lani had looked to the window, Rick took the opportunity to study her. What was it about the woman that interested him, more than anyone else he'd met?

Was it her velvety brown eyes? The way she blushed? When he'd embarrassed her, every bit of bare skin that he could see had gone pink, from the V of her blouse, to the tips of her ears. He wondered if the rest of her turned that attractive color.

What would it be like to kiss those full lips?

As skittish as she seemed, he'd probably have better luck kissing the old lady on his other side.

Lightning lit the sky outside and Lani gasped as the plane dropped and shuddered. She turned from the window to face forward, her eyes scrunched tight, her face as pale as his mom's lace tablecloth.

Over the intercom a man's voice drawled, "This is your captain. Y'all sit tight with your seatbelts fastened until we ride out this storm."

Poor kid, Rick thought as he studied Lani.

He couldn't stop himself. He eased an arm around her and pulled her head to his chest. She remained rigid, trembling. In a few moments, he felt her relax. A bit.

"Everything'll be fine," he whispered into her hair, and squeezed her cold fingers within his warm grasp.

His gut tightened at the smell of her and the feel of her soft body in his arms. Somehow he felt like he knew her. That he'd always known her.

The plane bounced and rattled among the turbulence, and she pressed her face closer. Tears soaked his shirt, and he fought the urge to slip his fingers into her hair.

Why was she so terrified?

He moved his thumb over the back of her hand and noticed a band of pale flesh against her skin, where she must've worn a wedding ring. A broken engagement? A divorce?

The rest of the flight to Tucson was one of the roughest he'd taken. The thunderstorm raged and turbulence tossed the plane like a toy caught in a dust devil. But Rick found himself glad for the storm, glad for the excuse to hold the young woman that he barely even knew.

A sensual caress, a deep passionate kiss…the cowboy touched Lani in ways she'd never been touched before. His slow hands were intent on exploring every inch of her naked body. He cupped her breasts and rubbed his thumbs over her nipples while he slipped his tongue into her mouth. The way he used that tongue amazed her. He tasted all of her as he moved from her mouth, along the column of her throat to her nipples and then on down the flat of her belly to her mons. He focused on pleasuring her like she'd never been pleasured before. Then the cowboy rose up between her thighs, his cock at her entrance ready to thrust into her –

Lani woke to a whisper in her ear. "We're here, Lani. We made it."

Disoriented, she blinked, then heat burned through her when she realized she had her head against the cowboy's chest. Her face flamed at the thought of what she'd just dreamed—about a total stranger who she happened to be sleeping on. She'd never had an erotic dream like that one, and it unnerved her.

When she pulled away from Rick, she couldn't think of a thing to say.

How could she have let a stranger hold her to begin with? But it had helped calm the terror that churned inside her like an earthquake in the heart of San Francisco.

James had never held her. *You're being stupid*, he would

say. *Get over it.*

But not this man. Rick didn't even know her, and yet he held her as though he truly cared.

"Such a sweet couple," the wispy lady croaked from the other side of him. She reached across with her frail hand and patted his, still covering Lani's. "You two remind me of my Wilbur and me. Sixty years of marriage and still dancing." She gave a watery smile and eased herself up to enter the aisle.

Rick grinned and Lani wanted to drop through the floor of the plane.

She ducked and reached under the seat in front of her to grab the laptop bag. When she looked back, her eyes kept going up, traveling those long legs in snug Wranglers and good lord, that very nice package... Her cheeks burned again at the turn of her thoughts.

He put on his cowboy hat and allowed her to go in front of him in the aisle. What did he think of her after that terrifying plane ride? Did he think she was some weepy woman who couldn't take care of herself?

Why did she care what he thought?

While she exited the plane onto the ramp, Rick strode at her side. "How long'll you be here, Lani?"

The way he said her name sent shivers throughout her. A gentle drawl, a husky tone.

"Three weeks." She chanced a look at him and saw his smile, a smile that caused something within her to burn. An ache, a wanting.

She didn't tell him that she was considering moving to Tucson. Too many memories shrouded her in the Bay Area.

As he stood next to her at the baggage drop, Lani tried not to think about the effect he was having on her. She was afraid he'd felt it too, and that was dangerous territory she had no intention of exploring.

With relief, she saw her bags tumble down the slide to the

conveyor. She snatched them one at a time and set them on the floor beside her. She turned to face Rick, and saw him grabbing his own suitcase.

"Thanks." She took a deep breath and met his intense blue gaze. "It was nice of you to—to—well, help me make it through that flight."

"Any time." In one swift movement, he gathered her two hefty suitcases along with his own and made it look like he was carrying a couple of hatboxes.

"What are you doing?" she demanded, hands on her hips.

"Helping you to your cab." He managed a small bow and sounded quite gallant.

"I can carry my own bags," she insisted to his retreating back.

But when they reached the security checkout, she presented her luggage ticket stubs and then trailed after him into the evening thunderstorm. The clean smell of rain hit her as thunder rumbled in the distance. An odd thrill tingled within her at the tension in the air. She loved thunderstorms—as long as she was safely on the ground.

He didn't stop until he reached the line of cabs and handed the driver her belongings while she stood under the awning. Rain rolled off his cowboy hat onto his shirt as he held the cab door open for her. "Where're you headed?"

"Tucson Grand Hotel," she replied as she dodged into the pounding rain and pushed her laptop case and purse into the cab's backseat.

Wrinkling her nose at the smell of stale cigar smoke, she scooted over the cracked vinyl seat, to the far side that had fewer tears in it. She wiped raindrops from her face and pushed her damp hair behind her ears.

Rick leaned in the cab door. "I'm staying the night at the Grand, too. Mind if I get out of the rain and share your cab?"

He was already soaked from the storm, and she hated to see him get any wetter. In fact, the thought gave her a little thrill. "Sure," she replied and then bit her lip as he disappeared again and she felt the trunk of the cab being slammed shut.

As the cab driver hopped into the front seat, Rick climbed in the back seat next to Lani. Her pulse rate picked up and she knew she should have told him to get his own taxi. Spending any time with a man who made her feel like taking a chance on romance was definitely not a good idea.

The cabbie pulled into traffic as Rick set his Stetson on his knee and studied the woman next to him. Lani was biting her lower lip, looking like she was having second thoughts about sharing the cab.

"I'm having breakfast at the Grand in the morning," he said, trying to set her at ease. "Otherwise I'd head home tonight."

Lani jumped as lightning split the sky, the crack of thunder not far behind.

"Scared of thunderstorms also?" Rick asked, hoping she'd need a shoulder to lean on.

"No." She shook her head. "I'm just not used to them."

He smiled. "If you're frightened, you could hold my hand again."

She pursed her lips, and he felt desire burn in him. So soft, so inviting, those lips.

"Listen, Rick." She hesitated. "You were kind to me on the plane. More than kind. But I don't let strange men hold me." She turned to the window, where he could see streetlights blurring in the rain.

"Lani," he said. She turned back with obvious reluctance. "I have no doubt that you would've made it through that flight without me lending a shoulder. There's nothing wrong with being insecure sometimes. We all are."

Sighing, she stared at her lap, reaching for her ring finger as if to twist a band no longer there. She thrust her hands to her sides and looked at him. "Someone always told me how weak I was for my fear of flying. He even knew what had happened."

The cab lurched to a stop in front of the Grand, and before he had a chance to respond, to ask what kind of jackass would say something like that to her, she flung open her door and darted out to the curb, into the rain. He followed, banging his forehead on the doorframe, and uttering a curse that was sure to turn Lani's pretty ears blue.

By the time he managed to get his bulk out of the cab, she'd stuffed bills in the cabbie's hand and was hauling her suitcases through the impressive doors of the Tucson Grand. Rick shoved his fare at the driver, grabbed his own bag and followed. He couldn't help but admire Lani's curves and the toss of her head. In a matter of a few strides, he'd caught up to her at the registration desk.

She tapped her nails on the marble countertop in a nervous rhythm that reminded him of rain falling on the cab's roof.

The clerk typed in a command and studied his computer. "Ah, yes." He handed Lani a key card. "Room 1110."

Rick moved beside her. "Wait for me and I'll help with your bags, darlin'." "McAllister," he told the clerk.

Lani frowned. "I'm not your darlin', cowboy. I can handle my own bags." She walked toward the elevators, across the acres of industrial carpet. But he had no doubt his ruse would get the results he wanted—at least with the clerk.

"Wedding jitters," Rick said to the young man, who gave a knowing grin.

"Hmm, let me see here, Mr. McAllister. Good. The room next to your fiancé is available. Room 1108."

Chapter Two

ဢ

"Come on, come on," Lani muttered, tapping her foot, anxious for the elevator to arrive before Rick caught up. Something about him was starting to wear down her defenses and she couldn't afford to let that happen with any man. No matter how kind and attentive he might be.

No such luck. The doors opened, and Rick darted in before they had a chance to close. It was a slow elevator, taking its sweet time to head up the eleven floors.

"Have dinner with me tonight." He smiled and she noticed a dimple in one cheek.

Lani's body heated and her nipples tightened beneath her blouse. *Why not? Why not spend one evening in the company of an attractive man?*

She gritted her teeth in an effort to fight off her attraction to the cowboy. *I'm not ready. I need more time.*

"It's just dinner between two new friends," Rick said, as if reading her mind.

The elevator groaned to a stop and the doors opened. *It's only dinner*, her thoughts echoed. What could happen?

Definitely not a good idea. There was no room for someone as handsome and charming as Rick McAllister in her life.

"Thanks, but no." She gathered her bags and stepped into the hall that had the same peculiar odor that all older hotels did. Like ancient carpet, mothballs and freshly laundered linens. It didn't surprise her that he followed. He was as tenacious as San Francisco fog.

"How about I make you a wager." He hooked his thumb

in his belt loop. "I'll guess something personal about you, and if I'm right, you have dinner with me. If not, then I'll eat by my lonesome."

She sighed and stared up at the popcorn ceiling, then shook her head and looked at Rick. "All right."

"If I'm right, you're having dinner with me."

Lani smiled despite herself. "Yeah, yeah."

He took her hand, and that strange energy jolted her at his touch, sending vibrations straight to her toes. His hand was much larger than hers and his callused palm was rough against her soft skin. She shivered and felt an ache between her thighs at just his mere touch.

"You're afraid to have dinner with me," he began, "'cause you just went through a rough time. I'd say you're divorced and your ex-husband was a real jackass. You deserve better, Lani."

A chill pebbled her skin and she snatched her hand away. "How did you know?"

With one finger he pushed up the brim of his Stetson, and grinned. "I won the bet."

Anger burned away the frost of her surprise. "How did you find that out?"

Rick gave a gentle smile that had the odd effect of relaxing her. "I noticed that you still have a line from where you wore a wedding ring, so it couldn't have been too long ago. You talked about a real idiot who treated you poorly, and you shy away from me like a horse spooked by a rattlesnake."

She took a deep breath and gripped her laptop bag tighter. "You figured it out just from that?"

"Like I told you, I'm in law enforcement. Figuring out clues is part of what I do." Rick's expression took on a more serious look. "I'll behave. Promise."

"I must be out of my mind." She shook her head and sighed. "All right. But it's not a date."

Rick strode to the start of the hallway, then stopped before the first door. "I'll meet you in fifteen minutes. I'm starving. Those dang airplane peanuts just don't tide me over." He stuck a key card into room 1108 and was through the door before she had a chance to reply.

Slick. He even managed to get a room next to hers. She stood before her own door and groaned. Should she take her bags downstairs and demand another room?

Instinct told her that he wasn't the type of man who would hurt or take advantage of her, and with the exception of the mistake she'd made with the man she'd married, her instincts were normally right on. She could always change her mind and ask for a different room if she felt it necessary.

And since Rick was in law enforcement, he spent his time protecting people.

Maybe she should ask to see his badge.

Despite her many misgivings, fifteen minutes later, Lani was ready. She'd managed to blow dry the rain from her hair, curl a few wisps with the curling iron and touch up her makeup. She'd changed out of her wrinkled blouse and skirt into a pink sundress and sandals.

When she was dressed, she dabbed honeysuckle perfume at her wrists and throat. Like the color pink, the scent made her feel feminine. James had hated it, and hated her in pink.

She wore pink and the honeysuckle perfume as often as possible.

A knock at the door interrupted her thoughts. Before she opened it, she took a deep breath and checked the peephole. It was Rick, and if that skewed image of him held true, he definitely looked too handsome for his own good.

When she swung the door open, she saw that he looked incredible in his black cowboy hat, his white teeth flashing against his deep tan, his navy shirt enhancing the disturbing blue of his eyes.

"Beautiful." Rick's gaze ran the length of her, and she

blushed. "Do you like Mexican food? They serve the best enchiladas north of the border in one of the restaurants downstairs."

She smiled despite the melting sensation in her bones. "Love it."

As he escorted her to the restaurant, she was intensely aware of him. What was it about him that sent jolts of hunger through her every time they touched?

When the hostess showed them to a corner table, Lani was surprised when Rick pulled out her chair before taking his own seat. James had never done those small gentlemanly things. She'd never considered it necessary, but she found the gesture touching coming from Rick. He seated himself, and then took off his hat and set it on the chair beside him.

Her stomach twisted. She hadn't been on a date since college.

No. It wasn't a date. Just dinner with a man she'd never see again.

When Lani finished studying the menu, she saw Rick watching her. He gave her a slow, sexy smile that made her heart stop, and she almost forgot to breathe. To her relief, the waiter arrived to take their order.

"You ought to try one of their margaritas," Rick suggested. "They're wicked."

She nodded. "Frozen with salt on the rim."

"*Gracias.*" The waiter hurried away with their orders.

The restaurant had the perfect atmosphere for a casual evening out. Mexican hats, serapes and decorated gourds adorned the walls, the floor a dark *Saltillo* tile. Mariachi music played in the background, and Lani found herself tapping her toe to the beat.

"You live in San Francisco?" Rick asked, drawing her attention back to him.

Lani tucked a strand of hair behind her ear. "All my life.

What about you?"

"I'm an Arizona native. A rare breed. Most folks you meet around these parts are from anywhere but here."

The waiter returned, placing a basket of chips, pots of salsa, and large margaritas in front of each of them.

"Goodness. It's enormous." She sipped her drink and smiled. "Delicious."

He took a swallow of his. "One of these things equals two and a half regular ones. It'll knock you on your ass if you're not careful."

Lani laughed and dipped a corn chip in salsa. "Were you on a business trip?"

Rick put a handful of chips on his plate. "Visiting my sister and her kids. I don't get to see them much, so I try to get out there at least once a year."

As soon as she bit into the corn chip, she knew it was a mistake. Her mouth flamed and her eyes watered. She grabbed her margarita and drank it, trying to cool the burning sensation.

"Careful," he said. "You'll be dancing on the tabletops if you drink that too fast."

Lani set the drink down and tried ice water instead, but her mouth still felt like it was on fire.

"Should've warned you about that salsa. Chips with salt might help."

She fanned her warm face as she ate a plain chip with no salsa. "I've had hot sauce before, but nothing like that."

Trying to get her mind off the fire burning in her mouth, Lani asked, "Were you with your sister at the Chinese restaurant?" Immediately she regretted opening her big mouth and admitting she had noticed him, and asking a question so personal that it might make it look like she was interested in him.

"So you do remember." Rick smiled. "Her name's Callie

and she's a pistol."

"Uh, yeah." Lani pretended nonchalance. "My friends and I have *dim sum* there regularly."

It wasn't long before the waiter arrived with their combo plates of enchiladas, tacos, refried beans and Spanish rice. Everything tasted fabulous, but there was so much food that Lani was only able to eat half of what was on her plate.

While they ate, she was surprised at how much she wanted to know about him. Definitely not a good idea. She purposely steered clear of personal topics, and was glad he didn't press her. He answered questions about Tucson, the best tourist attractions, and those frequented by the locals. She didn't bother to tell him she would be leaving Tucson in the morning.

In turn, he asked her about living in San Francisco. They talked about the areas he'd visited around the city, and she shared her favorite places.

Lani enjoyed how Rick focused on her when they spoke, like he was intent on hearing every word. The way his eyes lit up when he laughed. The infectious grin that held a bit of the devil himself in it. She enjoyed being around him too much, and had to remind herself that there was no room for a distraction or complication in her life like Rick McAllister.

"I'd better get to bed." She drained the enormous margarita and wondered at her reluctance to part with him. "I have an early appointment."

He agreed and called for the check. After they split the bill, which Lani insisted on, she stood and realized that he'd been right—drinking the entire margarita had been a mistake. Her head spun, and when Rick laced his fingers with hers, she didn't object—she was afraid she might fall. The feel of his hand sent tremors throughout her body, enhanced by the mellow, tipsy feeling the drink had given her.

On the elevator ride up to their floor, Lani's legs wobbled and she found herself leaning too close to Rick. She knew she needed to put distance between them, but when they reached her room, he took the key card from her hand and opened the door.

"Can I come in?" he murmured. "Two minutes."

"Okay." Where did that come from? Her heart pounded out a staccato that she could almost bet he was able to hear.

"I want to see you again." Rick flicked on a light as he drew Lani through the door, and it slammed shut behind her.

Her throat tightened and went as dry as the Arizona desert. "I—I…"

But her words vanished, her mind blank, as Rick took her face in his palms and captured her gaze with his.

"Rick, I—" But she no longer knew the meaning of up or down, and she melted against him, wanting him. His earthy scent intoxicated her, filling her senses, confusing her beyond the effects of the alcohol.

"Darlin', what you do to me," Rick said against her lips. "Let me taste you."

"Yes," she whispered.

He brushed his lips over hers. Just a whisper kiss. The light touch of his lips and the feel of his calloused fingers on her skin made her nipples pebble and her mons ache. A wave of longing crested, then crashed within her soul.

She pressed herself closer to him and heard a soft moan.

Coming from her.

The tip of his tongue outlined her bottom lip, a feather caress that sent desire spiraling within. She parted her lips and his tongue met hers, a velvet softness that she savored like golden honey. "You taste so good," he murmured.

Citrus from the margarita was still sweet on his tongue and she wrapped her arms around his neck as their kiss deepened. She smelled the light apple fragrance of his hair, and slid her fingers into the soft strands, knocking his cowboy hat off.

With a jolt, Lani became aware of Rick's erection against her belly. A voice inside her shouted, telling her she couldn't go any farther. Not with someone she barely knew. But her mind and body refused to listen.

As if he heard her thoughts, he let out a ragged breath and stepped back, putting distance between them — leaving her feeling cold and empty. Alone.

Rick traced one finger along her cheekbone and she shuddered with longing. "Say you'll see me again."

He looked so handsome, his chestnut hair in disarray, passion in his eyes.

"I — I don't know if that's a good idea." It took all her willpower not to throw her arms around him and tell him to spend the night. She had never been with a man other than James in a sexual way, and it frightened her how much she wanted Rick.

Right here. Right now.

Rick caught both her hands in his. "Have breakfast with me."

She shook her head. "I have a meeting, and then I'm going out of town."

He brought her hands to his mouth and trailed his lips over her knuckles, sending shivers throughout her, those intense blue eyes never leaving hers. "How do I reach you?"

Trying to regain even a modicum of self-control, Lani freed her hands and smoothed her hair. "I'll sleep on it. If I see you before I leave, I'll let you know."

"All right." He kissed her again, a soft lingering kiss, and she almost lost every shred of resolve. He smiled and caressed her cheek, then turned and slipped out the door.

And she was really alone then.

Dazed, Lani turned toward the bed and almost tripped over Rick's cowboy hat. She picked it up, wondering if she should take it to him.

No. Tomorrow morning would be soon enough.

Lani ran a shaking hand through her hair. What had she just done? She'd experienced the most incredible kiss of her life—from a virtual stranger.

She sat on the edge of the bed, then flopped onto her back, Rick's hat still cradled to her chest. She inhaled deeply, drinking in the intoxicating smell of him that clung to the felt Stetson. That masculine scent that made her ache for him.

What would it have been like to make love to Rick? Theresa would say *fuck* him, but Lani couldn't say that word aloud. Yet it had an erotic edge to it that caused a thrill to skip around in her belly.

She widened her thighs and with one hand pulled her sundress up around her waist. Lani imagined Rick would have slow gentle hands. She slid her palm down her stomach to her panties, then slipped her fingers beneath the elastic and into the soft curls of her mons.

Lani closed her eyes, still holding Rick's hat close to her chest. Her nipples were hard and tight against her sundress as she slipped her fingers into her folds. It had been so long since she'd given herself an orgasm, and right now she needed one. Sex with James had been mechanical and unfulfilling, and she'd always had to take care of matters herself afterward.

But she wasn't going to think about the jerk now.

No, she was going to imagine actually letting herself go and being with that tall, dark, sexy cowboy who managed to break through the ice of resistance coating her heart and soul since her divorce. She couldn't let him all the way in, but it wouldn't hurt to fantasize about him, right?

Rick stands behind her, the heat of his body burning through her thin cotton dress. Slowly he unzips it then slides the straps of her sundress down her shoulders, her arms, and over her hips until it drops in a swirl around her feet. He murmurs soft words while he kisses her shoulder, then unhooks her bra and lets it fall to the floor. Her panties go next as he pushes them down, leaving her entirely naked.

He turns her around and admires her with words and burning glances. He enjoys her curves, revels in her large breasts and voluptuous ass.

But he can't wait to have her. He unfastens his jeans and pulls out his cock…so big, so very big. Gently he pushes her onto the bed, her legs splayed wide. He moves between her thighs, his jeans rough against her soft skin, but the feeling is erotic and exciting.

Rick lowers his head and suckles her nipples, first one and then the other. His erection is teasing her folds, begging to slide inside her. With one hand he braces himself above her, and with his other he guides his cock to the entrance of her channel. She arches her hips up, begging for him. He smiles that slow sexy smile and then drives into her.

She gasps at the feel of him. The roughness of his denim jeans abrading the inside of her thighs. Rick leans down and kisses her as he drives her closer and closer to climax…

With a small cry, Lani came hard, jerking her out of her fantasy. Her fingers continued to circle her clit causing her body to shudder until she came a second time.

Heat filled her body and her cheeks flushed. Still clutching Rick's Stetson, she slipped her hand out of her panties and pulled down her sundress.

Good lord, what an amazing orgasm. I wonder what the real thing would be like.

No, no, no. Not going there!

* * * * *

Rick spent one hell of a sleepless night after leaving Lani. It must've been hours that he stared at the ceiling, remembering the scent of her, the way she looked with her hair mussed and her lips swollen from his kisses. To know she was in the room next door was sheer torture. His cock was still as hard as a steel rod, and it showed no signs of settling down.

Finally he decided to take a cold shower, but once he was

under the water he switched it to warm. He turned his back to the warm water and braced one hand against the smooth shower wall. With his free hand he stroked his cock, imagining Lani's sweet body beneath him.

His hands ached to caress her generous curves. He'd touch every bit of her body, run his tongue between her thighs until he reached her folds. He'd slide his hands under her soft ass and raise her up so that he could lick her pussy. He'd dine on her sweet flesh, licking and sucking her until she shouted out her orgasm. Then he'd rise up while she was still trembling and he'd drive into her core and fuck her. Yeah, he'd hook his arms under her legs and take her deep until she cried out again.

Rick groaned as his come spurted onto the tile of the bathroom wall relieving a little of his need for Lani. But not nearly enough. Hell, he'd jacked off before, but not like this, not right after just meeting a woman…a woman who he didn't want to let go of. And hell, he barely knew her.

One thing, though—he'd purposely left his Stetson in her bedroom so that she'd have to give it back to him in the morning. At least he hoped she would.

For awhile he'd stayed up, and even read her article in the magazine she'd given him. He'd been impressed with her writing style, and the way she'd presented a topic that she didn't have first hand experience in. A single father for five years, Rick was well-acquainted with the subject.

Yeah, this Lani Stanton was definitely worth getting to know.

* * * * *

The next morning Rick woke early, ready to find Lani before she fled.

What had come over him? The confirmed bachelor father. Hell, even if Lani did agree to see him again, what would she think of him having a son? He and Trevor were a package deal. Usually Rick talked about his son all the time, but for some reason he'd stayed away from personal subjects, much the same as Lani had.

At seven he knocked on her door, hoping she'd still be there. The door opened, rewarding him with the sight of Lani clad in a pink T-shirt and boxers, and a glimpse of her shapely legs.

"What are you doing here so early, Rick?" She ran a hand through her tousled hair.

He leaned against the doorframe. "You all right?"

"I'm fine." She gave a cute little yawn. "What time is it?"

"Seven."

"Seven!" She turned away, clearly distracted, and he caught the door with his boot. "Darn hotel drapes," she muttered. "Always make it too dark."

Rick followed her into the room, the door slamming behind him as she pulled open the drapes and flooded the room with sunshine. "Lani, we've got to talk."

She spun around, almost colliding with Rick, those dark eyes filled with emotion that he couldn't discern. "About what?"

"Us."

"There's no us." She raised her hands as if in amazement and sounded agitated. "You were nice to me on the airplane and we had dinner. That's it."

He reached up one hand and smoothed hair from her eyes. "What about the kiss we shared? You have to admit, it was more than a little peck."

For a moment, he saw yearning in her eyes, mirroring every desire in his soul. But she pulled free and pushed him away.

"No." She pointed to the door. "And you need to go."

Was she upset with him? Or did it have something to do with her ex?

"What happened?" he said softly.

She shook her head. "Nothing. I need to get ready for my appointment."

"Lani—"

"Please leave." Her expression looked both sad and distant. "I've really got to get ready for this appointment and I just don't have it in me for any kind of complications right now."

Rick stood there for a second, his thumb hooked in his belt loop. "Can I at least give you my card? I'll leave it up to you to get a hold of me. If you want to."

Lani sighed and nodded. "All right."

He dug out his wallet and pulled out one of his cards from the agency and handed it to Lani. She took it without looking at it and slipped it into a pocket of her backpack.

Well, at least she hadn't tossed it into the garbage.

Just as he was about to tell her goodbye, she said, "Hold on."

He paused wondering if she'd had a change of heart.

Her cheeks had gone a dark shade of pink as she leaned over and picked up his Stetson from a chair beside the bed. "You forgot this last night," she said as she handed him his hat.

He put it on and tipped the brim at her. "I hope you'll call," he said and then turned and headed out the door. She followed him and he stood and looked at her as she held the door open a moment.

Her eyes softened and she said, "Thank you for dinner. I had a nice time." And then she let the door close quietly behind her.

Well, hell.

Maybe she'd call him after all.

Chapter Three

ഇ

Rick realized that right now what he needed was to get his mind back on his job and start thinking about what he had to do to track down those damn *coyotes*. He knew he was getting closer to catching the bastards. He could feel it. Almost taste it.

He headed down to the hotel's restaurant and waited for Chuck to arrive. The sun shone brilliant through the beveled glass of the Grand and spilled onto the carpeted floor. Groundskeepers worked at cleaning torn palm fronds and other debris left from the previous night's storm, and housekeepers polished rain splatters from the windows and vacuumed dirt from carpets.

After he made his way into the restaurant, Rick was escorted to a table and let the hostess know he was waiting for another person to join him. He took a seat and tried to get his head back on the intelligence work waiting for him when he returned, but his thoughts kept turning to Lani.

"Howdy, Son." Chuck's voice brought Rick out of his thoughts about a certain blonde who'd given him the brush-off.

Rick smiled at his stepfather. "Mornin', old man."

"Old man, my ass." Chuck removed his gray Stetson, plunked it on top of Rick's, and took the seat across the table. After swiping his head with a meaty hand, Chuck eyed him with his penetrating stare, the same one that always could tell when Rick was up to no good as a kid. "You haven't been sleeping."

Rick leaned back and folded his arms. "Dad, I'm fine. Just had a restless night."

Chuck tugged at his turquoise bolo tie. "How're your sister and my grandkids?"

"Callie's doing great and the twins are ornery as all get-out." Rick laughed and shook his head at the thought of his niece and nephew. "Stevie takes more and more after his grandpa everyday. The spittin' image of you, and full of the devil."

"Humph." Chuck pulled his pocket watch out of his jeans. "Reporter should be here by now."

Raising an eyebrow, Rick asked, "What's this about?"

"Supposedly one of those in-depth feature type reports." Chuck took a drink of his ice water and settled back. "Didn't your mother tell you? This reporter fella will be staying with us awhile, talking with ranchers, showing our side of the story and not just those damn militants that make us all look like a bunch of uneducated red-neck yeehaws. He'll probably want to interview you and others from the department. He's supposed to be one of the best."

Rick's attention wandered from his step-dad as Lani entered the room, brushing her hair behind her ear as she spoke with the hostess. Fire burned in his gut as he thought of last night. Those lips. The taste of her.

Bright as a summer day, her honey-blonde hair tumbled loose to her shoulders, the soft pink blouse and faded jeans hugging her body, showing off her curves. He could almost smell her honeysuckle scent.

"What's the matter with you, boy?" Chuck turned and followed Rick's gaze. "Ah. A looker, that one."

The hostess grabbed a menu and led Lani straight to Rick's table. Her jaw dropped as she reached him, and her eyes locked with his.

"These handsome gentlemen are your party, Ms. Stanton." The hostess winked at Chuck. She set the menu in front of the empty chair between the men and left.

Chuck stood and took Lani's hand. "I'm Charles Turner.

You're the reporter, Lane Stanton?"

She moved her gaze from Rick to Chuck, and gave him a polite smile. "Please call me Lani."

What's Rick doing here? Lani thought, her body shivering with awareness.

"Call me Chuck." Charles Turner's hand swamped hers, and with his good ol' boy personality, she almost expected him to slap her on the back and offer her a chaw of tobacco.

He released her and gestured to Rick. "This is my son. Rick, this here is our reporter, who'll be staying a spell with us at the JL Star. It'll be right nice having a pretty lady as our guest."

"Your son?" That horrible flush rushed over Lani.

Rick's answering grin and the sweep of his eyes told her that he'd noticed. He stood and took her hand, and she felt that dangerous tingle skitter along her entire body.

Why does he affect me like that every time we touch? she thought, not sure what to think about anything right now.

She found her voice, and tried to sound like the professional reporter she was. "I thought your last name was McAllister, not Turner."

Rick gave a slow nod. "It is. Chuck's my step-dad."

Chuck lifted his bushy brows. "You two know each other?"

With only a little difficulty, Lani extracted her hand from Rick's. "We, ah, met yesterday on the plane."

"And had dinner last night," Rick added with a sparkle in his blue eyes.

Chuck's eyebrows shot up further. "Well then. Let's have us some breakfast."

After Chuck pushed Lani's chair in, they ordered from the waitress. Lani chose the fruit plate, not sure the butterflies inhabiting her stomach could handle anything stronger with Rick so close, pressing his leg against hers. When she tried moving the other way, she managed to ram into Chuck's knee. She flushed with embarrassment as she mumbled an apology.

When the waitress took their menus and left, Lani picked up her water glass and cut Rick a look that told him exactly what she intended to do with it. He chuckled and moved his knee, the remainder of the meal only accidentally brushing up against her thigh on occasion.

During the little knee waltz, Chuck explained how large the ranch was, and sure enough, Rick lived at the ranch, in the same house.

Wonderful. Lani groaned inwardly, wondering if she should say that she changed her mind, then flee back to San Francisco. But to what? The jerk? Her little apartment above the Italian bakery?

No. Not going to happen. She could keep Rick in his place, finish the feature, conquer the west, and be on her way.

As the waitress served their breakfast, Chuck launched into his concerns on the illegal immigrant situation and with his permission, Lani brought out her pocket recorder.

Chuck speared a sausage and gestured with it. "The problems have been there for years. They've got to get a handle on it, before more of those poor immigrant souls lose their lives, dying of thirst in the desert."

"What about the Border Patrol?" Lani asked. "Can they increase their efforts?"

"Ask Rick." Chuck waved his sausage at Rick. "He's on the patrol."

She raised her eyebrows. "You're a Border Patrol Agent?"

Rick gave her that easy smile. "I told you I'm in law enforcement."

"You didn't mention which branch."

He shrugged. "You didn't ask."

Chuck's chair scraped against the tile floor as he stood. "Son, I've got to go call your mother and let her know we'll be on our way in two shakes of a jack-a-lope's antlers."

When Lani was alone with Rick, she wiped her mouth with a napkin. "If I thought it remotely possible, I would bet you planned this."

"Who says I didn't?" he smiled. "You missed a spot."

As she speared a strawberry, she gave him a puzzled look. "What?"

He reached up and rubbed her chin with his thumb. "There, all gone." But he didn't stop, he continued on, trailing his thumb over her lips in a slow sensual movement.

She froze, trapped by the brilliant azure of his eyes.

No. No way could she allow herself to become vulnerable to any man again.

Lani pulled away. "Rick...that kiss last night was a mistake. I'm going to do this feature, and then I'm going to leave. There is no room for any kind of relationship with you in this equation."

"All right." His lips quirked. "If you say so."

Rick practiced keeping his hands off Lani as his stepfather maneuvered her into the front passenger seat of the SUV. Before she had a chance to argue, Chuck took the back seat. While Rick drove the hundred miles to the ranch, Lani turned and spoke with the rancher most of the way.

How the hell was he supposed keep his hands off her when she'd be sleeping down the hall every night?

Every night.

Well, hell. That thought certainly held promise.

Although being around her seemed to be short-circuiting his brain. He managed to keep forgetting the reasons he was still single. And his intent to stay that way.

Maybe he'd just been waiting for the right woman...and his gut told him Lani might be that woman.

The interstate cut through rolling hills dotted with prickly pear and *cholla* cactus, *palo verde* trees and mesquite bushes.

Rick had traveled the route so often he usually took it for granted, but Lani's fascination for the desert was like a drink of water to a parched man. He enjoyed the way her eyes lit up, the way she absorbed everything Chuck told her.

An hour and a half later, they reached the Border Patrol checkpoint just north of Tombstone, and Rick rolled down the window to say howdy to a couple of agents he'd known for years.

"'Mornin' Sal. Don," Rick said.

Don Mitchell nodded, but stayed at his post to speak to the next vehicle coming up from Tombstone way.

"What the hell you been up to, Rick?" Sal sauntered over and clapped a hand on his shoulder. "'Bout time you get your lazy ass back to work." His gaze flicked to Lani. His black brows rose and his mustache twitched. "Excuse me, ma'am. Didn't see you."

"Sal, this is Lani Stanton, a reporter from San Francisco. Lani, this is Salvador Valenzuela, one of the most ornery agents there is. "

"Nice to meet you, Sal." She reached across Rick to shake Sal's hand. Rick's gut tightened as she leaned close, the soft curve of her breast brushing his shoulder.

Sal tipped his hat, and Rick scowled. He didn't particularly like the way Sal's dark eyes roamed over Lani.

After Sal and Chuck exchanged greetings, Rick asked, "What're you and Don doing at this CP today? Get transferred while I was gone?"

Sal shook his head. "No. Short-staffed. Talk about one hell of a mind-numbing day."

"Any new leads on *El Torero* while I've been gone?" Rick asked.

With a shrug, Sal said, "The man's a ghost. I'm beginning to think he doesn't exist."

Rick checked the side view mirror. "Car coming. We'd

better head on out."

The agent tipped his hat and ambled back to the checkpoint.

"Do they use that huge trailer to detain illegal immigrants?" Lani asked, finally addressing a question to Rick.

"No. The UDAs sit on the ground until we can ship 'em back to the border to process."

"What does UDA mean?"

"Our politically correct term for undocumented aliens, sometimes referred to as illegal aliens, or just illegals."

Lani's look went scholarly, and Rick felt pretty sure she was making notes in her head. The shift was almost imperceptible, from wide-eyed girl in a new place to sharp-as-nails reporter, doing her job. She'd probably be a bear in an interview, if she had a mind to eat her subject instead of stroke their egos.

Tombstone eased into view, rising off the desert floor like a mirage. Lani smiled and looked out the window, still giving off that combination business-pleasure attitude. "How did Tombstone get its name?"

"Well now, Missy, that there is an interesting story," Chuck piped up as they drove through the town. "A prospector fella named Ed Schieffelin discovered mighty rich veins of silver in 1877, in the Goose Flats area. That old boy named his first mining claim 'The Tombstone,' after soldiers told him the only thing he'd find in those hills was Apache Indians and his own tombstone.

"That there on our left," Chuck continued, "is the Boothill Graveyard. They named it that 'cause so many of the folks buried there died sudden-like or were killed with their boots still on."

Chuck launched into a story about the town's first mayor and the gunfight at the O.K. Corral.

"Fascinating," Lani murmured then looked back out the

window. "Is that all there is to it? I think I missed the rest of the town."

Rick chuckled and said, "If you blink you miss it. From the highway there's not a whole lot to see of 'The Town too Tough to Die.'" He pointed to the gentle swells of land. "When I was a boy, and Mom and Dad would drive through here, I used to imagine a dusty road replacing the highway, and wagons instead of cars. I'd picture gunslingers on horseback, plodding along the gritty trails, and prospectors mining for silver."

"It's so...empty," she said. "So open and free." Rick glanced at her as she stared out the window and drank in the landscape. "I can almost picture it. Take down those telephone poles, get rid of the asphalt, replace the soil that was blasted out to make room for the highway, and nix the occasional passing car, and I bet it looks much like it did a hundred years ago."

He smiled. So, she could see it. She did get a sense of how it was out here, half-old, half-new—just from this little car ride. Ms. Lani Stanton wasn't just a big city girl after all.

And he still couldn't believe his luck, getting to bring her home with him.

When they'd walked out of the hotel that morning, the first thing that struck Lani was how warm it was, even though it was still relatively early. The air had been thick and humid from the previous night's rain, but she enjoyed it over the freezing chill that greeted her every time she set foot outside her apartment in San Francisco.

"What do you think of the wild west?" Rick asked as they headed deeper into rural country.

"It's beautiful." Southwestern Arizona had a rugged magnificence she'd never imagined, that captivated her completely. No wonder settlers came out west to start a new life in places like this. The land had a way of calling to a person's soul and claiming it.

Clouds had built up around the mountains, but the sky in between was an endless cerulean blue. The final road they took was paved, but they had to cross several washes, some full of mud from flash floods.

Lani still couldn't believe that she was in a car with Rick, and that it was his house she would be staying at. Her attraction to him was staggering, but she kept reminding herself that men were men, and the memory of James was still way too fresh.

No more mistakes. And no mixing business with personal, either.

Her heart rate increased when they finally drove up a dirt road to a sprawling ranch home—an oasis in the desert, surrounded by enormous weeping willows, cottonwoods, and junipers. Nothing but ground hugging mesquite bushes and tumbleweeds survived for acres and acres outside the fenced-off yard, but inside the yard everything grew lush and green from the expansive front lawn to the extensive flower and vegetable gardens.

As they reached the ranch house, a black Rottweiler bounded toward the vehicle, followed by a grubby boy. He was just a little kid. Lani studied him with a reporter's eye, sizing him up at around eight or nine. Rick parked the SUV, and as soon as he opened the door, the boy launched himself at the man.

"Dad! I missed you!"

Dad? Oh, my god. Lani's jaw dropped. Rick was a father? He had a son?

But of course. How could she have missed the resemblance? There was no doubt that boy was Rick's, from the vibrant blue eyes to the chestnut hair, to the dimple in one cheek.

Damn it, Stanton. Don't go wide-eyed over a cute kid and a dog. And a cowboy hunk. You're a reporter. A professional. You can do this.

She grabbed her purse and laptop, and followed the others out of the vehicle.

As she stood beside the vehicle, the Rottweiler sniffed at her jeans and slobbered on her shoes.

Even the friggin' dog is cute. Damn, damn, damn…

"Trevor!" Rick gave the boy a fierce hug and set him back down on the ground. "I missed you too, kiddo. Did you behave?"

"Yup." The child nodded so hard his hair flopped into his eyes. Lani wanted to groan. "I did all my chores, and helped Grandma in the garden, fed the pigs, and found a rattlesnake, but I didn't get close to it, I ran and told Grandma and—"

"Slow down there, Pardner." Chuck crouched down, eye level with Trevor. "What's this about a rattler?"

The boy squirmed. "I found it this morning and told Grandma and she chopped its head off with a shovel, and she gave me the rattles. They're really long and so cool, you wanna see?" He grabbed his dad's hand and tried to pull him toward the house.

"Hold on," Rick said. "Trevor, this is Lani. She's the reporter who'll be staying with us."

The adorable little dynamo actually slowed down for a second and looked at her. "Whoa, you're a girl. We thought you were a boy. Isn't Lane a boy's name?"

Lani forgot about why she didn't want to love the child instantly, grinned and extended her hand. "It's nice to meet you, Trevor. My real name is Lani but I go by Lane E. for my work."

He gave her a gap-tooth smile and shook her hand, and she noticed he smelled of bubblegum and dog. He would easily be as handsome as his dad when he grew up. "You wanna see my snake rattle?"

Chuck patted Trevor on his shoulder. "Show Lani to the guest room, and then you can show her the rattle."

"Okay!" The boy grabbed her hand and started for the house, hauling her along like he probably hauled his dog around when the big brute was a puppy. "How old are you? I'm nine. Well, almost nine. My birthday is in three days on the fourth of July. It's summer, so we don't have school now. Grandma says that there's six more weeks until school starts and she can't wait, 'cause then she'll get some peace and quiet. She calls me Taz. She thinks I'm like the Tasmanian Devil. Ever heard of him? He's on Bugs Bunny. I watch it all the time on Cartoon Network."

Lani laughed out loud. "I'm twenty-five and I think Taz is a good nickname for you."

"My dad's old 'cause he's thirty-four now. But Grandma and Grandpa are lots older."

"Now what's this about your Grandma being old?" came a voice from the porch, then a youthful woman stepped through the screened door. She had the same blue eyes as Trevor and Rick, though her brown hair was graying at the temples.

"Grandma! This lady is Lani, the reporter who's staying with us. She's not a man, though, and she's twenty-five. I'm going to show her my snake rattle after I show her where the guest room is."

The woman clasped Lani's hand in a firm grip. "I'm Sadie Turner. I see you've met the welcoming committee."

Lani returned the woman's warm smile and thanked her for her hospitality. "You look much too young to be Rick's mother," she added, "and certainly not a Grandmother."

Sadie laughed, a genuine sound that made Lani feel comfortable at once. "I like you already. I'm plenty old enough, and have the battle scars to prove it."

Trevor nodded solemnly. "Grandma's real old, 'cause she's over fifty and Grandpa's really, really old 'cause he's older than that."

"Off with you now, and show Lani her room." Sadie gave

Trevor a playful swat on his behind. "And wash up. You're filthy."

"Okay." He pulled Lani through the screened-in porch, then the glass and oak double doors of the house, jabbering all the way. Lani could tell he would be the kind of kid who would wear a person out with his enthusiasm and chatter, but he'd already won a place in her heart.

The house was spacious with exposed beam ceilings and acres of unglazed *Saltillo* tile. The furnishings were southwestern and casual, the type of home where a person would immediately feel comfortable. Country western music played on a stereo in the family room, and they even passed a wood-burning stove that she assumed would work in the winter since the stovepipe climbed into the ceiling.

Trevor pulled her through a spotless kitchen that smelled of fresh-baked cinnamon rolls. They headed around a corner, then down a long hall and he stopped at the first room.

"This is the guest room. Dad's is that one right next to yours, and the one at the end of the hall is my mine. Grandma and Grandpa's room is way over on the other side of the house. Do you wanna see mine now?"

"Sure." Lani tried to calm the nervous flutter stirring in her belly at Trevor's words.

Rick's room, right here?

"I think he'll be a good chaperone, don't you?"

Rick's voice startled Lani, so close his breath tickled the back of her neck, and she caught his earthy scent. She whirled, sending her elbow into his hard stomach. "Oh! I'm sorry. No—no I take it back. You deserved that."

He rubbed his side. "It's dangerous startling you, darlin'."

"Next time you might not be so lucky, cowboy." She couldn't help but be mesmerized by those blue, blue eyes. She wanted to kiss him again, to taste him.

She shook her head, shaking the thoughts from her mind and turned away. "Hold on, Trevor, I'll take a look at your room once I put my bag and purse in here."

Antique furniture of a deep mahogany filled the guest room. Cream brocade with a rose design covered the bed, matching drapes hung at the windows, and a beautiful Victorian lamp perched on the nightstand. It looked like a picture-perfect room at a bed-and-breakfast. A four-poster bed occupied the far side of the room, and she plopped her belongings beside it.

Rick followed, set her two suitcases on the rose-colored throw rug as Lani turned to face him. For a moment neither of them moved. The tension in the room had just tripled and Lani wasn't sure what to do. Kiss him or kick him in the shin and make a run for it.

He winked then turned and headed back out the door. "Let's see that snake rattle, Trev."

After they checked out the snake rattle, Trevor grabbed Lani's hand and took her on a tour outside. Warmth stirred in Rick's gut as he observed Lani with his son. She listened to Trevor's non-stop jabbering and looked suitably impressed at everything he presented to her, including Roxie the Rottweiler, a dead June bug, and Rock, his pet turtle.

When Trevor dashed off to search for one of the barn cats, Lani grinned at Rick. "You have a wonderful son. So much energy and utterly honest."

"To a fault," Rick agreed. "The kid doesn't know how to lie—not yet anyhow. I wonder how charming you'll find him once you've been around his endless gab for awhile."

"He might wear me out, but I can tell he's one great kid. I've always loved children, and wanted to have at least a couple." Her voice went soft and her thoughts seemed far away. "But James insisted we weren't ready, and he worried that I would get fatter." She bit her lip and blushed, like she felt abashed, like she'd let something slip she hadn't intended to.

"Sounds like a stupid ass, this James. Because you're

perfect." He put his hand on her shoulder and looked into her sensual brown eyes. "I wouldn't want you any other way."

"Thanks." She shrugged away from his touch. "I'm not sure any man could truly love a woman as she is. I heard more than enough lies from James to convince me of that. Not to mention all the lies my father told my mother."

Rick caught her hand, bringing her eyes back to him. "I'm not lying, and I'm not James or your father." He squeezed her fingers. "They both sound like bastards."

Lani looked startled, then laughed. "That's them all right."

He dropped her hand before she could pull away, and they walked through Sadie's apple and peach orchard toward the barn. The air was completely still, a prelude to a monsoon storm. Thunderheads had built up all around, and it smelled of rain.

"How long have you lived here?" she asked.

"I grew up in this house." He sidestepped a watering hose and sprinkler head hidden in the grass and made sure Lani didn't stumble over it. "When I graduated high school, I moved to Tucson to attend the University of Arizona, then went into the Border Patrol Academy. After that, when I became an agent, I was stationed along the Texas border."

Lani ducked under the branch of an apple tree. "How did you end up back on the ranch?"

"When Trevor's mother died five years ago, I felt he needed his grandparents. So I managed to get a transfer here and we moved in with Mom and Chuck."

"I didn't mean to pry." Embarrassment flashed across her face.

He smiled and squeezed her shoulder. "You didn't."

"Dad Dad Dad Dad!" Trevor charged toward them. "Come see! Come on, come on!" He grabbed Rick's hand.

Trevor led the way, pulling his dad toward the barn.

"Wait 'til you see!" When they entered the dusty barn, Lani sneezed, and Trevor said, "Bless you. Come on now and see." He pulled Rick around the saddles and tack to a cardboard box in one corner. "Look, Barny had kittens. Lots of kittens. It took me a long time to find her, but I did and I counted five kittens, and one is orange like her and two are black and I think one is calico, and the other is white."

"Cute babies." Lani crouched next to the box and sneezed. "The mama cat is beautiful." Her eyes watered and she sneezed again.

"Those are some fine kittens, Trev." Rick stroked one of the rat-like things as the mama cat kept a watchful eye on him. "I think Lani is allergic to cats or the barn, so maybe we'd better scram."

"I'm—" She sneezed. "Fine. Really—" Sneeze. "I am." Sneeze.

With a laugh, Rick grabbed her hand and pulled her up. "Come on, Sneezy."

"Lani's like Aunt Callie. She always sneezes when she comes out to the barn, too. Come on and let's tell Grandma and Grandpa about the kittens." The boy charged out the door and headed back to the house.

"I don't think I've—" Lani sneezed. "Ever sneezed so many times in my life." Sneeze.

"Let's get you some allergy medicine." Rick nodded toward the house. "And I think I smell Mom's tacos. They're the best in the west."

Sure enough, tacos it was for dinner. It amazed Rick how comfortable Lani was with his family. After dinner, she insisted on helping clean up, and he joined her in washing and drying the dishes.

"I'm going to sleep like a baby," she said after Trevor was tucked in bed, and Sadie and Chuck had retired for the night. "Those allergy tablets are making me drowsy."

"I'll call it a night, too." Rick kicked off his boots at the front door, next to Trevor's. "Back to work tomorrow."

She walked ahead of him, then stopped before the door of the guest room, looking at him with those sensual brown eyes that made him burn. "There is a lock on this door, isn't there?"

He slid his hands into his front pockets and studied her face, remembering how soft she'd felt in his arms the night before. How delicious her lips had tasted. His voice was husky as he replied, "You'll be glad to know that I have the only key."

"Rick!" She narrowed her gaze and gave him a mock frown.

He chuckled and moved closer to her. "The door locks from the inside." A strand of her honeyed hair fell forward, and he brushed it behind her ear. "You have one hell of an effect on my self-control," he whispered, his lips nearing hers.

"Dad!" Trevor's voice shattered the quiet, and Lani jumped. The boy peeked around the corner of his room. "I can't sleep. Will you read me a story?"

Rick stepped back and nodded to his son. "Sure, kiddo."

"Goodnight Trevor," Lani said with a smile to him. She turned to Rick and blushed.

"Sweet dreams," Rick said.

"Ah, right." She closed the door. He heard the lock click and he grinned.

Chapter Four

ॐ

Emotions raged within Lani, holding her on the edge of sleep. She couldn't stop thinking of last night when Rick had kissed her. His earthy, enticing smell. Her fingers against his muscled chest, and his lips burning hers...so sensual. Everything about him was sensual.

Lani's eyelids fluttered. Rick's arms, holding her to him...the hammer of his heartbeat against her chest...wanting him, so much. Such warmth. Fire, burning her skin wherever his lips trailed. Her breasts aching beneath his slow and deliberate touch. Rick's mouth upon her nipples, his tongue swirling across one and then the other. His naked body pressed against hers, his arousal melting her resolve.

She surrendered, losing herself—

Lani woke with a start. She blinked away the sensual dream and stared up at the ceiling. Moonlight and shadows flickered and danced across the white surface and her heart pounded an uneven rhythm.

Losing myself. That's exactly what would happen if she surrendered to any man, and exactly why she couldn't allow it to happen with Rick.

And yet, how she wanted more of him.

Damn. Even her dreams betrayed her.

Rick's words whispered through her mind. *I'm not lying, and I'm not James or your father.*

"I can't believe I slept so late," Lani told Sadie as she sat at the breakfast table in the copper and verdigris kitchen. The aroma of baked bread and cinnamon met her nose, and her stomach growled. "It must have been those allergy pills."

"You probably needed it." Sadie handed Lani a glass of orange juice. "Nothing like country air to give you a good night's sleep."

"Thanks." Lani took a long drink then set the glass on the table. "Must be true. I don't think I've ever felt so relaxed. Where are Rick and Trevor?"

"Rick left early for work." Sadie grabbed a set of oven mitts, then pulled a shallow pan out of the oven.

A strange wave of disappointment flowed through Lani. Why should she care that Rick left before she could see him? She didn't need an adolescent obsession and she refused to think about him another second. Not one.

"Trevor's out feeding the pigs." Sadie set a pan on the stove and nodded toward the window. Lani could see sunshine warming a rose bed, and willow branches dancing in a breeze.

Sadie blew a strand of chestnut hair out of her face as she wrapped up a square of cooled coffee cake and added it to a growing stack. "Would you like some Polish coffee cake?"

"Absolutely." Lani's mouth watered as she breathed in the aroma. "It smells heavenly."

Sadie handed her a plate with a thick slice. As soon as Lani tasted it, she realized it was more than heavenly. Thin yeast bread with anise seeds baked in, then a cinnamon, sugar and butter topping crumbled on top, and another topping drizzled over that.

"It's to die for." Lani sighed around a mouthful of the treat. "I'm going to gain ten pounds just from the smell of your cooking."

Laughing, Sadie whisked off her apron. "I wouldn't worry about pounds around here. Lots of walking. Good for the body—and the mind and soul. What're your plans for today?"

"I'd like to start with interviewing you."

The woman plopped a wide-brimmed hat on her dark curls. "Just holler when you're ready. I'll be in the garden." She grabbed a metal bucket from the counter. "I'm dumping these scraps in the compost heap. Nothing goes to waste here, so don't throw away any leftovers."

"No danger of a crumb of it going to the compost." Lani smiled and rubbed her stomach. "Only problem is, it'll be going to my waist."

"I told you, no worry about your waist. You'll see how much exercise you get, just hanging around this place." Sadie laughed and headed out the back door with the scrap bucket.

Lani couldn't help but like Sadie, not to mention Chuck and Trevor. What a wonderful family Rick had.

Her heart gave a twinge. A family like she'd had before her parents and sister were taken away. A family like she could've had, if James loved anyone besides himself. If he'd been the person she'd thought he was.

A son like Trevor, energetic and bright—they might have built a tree house, or played soccer. He would have hugged her each night, after a bedtime story. *Mommy, I love you…*

Oh, enough! It was better that they had no children. The divorce would have been an even greater nightmare, and no son of James could have grown up healthy.

She decided to start with a shower, and in the bathroom, she discovered Rick's apple-scented shampoo and smiled. No wonder he smelled of apples.

While she washed her body she couldn't help but imagine what it would be like to have Rick soaping her…touching her. She slipped her hand between her thighs and slid her fingers into her folds as she imagined Rick would.

He was soaping every inch of her, paying close attention to her breasts and her mons. While the shower washed away the soap, Rick bent his head and sucked her nipples, first one, then the other. He was heedless of the water pouring on his dark hair, slipping his fingers into her folds and stroking her clit as he continued to pay close attention to her breasts.

Just when she was on the edge, the very edge, he backed away and handed her the soap. Her body was crying for release, but anxious to touch every inch of him. He smiled as he watched her lather the soap and then rub it through the light sprinkling of hair on his chest. Warm water pounded on her back while she worked her way down. She knelt before him and lathered his abs and his hips and then the dark hair around his cock. Her fingers trembled as she forced herself to move to his thighs and ignore what she wanted to touch most.

When she finished soaping him and started to rise, he cupped the back of her head and brought her mouth close to his erection. Willingly, she slipped her lips over the head of his cock, licking him and sucking him the way her friends said was the best way to give a man fellatio. She used her hand along with her mouth, enjoying the way he gripped her hair and the way he groaned as she sucked his cock.

Just as she felt him near that point where he was ready to climax, he drew her up and ordered her to change positions with him, to turn her back and place her hands against the tile. The ceramic was cold beneath her palms, but Rick was so hot against her backside. He leaned over her and palmed her breasts at the same moment he rubbed his cock against her ass. He slid two fingers into her hot core to find it slick, waiting for him.

Rick held his cock in one hand as he gripped her hip with his other. In the next instant he drove inside her and it was all she could do not to scream, it felt so good. Slowly he began thrusting in and out, driving her beyond all reason until she was so close to the edge that one more thrust pushed her over.

She cried out unable to hold it back any longer. Rick continued pumping in and out of her, drawing her orgasm out until he came, shooting his hot fluid into her.

Lani bit her lip to restrain her cry as she surfaced from her fantasy. Her fingers continued to work her clit and her body jerked with aftershocks until her legs trembled.

With a groan, she sagged against the cool tile behind her

as warm water sprayed down on her chest. If fantasizing about Rick gave her such great orgasms, she was in big trouble. How would she manage to keep her hands off him during her stay at the ranch?

She just had to keep in mind that she would only be here three weeks and she didn't do short-term relationships.

After showering, then dressing in jeans and a blouse, Lani tried not to think about Rick any longer and headed to the den. The country air certainly did relax her, as if there was no hurry in the world to get to work. That's probably what Theresa had in mind when she'd agreed to giving Lani the assignment.

With a sigh, she sank into a swivel chair in front of a roll-top desk. She slid on her glasses, then plugged her laptop into the phone jack and dialed her e-mail account. The only sound in the room was the ticking of the wagon-wheel shaped clock, and the click-clack of her laptop keys.

Outside chickens clucked and Rainbird sprinklers went *ch-ch-ch-ch*. A wave of memories washed over Lani. The lazy sound of the sprinklers took her back to her childhood, when she and her sister Naya would run through the water in their underwear. Lani could smell fresh-cut grass and feel water splashing her legs.

She rubbed the scar on her thigh as she stared out the window. How she missed Naya, and her mother. If only…

A chime came from Lani's laptop, indicating her e-mail account had come up, and she jerked her attention away from things that couldn't be changed. She wanted to shut down the computer as soon as she saw the hundred plus e-mails that had accumulated in the two days since she'd last checked. Several were responses on her recent feature on the former California governor, a couple were from friends, and two from her editor, and the rest were SPAM. She deleted all the unsolicited mail and responded to the rest.

After she finished her replies, Lani leaned back in the swivel chair and closed her eyes. Her thoughts turned back to

Rick. His was a powerful presence, yet he was so gentle with her. Definitely a man she could lose her heart to, and it would make it all the harder when it was time for her to head back home.

* * * * *

"They're not suffering, Rick," Don Mitchell said. "Just a bit of dehydration."

Rick nodded and wiped sweat from his forehead with the back of his hand. The merciless sun cooked the desert as agents rounded up a group of thirty-three undocumented aliens at the Ford Ranch, at the foot of the Mule Mountains. Men, women and children made up the miserable group, but they were too beaten by the heat to do more than crouch in the dust and wait to be processed.

Ford had reported the group when they stopped at his ranch for water. The rancher was a good man, and had allowed the UDAs to drink from his irrigation hose.

The stench of sweat and body odor was almost unbearable, and the heat only intensified the smell. It was obvious they'd been on a long and difficult journey, not uncommon for illegals trying to cross the U.S. border. Rick was not usually called in on a routine process, but one of the UDAs had claimed to have information on a key smuggler Rick was after.

In Spanish, Rick questioned Juan Dominguez, who'd insisted he knew the smuggler.

"Gordo," Juan said. He continued rattling in Spanglish, the border version of Spanish and English. The *coyotes* had left the UDAs to die, and Juan was angry. Gordo was the name the *coyotes* had called the smuggler. Juan gave Rick a description that matched what he knew of the man.

"Gordo," Rick muttered as he pushed his Stetson back and scratched his head. The name kept coming up, and in his gut he knew he was closer to tracking the bastard down.

Sal Valenzuela strode toward Don, looking like he was sweltering in his rough duty uniform. "The kid on the end says an old guy couldn't keep up and they had to leave him behind. I'll call it in."

Don Mitchell radioed for a transport van after he and Sal determined that all the members of the group were indeed UDAs, advised them of their administrative rights, and took down their biographical information.

The helicopter searched for the missing man. The agents finally located him where he'd crossed Sweetwater, the ranch of the former county sheriff John "Bull" Stevens. The UDA was evacuated to Douglas Hospital, but he died from dehydration during the flight.

"Damn *polleros*," Rick cursed to Sal and Don. He tossed his hat into his truck as they got ready to leave the ranch.

"To hell and back," Don replied. "Those *coyotes* deserve to die in the desert, instead of the people they leave stranded."

Sal nodded.

Rick rubbed his hands over his face, trying to wipe away some of the exhaustion and frustration. "Only getting worse."

With a shrug, Don walked back toward the group of UDAs. "The *coyotes* run people and drugs. Both are profitable enough to be worth the risk."

"Need any help here before I take off?" Rick asked.

"We've got it handled," Sal replied.

"I've got to head on home." Rick climbed into his truck, lowered the window, and slammed the door.

"How long is that pretty gal staying with you?" Sal's dark eyes gleamed.

The possessive feeling that grabbed Rick surprised him. "Not long enough." He buzzed up the window, his friend's low whistle fading as the glass rose.

* * * * *

After Lani settled at the dining room table for their interview, Sadie stretched a block of fabric across a hoop. "I hope you don't mind if I quilt while we talk."

"Not at all." Lani pulled her recorder out of her bag and set it on the table's surface.

She admired the furnishings, including an oak china cabinet filled with crystal glasses, goblets and decanters. It surprised her to see crystal on a ranch, one of her many preconceived notions of life in the country to be shattered since meeting Rick's family.

Margarita glasses caught her attention. Heat rushed through her at the memory of what her last margarita had led to. How could she be thinking of that in front of his Mother?

Lani shoved thoughts of Rick from her mind, praying his mother wouldn't notice the flush in her cheeks. She ran her hand over a quilt block, admiring Sadie's work.

"Incredible." Lani traced one of the circles designed with small blocks of cloth. "I love the materials you've chosen and the way the rings loop together."

"You're sweet." Sadie slipped on a pair of half-glasses, adjusted the hoop, slid a thimble on one finger, and started stitching. "It's a wedding ring quilt, and the materials are hand-dyed."

Lani picked up a corner. "The circles do look like wedding rings intertwined."

"I've been working on it for years, off and on. I keep hoping Rick will find a young lady he wants to settle down with, so that I can give the quilt to him and his bride as a wedding gift." She glanced up and smiled. "There's been no shortage of women who've been interested in Rick. He's just never fallen in love with anyone."

Lani snatched her hand away like it had been scalded. An image of Rick's kiss came to mind and a furious blush engulfed her to the soles of her feet.

"Can you tell me about your ranch?" she asked, trying to

keep her voice steady as she steered the conversation to safer ground.

Sadie quilted with deft strokes as she spoke. "Since Rick had no interest in going into the business, Chuck sold off all the commercial cattle a couple of years ago when we retired. We keep enough livestock for personal use, and raise most of our own vegetables and fruit."

Lani shifted her notebook. "Do immigrants travel through your land?"

"We're fortunate that illegals don't cross our property as often as they cross the MacLeod's, or the Grand's." Sadie adjusted her glasses and continued stitching. "And oh, heavens. Then there's the Mitchell's ranch—why, Don estimates five hundred or more go through their back pasture every night. Like a highway. Kitty put bars on her back window 'cause she's worried for her granddaughter."

She sighed and shook her head. "That's why Kev Grand bought himself a shotgun. Shoots up in the air, just to scare them. That, I don't agree with."

"By MacLeod are you referring to Trace?" Lani asked.

"One and the same gal who arranged for you to stay here." Sadie nodded. "Although she's Trace Lawless now. Married a fine man, a DEA agent with a rough edge that more than earns that Lawless name. And Dee, she married Jake Reynolds who's with Customs, but she goes by Dee MacLeod Reynolds."

Lani smiled. "Trace is a terrific friend, and I'm so thrilled for her and her sister."

"Trace off and moved to Texas with Jess, but she gets back every now and again," Sadie said.

"Yeah, that's what she told me in her last e-mail." Lani twirled her pencil. "She hopes to make it here for a visit before I leave."

Sadie clipped a loose thread and started to rethread her needle. "Do you have any more questions?"

"A few." Lani glanced at her notes again. "Do you come in contact with these people—the UDAs—often?"

"The illegals we get, most of them just want water," Sadie said. "Not too long ago, we discovered a hole cut into our fence beside a water trough. Rather than reaching over the fence to get water, they cut right through the wire."

"Sweetwater Ranch has sustained the most damage that I know of." Sadie adjusted the quilting hoop in her lap. "Bull—that's John Stevens, who owns Sweetwater—lost thousands of dollars in cattle when *coyotes* tore down his fence to run illegals through."

Lani frowned and stopped taking notes. "*Coyotes?*"

"The smugglers, also called *los polleros*, who are paid to sneak illegal immigrants into the U.S."

Lani tapped her pencil on her notepad, her thoughts whirling. "What do you do when illegals stop by?"

Sadie glanced over the rims of her glasses. "We call the Border Patrol and give them water."

Lani looked at the dog at her feet and smiled at the large sad-eyed Rottweiler. "I'm sure Roxie is a good watchdog."

"Nothing like a Rottweiler to keep folks at a distance." Sadie chuckled. "'Course she'd as likely slobber all over your shoes than bite you, but we'll keep that to ourselves."

Lani and Sadie talked for about an hour longer. Sadie explained how deep passions ran among people when it came to the subject of illegal immigrants, no matter which side of the issue the person might be on.

"When does Rick get home?" Lani asked when they finished the interview. He'd been gone since at least six a.m., and it was closing in on a full twelve hours from the time he'd left the house until this moment.

"Anytime now." Sadie glanced out the front window. "Looks like he's here."

A low thrill invaded Lani's belly, and when Rick walked

through the door, her senses ran sky high. His presence filled the room, and the tired smile he gave her made her knees quiver.

"Mom. Lani." Rick hung his Stetson on the hat rack, then kicked off his boots and left them beside the front door. He wore a faded blue shirt over a black T-shirt, and snug jeans.

"Shower?" Sadie asked as he strode by.

"Uh-huh." Rick walked past, straight for the laundry room.

"He usually won't say two words after work until he's had his shower." Sadie began folding her quilt and packing it away. "At least on days when he's detained illegals."

"Why is that?" Lani asked.

Rick stepped out of the laundry room, his shirt off, and he was removing a black vest. Her skin chilled as she realized it was a bulletproof vest—it had never occurred to her that Rick would ever be in that kind of danger.

"I come in contact with hundreds of people a day from all over the third world." He walked to an oak cabinet and opened one of the doors with a key. "Due to the conditions of their trip, who knows what viruses or diseases they could be carrying. I've seen HIV, HEP, Plague, Malaria, Typhoid, Cholera, TB…you name it."

Lani checked to make sure her recorder was running, forcing herself to take her eyes off Rick's muscular chest and the dark triangle of hair that ran into the waistband of his jeans. "That's something that never occurred to me," she said, her eyes drawn back to him.

He withdrew his gun from a holster at his back and placed the weapon in the cabinet, followed by a small canister, then locked the cabinet. "In Douglas, a few agents a year contract TB at work and someone always ends up sick. The last thing I want to do is bring anything home to my family."

"I see." Lani chanced a glance at his face. "Why aren't you wearing the green uniform that Border Patrol agents usually wear?"

He gripped the back of a chair and eyed her with that intense blue stare of his. "I work intelligence, so I wear civilian clothing. It's easier to obtain information when I don't look like law enforcement."

"Ah." She struggled to think of something to say, her brain seeming to have gone on vacation with him standing so close. Half-naked at that. "I-uh, I'll have to pin you down for an interview."

He winked. "Darlin', you can pin me down any time."

A hot flush seared Lani, and with Rick's mother sitting next to her, she could think of no suitable reply.

"Time to finish dinner." Sadie chuckled and slid her glasses into a case as she stood. She settled her quilting materials into a corner and headed into the kitchen.

Lani pushed back her chair. "I'll help."

Her gaze followed Rick as he headed into the laundry room, noticing the powerful lines of his naked back. With a mental shake, she followed Sadie into the kitchen, trying not to think about how good Rick looked without his shirt on. Trying not to imagine what it would feel like to run her palms over his chest and down, down the flat of his hard stomach, down—

Lani! She clenched her hands and took a deep breath. *Enough of that.*

"What can I do to help you?" Lani asked Sadie.

"Why don't you peel the potatoes?" Sadie gestured toward several brown-skinned potatoes on the countertop, and then reached up in a cabinet filled with jars of spices. "Now where is the oregano…"

Lani heard the washing machine start as she grabbed the potato peeler off the counter. She almost dropped it when Rick walked through the kitchen clad only in his underwear. He winked at her, but didn't pause and went straight to the bathroom.

He had one of the most gorgeous male bodies she'd ever seen. Hard, muscular thighs and calves. Powerful arms, and definitely a tight ass she could just bite.

Lani blushed, realizing that Rick's mom was right behind her. If Sadie hadn't been there, she probably would have stood with her mouth hanging open.

A while longer.

Chapter Five

ॐ

During dinner Rick sat beside Lani. The family chattered and laughed, but Lani could scarcely think with the hair on his forearm tickling her arm every time he moved. He pressed his leg to hers beneath the table, and even when she shifted in her seat he still managed to brush up against her.

She was so turned on by the brief contact she could only pray that no one would notice her rigid nipples beneath her blouse. It was almost a relief when dinner was over and she could escape his constant presence.

After they all helped Sadie clean off the table and straighten the kitchen, Trevor grabbed Rick's hand and tugged him toward the back door. "Come on, Dad. Let's show Lani my hideout."

"You game?" Rick asked, looking at Lani in a way that made her heart skip a beat.

She smiled and shrugged. "Sure. I'd love to see your hideout, Trevor."

"All right!" The boy snatched her hand and pulled her and Rick out the door.

She laughed and looked over Trevor's head at Rick. "You have quite the dynamo here."

"You have no idea." Rick's dimple appeared when he smiled, and her stomach flip-flopped.

The boy's hand felt small and warm in Lani's as he dragged them through Sadie's orchard and into the windbreak. The late afternoon sun hung just above the mountains and the air smelled of cut grass and marigolds. A breeze cooled her cheeks and leaves crunched underfoot as they walked through cottonwood, eucalyptus, and juniper trees.

When they reached a grassy area, Trevor pointed to a muddy pool of water. "That's Grandma's duck pond." It smelled of moss and algae, and the sounds of quacking ducks filled the clearing. "Don't they sound like they're telling secrets? That's what Grandma always says. And look, there's Momma duck and her babies."

Lani smiled. "I bet Momma duck is chatting about how adorable her babies are." They halted as the duck family waddled in front of them, about a dozen fuzzy ducklings trailing the mother.

"Come on." Trevor pulled Lani's hand and led her further into the windbreak. "Here it is!" he announced when they came upon a playhouse painted in cheerful primary colors. "My dad made it for me when I was five and he painted it in my favorite colors. It's on the ground 'cause the trees around here aren't big enough to build it up high, so it's not a tree house, it's a ground house, but I call it my hideout."

The yellow house stood about five feet tall, had a green chimney, scarlet door, and bright blue trim around the windows and eaves. It was perfect for a kid to have loads of adventures in.

"The craftsmanship is beautiful." Lani glanced at Rick. "Your father must be talented with his hands."

The second she said it, a hot flush swept over her, and it was all she could do to not clap her hand over her mouth. Instead she studied the playhouse, trying to regain her composure.

Rick chuckled and leaned close. "Why, thank you, darlin'."

"Come inside!" Trevor dodged through the door. "I want to show you all my stuff."

Lani followed, doing her best to ignore Rick. No easy feat considering the effect his presence had on her erratic pulse.

The playhouse was snug, but the three of them managed to squeeze inside and sit on the green floor. She scooted beside the child-sized table and chairs, and she was sure Rick made a point to press as close to her as possible.

The warmth of his skin seared her as his arm rubbed against hers, and his jeans were rough against her bare thigh. His masculine scent surrounded her. She considered telling him to move away, but she was afraid her voice would betray the wanton feelings he stirred inside her.

"This is a great place to hide, so that's why I call it my hideout." Trevor pushed open blue shutters and pointed out the window. "You can see the driveway from here and the front door, but no one can see us. So if I want to be a spy, I can check out things from here." He dug in a toy chest under the window, tossing out toys left and right. An orange ball bounced across the room and action figures clattered to the floor. "I have these old binoc—binoco—how do you say it, Dad?"

"Binoculars."

"Oh, yeah, binoculars. Anyway, I can see really far with these. Grandpa gave them to me. I've got all kinds of spy stuff. Dad said that if something ever happens and I need to find a hiding place, to come here and he'll know where I am."

Lani captured the orange ball with one hand as it rolled across the floor. "Do you play out here a lot?"

Trevor nodded, his brown hair flopping into his eyes. He swiped the hair away with his grubby hand. "Mostly when Grandma says her ears need a break."

Lani giggled and Rick grinned. He said, "Why don't we show Lani around the ranch?"

"Sure!" Trevor started to head out the door.

"Hold on, Pardner," Rick said. "Aren't you forgetting something?"

Trevor turned back. "What?"

"Your toys."

"Do I have tooooo?" the boy whined.

"Yes."

With a sigh, Trevor scooped up all his toys and tossed them into the box, the crash loud enough to bring the roof down. He whirled and scampered out the door and vanished into the windbreak.

Lani pitched the orange ball into the toy box and went next, wondering where Trevor had disappeared to.

As she went through the little doorway on her hands and knees, she felt Rick's gaze on her backside. She didn't know what got into her, but she paused for a moment, her knees wide. She imagined Rick's palm on her ass, a slow rub that made Lani want to moan. Heat burned her and she scrambled out into the trees.

After Rick crawled out, he shut the door and stretched his limbs. His muscles rippled beneath his snug T-shirt, and she couldn't help but remember how good he had looked earlier, clad only in briefs.

Trevor came crashing through the windbreak, grabbed Lani's hand, bringing her attention back to the boy. "Dad, let's show her the plane."

"Plane?" She heard the nervousness in her own voice as she glanced at Rick.

He shrugged. "I told you, I'm a pilot. I have a twin-engine Cessna."

"And it's really, really cool!" Trevor pulled her arm. She forced herself to go with him through the trees until she saw the small craft sitting on the dirt landing strip.

Lani stopped abruptly and Trevor almost fell backwards. "It's, uh, nice." As she grabbed the boy's shoulders and steadied him, her heart pounded and she felt blood drain from her face. She swallowed, trying to force the lump out of her throat. "Ah...anything else you want to show me? Your grandma's garden?"

Trevor pulled her hand. "I'll show you the inside of the

plane."

Panic gripped her. "Oh. Well, I—"

"Trevor!" Sadie's cry came from the house. The woman had a mild easygoing manner about her, but could she ever yell.

Rick watched Lani as he patted his son's shoulder. "Better see what Grandma wants."

Trevor frowned and put his hands on his hips. "But, Dad. I wanna show Lani the plane."

"Go." Rick's tone was one that meant he didn't expect any further argument. "You know your grandma doesn't like it when you don't answer right away."

"Trevor!" Sadie called again.

"But, Dad!"

"Now."

"All right," the boy grumbled and took off for the house.

Rick studied Lani for a moment before he said, "You like small planes less than commercial airlines."

"Far less." She smoothed a strand of hair behind her ear and tried to stop her hands from trembling. She turned her back to the plane and gestured toward the house. "Why don't you show me something else?"

"Want to talk about it?" His voice was calm. Grounding. And she almost wished she could tell him.

She shook her head and started walking through the windbreak. "No."

His eyes were dark, concerned. "All right."

Gradually, her tense muscles relaxed as he took her on a tour of the ranch. The farther she got from the plane, the easier it became. He showed her Sadie's greenhouse and garden, then the henhouse and corrals. Lani laughed when she saw Trevor's family of potbellied pigs, and at the antics of Sadie's baby Alpine goats.

When it was dusk, they strolled back toward the house. "Enjoying your stay?" Rick asked, watching her with hooded eyes.

"Very much." She smiled and nodded. "It's wonderful here."

"Have dinner with me." His voice was low and husky, sending shivers down her spine. "We'll head into town to a nice little restaurant I know. Just you and me."

A fluttering sensation gathered in her belly and she struggled to calm it. She took a deep breath of clean evening air and said, "I—I don't know."

They halted in front of the house, just outside the porch. Light poured through the windows and teased the gold in Rick's chestnut hair. An overwhelming urge came over her, to run her fingers within that thick hair, to press close against his hard body and kiss him like the world was on fire. Like there was no tomorrow, only today. Only the two of them.

Rick trailed his finger down her arm and she gasped at the sensual contact. "It's just dinner, Lani."

She stepped back, away from his disturbing touch. "I'll think about it." She forced herself to turn from him, and hurried into the house.

Even as she left him outside, she wondered why she couldn't just let go and spend some time with this man.

What's wrong with me?

Why don't I just go for it?

And the answer came to her clear as day.

She didn't want to lose her heart, and with Rick, that was something that would be only too easy to do.

* * * * *

Lani tucked her glasses into their case, then rubbed the bridge of her nose. Her temples throbbed from spending the afternoon transcribing notes from her interview with Chuck.

Since her deadline was a couple of weeks off, she had time yet to start writing the feature.

She closed her eyes and relaxed in the study's leather chair. Against her will, her thoughts wandered to yesterday evening, when Rick had suggested they go to dinner. Alone.

No matter how much she tried to tell herself it would be a mistake, she couldn't help wondering what it would be like to be with him. That one kiss she'd shared with Rick had unraveled her more than any amount of intimacy she'd shared with James.

With James it hadn't been making love, it had just been sex, and she'd never enjoyed it. He'd called her a cold fish. Told her she was terrible in bed. She'd never known what to do, and with him it was over before it started. No foreplay. No cuddling. Just James relieving his needs.

She'd thought that was all there was to sex until Theresa and her friend Calinda had started in on the topic one day at lunch. Lani started wondering if she'd been missing something. Perhaps James had been not only a sorry excuse for a husband, but a poor sexual partner as well.

Why did she believe it would be any different with Rick?

Well, let's see. The way he'd kissed her, as though he wanted to taste her everywhere. The way he touched her, and how careful and protective he was with her. The way that he looked at her, like she was the only woman on Earth. The way he made her feel, like a fire burned deep within her soul—an ache, a need that only he could fill…

And she could imagine him filling her in every possible way.

With a shiver and a sigh, Lani opened her eyes and looked out the window. It was a beautiful day, and she was tired of being cooped up. She stood and stretched her stiff limbs, then wandered out of the study and into the kitchen. Delicious smells filled the room, apparently coming from a pan of ground beef simmering on the stovetop, next to a pot of bubbling red sauce.

"Need help?" Lani asked when she saw Rick's mom at the counter shredding a head of lettuce.

"You betcha. You grate the cheese." Sadie pointed to a block of cheese on the counter as she scooped lettuce into a colander. "I'm making a batch of enchiladas for the Frontier Homemakers' dance and potluck tonight."

After Lani washed and dried her hands, she started grating cheese onto the plate Sadie provided. "Sounds like fun."

Sadie took a bunch of green onions and chopped them into small pieces on a wooden cutting board. "I was hoping you might like to join us."

Lani glanced up from the growing mound of cheese. "I don't know how to dance to country western."

"Nothing to it." Sadie shrugged and scraped onions into a small bowl. "If Rick's not too tired after work, I'm sure he wouldn't mind showing you how to two-step."

Heat warmed Lani's face at the thought of dancing with Rick. "I wouldn't want to impose." She finished her task and set down the grater. "What else can I do to help?"

"Would you mind chopping these?" Sadie handed Lani two plump tomatoes. "And nonsense about imposing. I'm sure Rick would enjoy it. He's quite good."

"I'm sure he is," Lani murmured as she took the knife and cutting board Sadie handed her.

Sadie scooted an enormous baking dish onto the counter. "Besides, you'll have a chance to meet some folks you'll be interviewing."

"True." Lani nodded as she sliced one of the tomatoes. Who knew, she might enjoy herself. An image of Rick holding her close flashed in her mind, and her hands trembled. The knife slipped and she barely avoided cutting her thumb.

She needed to get her mind off Rick or she'd end up

slicing off a finger.

But before she could think better of it, Lani asked, "Does Rick usually go?"

"When I can convince him." Sadie began filling and rolling tortillas and placing them into the pan. "He tends to shy away from these things."

Lani gave an inward sigh. Why did she feel such a keen sense of disappointment to learn that Rick might not go to the dance? Wasn't that what she wanted? To keep her distance from him?

Yes. It was for the best. She couldn't allow herself to trust so easily and to want so much so soon. Especially a man who continually invaded her thoughts and made her feel like she was melting inside every time he looked at her. She was only there for three weeks and then she would be gone.

And Rick would be out of her life forever.

Why did that thought make her feel so hollow?

After debating over whether to wear a skirt or slacks, Lani opted for a new pair of jeans and a silky blouse in shell pink.

Her stomach clenched at the thought of Rick asking her to dance with him—if he went. She could almost feel the warmth of his body close to hers, his arms wrapped around her, his lips brushing her ear…

For goodness sake! She was acting like she was in high school again, getting ready to attend one of the functions where boys lined one wall and girls grouped together against the other. Memories of her younger sister's first school dance abruptly came to Lani. She closed her eyes, remembering how pretty Naya had looked in her indigo dress. How her brown eyes had sparkled and how nervous she'd been the first time a boy asked her to dance.

Lani had been fiercely protective of her younger sister and had refused to let Naya out of her sight that night. But in the end, just a couple of years later, Lani hadn't been able to protect her. She hadn't been able to do anything to prevent her sister from dying.

Wiping away a tear, Lani forced the thoughts from her mind. It didn't do any good to dwell on the past. No good at all.

While she jerked a brush through her hair, she studied her reflection in the mirror. She couldn't help but see herself as James did, remembering all the times he told her how fat she was.

Stop it! She took a deep breath and tried to relax. Funny that he used to tell her she was beautiful before they were married. But how quickly things changed, and how controlling he'd become. She'd been stupid. Naïve.

She slammed the brush down on the bureau and clenched her fists. *Get a grip.* She'd finally come to her senses and ditched the jerk. Taking several deep breaths, she cleared her mind of all unwanted memories.

The only problem was that the image that filled her mind next was of Rick walking through the house in his underwear yesterday. God, but he was good to look at. Not to mention good to taste.

With a groan, she touched up her makeup, going to a little extra effort on her appearance. At the last minute, she decided to paint her toenails bright pink with quick-drying enamel polish. When she finished, she tucked her blouse in her jeans, slid on a pair of sandals and headed to the kitchen.

"Well aren't you a purdy sight," Chuck said when she entered the room.

Lani smiled, enjoying his country charm. "You're quite the dashing gentleman."

"Hey, Lani." Trevor whirled into the room. His hair was combed and parted on the side, and he wore jeans and a western shirt. "Are you going with us?"

"Yes, sir." She put her hand on his shoulder and smiled. "You're so handsome. Will you save a dance for me?"

"Okay." Trevor bounced on his toes and turned to his grandma. "Is it time to leave? Bobby Torres is coming and I wanna show him my snake rattle. I've got it in my pocket."

"We're ready." Sadie picked up the foil-covered pan of enchiladas. "Chuck, will you take this out to the car?"

"Sure thing, sweetheart." He kissed Sadie and took the pan.

Sadie grabbed a pen and notepad off the counter and scrawled a quick note, then laid it on the table. "I'm letting Rick know where we'll be. Who knows if he'll remember about the dance tonight. Since he's late, it's possible he'll be too tired."

Lani just nodded. What difference did it make to her if Rick showed up at the dance or not?

They all piled out of Sadie's SUV after they drove the two miles to the clubhouse. It was early evening and lights were blazing through the windows, the dirt and gravel parking lot filled with vehicles. The clubhouse wasn't much to look at from outside—a long, narrow building that must have been at least fifty years old and had the scars to prove it. Scraggly trees grew behind the clubhouse, and if Lani wasn't mistaken, there were "hers" and "his" outhouses in the back.

She hid a smile as she followed the Turners up the concrete steps to the clubhouse. Country western music blared into the night, along with laughter and conversation. As they walked into the building, everyone they passed greeted Sadie and Chuck, and Lani's head spun with the names of all the people she was introduced to. The clubhouse smelled of fried chicken, sawdust and sweat. Couples danced on the sawdust covered hardwood floor, people were laughing, talking and eating, and children dodged underfoot. In the corner a band was set up with a couple of bales of hay around them, for atmosphere, she supposed.

"This is Sal, a Border Patrol Agent and friend of Rick's," Sadie said when the dark-haired man walked up to them. "Sal, this is Lani, the reporter who's staying with us."

"Hello, Sal." Lani had to raise her voice to be heard over the toe-tapping song the band was playing.

"*Buenos Noches.*" His mustache curved upward as he squeezed her hand.

Lani turned to Sadie and explained how they'd met at the Border Patrol checkpoint outside of Tombstone. The song ended, and the band started another tune. "Would you care to dance?" Sal asked Lani.

Her cheeks grew hot. "Ah—"

"Get on out there." Sadie chuckled and ushered them toward the dance floor. "I'm gonna make sure Chuck set the enchiladas on the buffet table. I wouldn't be surprised if that man decided to keep the whole pan for himself."

Lani's gaze darted from Sal to the dance floor and back. "I, ah, don't know how…"

"It's easy enough." Fine lines at the corners of Sal's eyes crinkled and his mustache twitched as he guided her onto the floor.

Sal turned out to be an excellent teacher, and didn't seem to mind Lani stepping on his boots at least half a dozen times. Soon she was getting the hang of it and actually enjoying herself. Every now and then, though, she couldn't help but glance at the door, wondering if Rick would show.

When they stopped to drink some punch, Lani was asked to dance by a man who was chewing on a toothpick. Before she knew what was happening, she was swept onto the dance floor again.

John Stevens introduced himself as they danced around the room. A pleasant-looking man, he was built like a bulldozer, had hazel eyes, a slight receding hairline and long sideburns.

He leaned close and said over the music, "I hear you're staying with the Turners."

Lani smiled and tilted her head, trying to avoid getting jabbed by the toothpick. "Sadie mentioned you. Don't you own a ranch by the name of Sweet..."

"Sweetwater." He drew her out of the way of a couple twirling into their path.

"I'm interviewing ranchers about the illegal immigrant situation. Would you be free to chat with me?"

A flicker of something passed across his features, but it was too brief for Lani to get a feel for what it might be. He shrugged and said, "You're welcome to come on out to Sweetwater any time. Just give me a heads-up."

By the time she finally made her escape to grab something cold to drink, Lani had danced with a few men after John Stevens, as well as once with Trevor. Her face was warm, droplets of sweat trickled between her breasts, and the backs of her heels surely had blisters.

Sal eased up to her as she ladled punch into her cup. "All danced out?"

Lani laughed and sipped her punch. "I haven't had this much fun in ages."

She agreed to one more dance, but when he led her to the floor, she realized the band was playing a slow tune. A twinge of nervousness gripped her stomach. It had been fine dancing to fast numbers, but being too close to any man made her uncomfortable.

Any man but Rick, her thoughts amended, and then she immediately chastised herself. What was with that man, that she couldn't get him out of her head?

Fortunately, Sal held her at a respectable distance, one hand on her shoulder and one at her waist, with plenty of room between them. "I'm surprised Rick isn't here," Sal said as they moved across the floor.

Lani shrugged, pretending it didn't matter. "Apparently he had to work late. He's probably too tired, anyway."

Sal winked. "I'd bet next month's paycheck that nothing

would stop him from coming, just knowing you're here."

Blushing, she shook her head.

Tingles erupted at the base of Lani's neck. She cut her gaze to the doorway and caught her breath. Rick had his shoulder against the doorframe, his arms folded across his chest. His blue eyes were focused on her, his expression unreadable. He looked so good, dressed all in black from his western shirt and jeans to his boots and cowboy hat.

Good enough to eat. *Whole.*

Sal leaned close, and she forced herself to turn away to hear what he'd said. When she glanced back to the doorway, Rick was gone.

Chapter Six

&

Fire simmered in Rick's gut. He clenched his jaw as he watched Lani dancing with Sal, her face flushed and her eyes bright. Watched her smile and blush at something Sal said. She was obviously enjoying being with him. She'd barely been giving Rick the time of day, yet there she was, dancing too damn close to his friend.

He'd studied Lani a while before she noticed him, and then their eyes locked. Until Sal said something in her ear.

Even though Rick knew he wasn't thinking clearly, at that moment he would've liked nothing better than to smash his fist into Sal's jaw. With grim determination, he tossed his Stetson onto a hat rack, then moved through the dancers until he was behind Sal. Lani was looking to the doorway, where he'd been standing.

He touched Sal's shoulder, trying to not look like he was ready to kill him. His friend looked up and with a nod, let Rick cut in. Lani turned her gaze back from the door just as Rick replaced Sal, and her jaw dropped.

"Rick," she said, her eyes wide.

"May I cut in?" he murmured, studying those incredible dark brown eyes. "Or do you prefer Sal's company?"

"No. I mean yes." Lani shook her head and turned a pretty shade of pink. "Yes, I would like to dance with you, and no I don't prefer Sal's company."

"Good." He smiled and eased his hands around her waist. "I'd hate to be out here all alone."

The song ended, but they remained at the center of the floor as a mellow tune began. Rick drew Lani to him, her head under his chin, her body close to his.

She pulled away enough that she could look up at him. "I don't know if this is a good idea." Her voice was low and trembling.

"Trust me." Rick leaned close to whisper in her ear. "It's a great idea."

She remained stiff in his embrace as they moved in time with the music, but gradually she relaxed, her head against his chest, his arms secure around her. He drank in the scent of her, reveled in the feel of her soft body against his. The swell of her breasts against his chest, the curve of her waist beneath his hands. Her hips and thighs were so close to his he was all but making love to her on the dance floor.

Well, hell. Damn if he wasn't getting rock-hard just dancing with her. He muttered another curse under his breath and eased away from her as the song ended and the band stopped to take a break.

"Did you say something?" she asked as they parted.

He took a deep breath and willed his body to behave. "Would you like a cold one?"

She nodded, her honey-blonde hair brushing her shoulders.

Rick put his hand to her elbow and guided her to the buffet tables. "Looks like the folks are getting ready to leave with Trevor." He inclined his head toward where his parents stood talking to Stan and Marnie Torres, and their son Bobby. Sadie was holding her empty enchilada tray and Trevor was showing Bobby his snake rattle.

"Would you like to stay?" Rick asked, hoping she'd say yes. "I'll drive you home."

Lani glanced at him for a second before looking away. Was that fear mingled with desire in her eyes? "I should be getting back with everyone else."

"Why?" Rick tilted his head and gave Lani that sexy smile that made her toes curl and her insides melt into pools of liquid silver. "Afraid of being alone with me?" His tone was low and husky.

Lani sighed. "Yes. I am."

"Don't be." He took her hand, his incredible blue eyes looking at her like they were the only people who existed. "I'll be the perfect gentleman."

"I know. But..." Her heart pounded as she glanced toward his parents. "It's late."

He squeezed her hand, sending shivers throughout her body. "The dance won't last much longer. I promise to take you right home."

"Are you two staying?" Sadie asked as she came up behind them.

Lani jumped and snatched her hand away from Rick, and was sure she managed to turn ten shades of red for the umpteenth time.

"I was just convincing Lani to stay," Rick said, never taking his eyes from Lani.

Lani glanced from Sadie to Rick. "Maybe a little longer," she replied, despite her misgivings. "But not too long. I—I'm worn out from all this dancing."

"Wonderful." Sadie patted Lani's arm and smiled. "We'll leave the light on."

"Thanks," Lani murmured as Rick laced his fingers with hers and led her to the buffet.

He released her to ladle punch into a plastic cup and then handed it to her. She accepted it, her hand trembling a little as she swallowed the drink that tasted of pineapples and sherbet. When she finished, he tossed their cups into the garbage, then led her onto the dance floor.

A song with a fast beat was playing, and she said, "I just learned to dance to country western tonight, so I'll probably stomp on your toes a few times."

He smiled and slid his arm around her waist. "You can

step on my toes all you want."

"Stomp." Lani gave a mischievous grin as they started to two-step. "I figure I owe you."

Rick chuckled. "Thanks for the warning."

By the time they'd danced to a couple of songs, she was relaxed and enjoying herself. Rick was an excellent dancer and teacher, even better than Sal, and she managed to only stomp on his boots two or three times.

At the end of one particularly fast number that she'd had a hard time learning, Lani was laughing so hard she stepped on Rick's foot and she almost fell. He caught her and slid his arms around her waist. Her laughter died in her throat as the lights dimmed and a slow tune started, and she saw the look in Rick's eyes. So intense. Burning with desire. For her.

She tried to back away, but he held her tight. "I—I'm all sweaty, Rick."

"So am I." He moved his lips to her ear and murmured, "Just relax and enjoy the dance."

Lani nodded, the top of her head brushing his chin. She allowed him to hold her snug against him and rested her head against his chest. Rick felt solid and warm, his masculine scent so earthy, so potent to her senses.

His breath feathered her hair as her body merged with his and the heat of his body burned through her blouse. Her nipples ached as they brushed against his chest and a low thrill settled between the junction of her thighs.

If she wasn't mistaken, he was very attracted to her, judging by his erection against her hip. Heat rose in her cheeks and she was glad he couldn't see her face. Despite his obvious desire, she didn't feel threatened. Deep within she knew he wouldn't push her. He could have the one time they'd kissed—but he'd been the one to back away.

When the song ended, Rick lifted his head and lightly caressed her shoulders. "Ready to head on home?"

"Yes." Lani let him take her hand and he linked his

fingers with hers and smiled.

He plucked his cowboy hat off the hat rack as they left. A single light illuminated the small parking lot as he led her to his truck. Gravel crunched underfoot and music from the clubhouse filled the night. He opened the passenger door and helped Lani in, then closed the door behind her before getting in on his side and starting the vehicle.

Lani studied Rick in the amber glow of the dashboard lights as they headed back to the ranch. She was fascinated by the strength of his arms as he drove, the dark hair curling from his wrist along his forearm. His masculine profile, his strong jaw.

Yearning curled in Lani's belly. It was more than lust. It was the desire to be wanted, needed and loved.

No. She knew better than to start thinking that way.

Warmth crept over her when he caught her watching him. "I had a great time," she said, her voice slightly husky.

He reached across the seat to squeeze her hand, his touch electrifying her.

Releasing Lani's hand to take the wheel, he brought his attention back to the road and the short drive to the Turner Ranch. When they drove up to the house, Roxie bounded out to the driveway. Rick parked the truck and Lani climbed out, only to be waylaid by the Rottweiler snuffling her greeting over the seat of her pants.

"Gee, thanks," Lani muttered. "Just what these jeans needed. Dog slobbers."

With a soft laugh, Rick came up beside her and leaned down to scratch the dog behind her ears. "Roxie's a regular slobber monster."

Rick took Lani's hand before she could get away from him, and they walked hand in hand to the front door. He stopped beside the screen door, leaned against a pillar, and brought Lani into his embrace. "You drive me crazy, woman."

She relaxed for a moment and then looked up at him.

"I'm only going to be here a few weeks."

He didn't bother to answer. Instead he lowered his face, slow enough that she could turn away if she didn't want what he was offering.

"Rick," she whispered before he kissed the corner of her mouth and she sighed. He lightly nipped at her lower lip and she gave a little moan. She smelled of honeysuckle and her own unique woman's scent and he wanted her so badly now it was all he could do to rein himself in.

He slipped his tongue into her mouth and she readily took him. He enjoyed Lani's sweet taste mixed with the pineapple flavor of the sherbet punch she'd had before they left the dance. She leaned into him, her arms gripping his biceps like she was hanging on for dear life.

Damn but he wanted to palm her firm breasts, to suck them into hard peaks while he slid between her thighs. How could he keep his hands off her, as badly as he wanted her?

Lani suddenly pulled away, her lips parted and moist from his kiss, her eyes glittering in the dim light. "I can't do this, Rick," she said as she released him and backed away.

He hooked his thumbs in the belt loops of his Wrangler jeans. "Do what, Lani? Kiss?"

Even in the near darkness he could see a dark flush staining her cheeks. "A casual relationship. I'm just not a casual kind of gal."

"And I'm not a casual kinda guy." Rick tried to step toward Lani but she stepped back. "All right, darlin'. First things first. Let's get to be friends and see if it takes us anywhere. Is that fair?"

"Friends." Lani raked her hair away from her face. "O-okay."

Rick held the screen door open. "Have you thought about dinner with me?"

"No." Avoiding his eyes, she ducked past him and entered the house.

He shut the door carefully, keeping it from slamming. "Why not?"

Lani watched Rick kick off his boots and toss his hat onto the rack. "It's not a good idea."

"You keep saying that." He caught her hand and pulled her to him. "But I haven't heard a single good reason. We can go as friends."

Lani studied her pink-painted toenails, struggling to calm her raging desires. She had to remember why she couldn't develop a relationship with him.

He lifted her chin with his finger, forcing her to look into his azure eyes. "What does it take to cross your border, Lani?"

With a slight shiver, she stepped back and pulled her hand away from him. "This border is closed. Indefinitely."

Rick smiled and gazed at her with a look that turned her heart inside out. "I can wait."

* * * * *

Douglas had seen its better days, at least three decades ago. Memories from Rick's childhood flickered through his mind like a series of postcards as he sauntered toward the place that had once been the town's only drugstore.

The building had changed—hell, the whole town had changed—since those times he'd perched next to his father at the drugstore counter, drinking a malted milkshake. Every Saturday when he was a kid it'd been their routine, when the man who fathered him was still around.

Smoke and sour beer filled his nostrils as he stepped into the dim recesses of Mario's Cantina, the drugstore-turned-bar. He waited for his eyes to adjust, and forced himself to focus on the upcoming meeting with Jorge Juarez, a flighty contact he'd been developing.

The seedy tavern/discothèque bore no resemblance to that sunny milkshake bar of Rick's childhood. Bright red and chrome chairs had been replaced by black vinyl bar stools, cracked with neglect and pitted by cigarette burns. It was mid-afternoon, and the only denizens were a couple of habitual barflies he recognized from previous visits, who crouched on stools and nursed beers.

Rick slid into a corner booth where he could keep an eye on the front door, yet remain close enough to the bar's back room, so that he could slip out the rear door if necessary. He laid one hand on the scarred tabletop, the waxy buildup under his palm a good indication the surface hadn't received a decent scrubbing in a long time.

The waitress was new, younger than the woman who normally worked the day shift. With a practiced eye for detail, he sized her up in one glance—young and accustomed to using her body to get what she wanted.

Not much over five feet, she wore a tight blouse, unbuttoned just far enough to expose the tops of her full breasts. Her skirt stopped at her upper thighs and hugged her hips so high that little was left to the imagination. Black hair flowed to the middle of her back, and she'd applied her makeup with a heavy hand. If Rick didn't know better, if he hadn't noticed the fine lines at the corners of her eyes and mouth, he would've wondered if the woman was old enough to be employed in the bar.

She tossed her hair back and stood with one hand on her hip and her breasts pushed forward. "A drink?"

He nodded. "Give me a beer."

Within a couple of minutes, the waitress returned with a hefty mug and slid it in front of him, her rows of gold bracelets clattering as she moved. She stood so close, he could smell the cheap perfume she wore. "You are alone?"

"Yeah." With his drink in his left hand, Rick leaned back in the seat and felt his gun dig into his lower back. Out of habit, he kept his right hand close to his hip, within reach of the weapon concealed beneath an unbuttoned denim shirt that he wore over his T-shirt.

"Mari!" a man shouted from the back room.

The woman called Mari scowled but managed to brush one hip against Rick as she turned away. Amusement flickered within him at the not-so-subtle message.

His thoughts turned to Lani and he smiled. Damn, but she'd felt good in his arms when they'd danced. Too bad he'd had to work so late last night before dropping by the clubhouse. He would've liked nothing better than to have been with her the whole evening. She was fighting it, but he knew she was attracted to him. He could see it in her eyes, and the way she watched him when she didn't think he was looking.

He glanced at his watch, and just as he wondered if his contact would show, Juarez slunk in through the open door.

With a nervous glance around the bar, the slight man hurried to Rick's booth.

"Juarez." Rick took a sip of his beer.

The man answered in Spanish, his black gaze darting around the room. "This is too dangerous. I could be killed."

"Tell me what you know," Rick replied in the same language, keeping his voice level and never taking his eyes off his informant. The man owed him too much to back out now.

Juarez shifted in his seat. "The smuggler is someone who has long been known in this town. I do not yet know his name, but I am afraid. I've heard too many stories of how he deals with those who cross him."

"What do you know?" Rick repeated as he saw Sal Valenzuela and Don Mitchell walk into the cantina. Neither man did more than glance in Rick's direction before taking seats at a table in the far corner of the bar. Both knew better than to acknowledge Rick and take the chance of disrupting his work.

Juarez licked his lips. "This man. He owns a business and has many friends. Few enemies because no one knows what he truly is." He clenched his fist, and his dark features contorted, but he kept his voice low. "A monster who cares little if the people he smuggles die. Like they are nothing more than animal skins to lay upon the floor and trample."

Rick gripped the handle of his still full beer mug. "I can't bring back Maria, but I can bring this scum to justice. What else have you got?"

"One of the *coyotes* called him *El Torero*," Jorge whispered. "The matador, a killer. I am very afraid, *amigo*."

"What else?"

"*Nada*."

The tap of heels on the scored linoleum alerted Rick to Mari's return. Before Rick could thank him, Juarez slipped out the front door to vanish into the hot summer afternoon.

Mari stopped at Rick's booth and pressed her pelvis to the edge of the table. "Do you need anything else?" The brazen look in her eyes told him exactly what she meant.

He stood, towering over the petite woman. "No thanks." He dropped a ten on the table and headed out the door.

Later that evening, when Rick arrived home, he was disappointed to find Lani wasn't back from her interview. He hadn't realized how much he'd been looking forward to seeing her.

When he climbed into the shower, he ran it as hot as possible, cleaning the day's grime from his body. All he could think of was Lani. That kiss the night they met and then the one after the dance. The flames that raged beneath her skin and set him on fire.

He had to switch the water from hot to cold. That or take care of business in the shower. Again.

After he'd gotten it about as cold as he could take, he finished up then toweled off. His thoughts never strayed from Lani, and his cock was standing at attention as he squared off in front of the mirror to comb his hair. He was buck naked when the door opened and Lani walked into the bathroom.

She froze, her gaze riveted below his waist and the erection he still had from thinking about her. Her eyes shot up to his face and she turned a deep shade of crimson.

Rick raised an eyebrow, and tried to hide a grin.

"Oh, my god," Lani said with a horrified expression. "I— I'm so sorry." She backed out the door and shut it behind her, and then he heard her own door close across the hall.

Rick dressed in clean jeans and a T-shirt, and felt a whole lot better—not to mention a whole lot more turned on after Lani had walked in on him. He was still smiling when he walked into the kitchen and saw Lani at the table. She had her gold-rimmed glasses on that managed to make her look even sexier.

He hitched one shoulder up against the door frame and just watched her as she scribbled notes into a notebook. A strand of golden hair fell across her forehead and her lips were pursed as she concentrated. Her nipples were hard beneath her pink blouse and he wondered if she was thinking about seeing him naked.

"Rick." She glanced up from her notebook and turned red again. "I'm sorry. I didn't hear the shower and I expected it to be locked if it was occupied."

He gave her a lazy smile, taking in her curves and sensual lips. "No problem."

"Another tough day?" She seemed desperate to change the subject.

"Yeah, but it's been getting better by the minute." He winked.

Biting her lip, she grabbed her notebook and recorder from the table and pushed back her chair to stand. "Do you have time for our interview?"

"I always have time for you, darlin'." Rick moved away from the wall and stepped so close to Lani that she had to look up to see his face.

She placed her hands on her hips and narrowed her velvety brown eyes as if she was angry. "Listen, cowboy. You'd better behave." But he saw the warmth and humor that warred with her desire to keep him at a distance.

"Come on outside, and I'll show you Mom's goldfish pond." He jerked his head toward the front door. "We can sit in the swing, and you can ask whatever you'd like."

She hesitated, then nodded. In comfortable silence, they walked through the house and out the front doors, and then the short distance to the pond.

The sky was overcast and the air was muggy and warm, the sun just settling above the Mule Mountains. Cattails and flowers sprouted from Sadie's pond, and lily pads floated on the surface. Rick and Lani stopped before the small waterfall that tumbled into the pond, and water splashed over their shoes.

Lani knelt beside the pond. "I didn't know goldfish grew to be that large."

Rick squatted next to her and pointed to an almost translucent fish speckled with bluish-black. "That one and the black with gold stripes are Japanese koi."

"This is all gorgeous." She took a deep breath and sighed. "I love it here on the ranch. So relaxing and peaceful. What a difference from living in the city."

With his head cocked to one side, Rick studied her. All he could think of was how much he'd wanted her from the time he caught her watching him in the Chinese restaurant. This wasn't a woman to simply enjoy sex with. This was a woman to spend a lifetime with.

"Think a city girl like you could get used to living in the country?" he asked.

"Who knows." Lani seemed oblivious to the desire that burned beneath his words, beneath his skin. She shrugged and stood. "I've only been here a few days, but I think I could easily fall in love with this part of the world. Though I'd probably miss shopping in the Embarcadero and going to the wharf for clam chowder and sourdough bread." She ran her tongue along her lower lip, and it was all he could do to keep from leaning over and kissing her.

Rick more than liked the thought of Lani staying in Arizona. "Thinking about moving away from Frisco?"

Lani didn't answer for a moment, as if deciding how much she should say. "Before I left, I considered moving to Tucson, but I wasn't sure if I would like Arizona. Now that I'm here, I know I would, and I'm ready for a change. When I finish this feature, I plan to interview with *Tucson Today Magazine*."

With a sigh, she turned to Rick. "Now about my questions for you…"

"Why don't we sit in the swing and you can fire away?" He hooked his thumbs in his belt loops, forcing himself to keep his hands off Lani. He'd probably only scare her off, and that was the last thing he wanted.

She glanced to the swing and back to Rick.

He smiled. "I promise I don't bite."

Chapter Seven

❧

"I know for a fact you do bite," Lani retorted, then heat crept up her face as she remembered his kisses and how he'd nipped at her lower lip.

"Got me there." With a chuckle, Rick eased his big frame into the swing that was wide enough for three grown adults. "How about I promise I won't bite…for now?"

She tried to glare at him, but the mischievous glint in his eyes disarmed her.

His face grew serious as she settled into the cushioned swing. "I can tell you about the Border Patrol, and some of what we do, but due to the nature of my job you can't use my name."

"Do you mind if I ask why?"

"I work in intelligence," he replied. "A lot of what I do is classified."

She nodded. "I understand."

Rick stretched out his long legs. "I can put you in touch with Miguel Martinez, Special Operations Supervisor. You can talk to him on the record."

"Thanks." Lani turned on her recorder. "What did you do today?"

"Among other things, tracking and cutting sign," Rick replied.

Lani adjusted her glasses as she glanced at him. "Can you explain?"

"A trail begins when we locate sign of people crossing the desert. We usually start our search along roads the Border Patrol maintains."

"What types of sign?"

"Sign can be footprints, a scrap of clothing, or garbage that's been discarded."

Lani scrawled a note on her pad of paper. "How do you maintain the roads?"

"By pulling tires behind the vehicle. That makes a relatively smooth surface to enable us to easily see footprints. Even if the UDAs try to eliminate their sign by walking backwards, or by using other methods, we can usually determine where they've crossed."

"When you locate sign, how do you know how old it is?"

Rick raked his hand through his thick hair. "By a variety of factors. We look to see what effect the weather may have had on the tracks, such as raindrops and wind. If it's been awhile, detail will diminish. We can even tell if the UDAs are walking in daylight or after dark."

Lani glanced from the note she'd written on her pad. "How on earth would you do that?"

"If the tracks head up to a bush, even though the person could've walked around it, more than likely they were walking at night."

She chewed the end of her pencil, staring at her notes. "Any other methods?"

"Animal tracks assist in aging the trail. Most desert animals move around at night, so if we find animal sign on the trail at five o'clock in the afternoon, it may not be fresh."

"What happens once you find a trail?"

"We have to describe it to other trackers who haven't seen it." He shifted and put his arm on the back of the seat. "Rather than relaying several types over the radio, we locate the most distinct tracks and describe them. Other agents work ahead to find the trail on roads that intersect the path. If an agent picks up the trail, he'll attempt to match the sign described by the agent who originally cut the sign. We continue until we catch the UDAs, or until we can't follow the tracks any longer."

She paused while she made a note. "How large are groups that come across the border?"

"These days twenty to thirty UDAs at a time is normal."

For quite a while, Rick continued answering Lani's questions, giving her a better idea of what the Border Patrol was about.

Somehow the interview itself faded away, and they moved on to other topics. He shared information with her about the southwest and his family, and she chatted about her job and living in San Francisco. She was amazed at how easy it was to talk with Rick, and how much she enjoyed his company.

A door slammed and then Trevor tore around the corner of the house, waving a piece of paper. "Lani Lani Lani!" he yelled, then skidded to a stop. "Look what I drew."

She smiled and caught the paper Trevor thrust in her lap.

"It's a picture of you and Dad that I drew all by myself. Do you like it?" He hopped up and down on one foot, blue eyes flashing and brown hair flying in time with his movements. "Do you, do you?"

With one finger Lani traced the crayon figures, surprised at the detail the almost-nine-year-old had drawn. In the picture, Rick wore a blue shirt and jeans, with Lani in pink, and they stood side-by-side. "It's wonderful." She looked from the drawing to the boy. "You're very talented."

Trevor grinned from ear to ear. "You really like it?"

"Love it."

Rick reached for the picture. "Let me see, Son." He studied it with the seriousness of a true connoisseur. "A fine work of art."

"I drew it for Lani. I can make you one too, Dad."

"When you do, I'll hang it on my wall." Rick wrapped his arms around Trevor and brought his son onto his lap.

After giving his dad a quick hug, Trevor wriggled free.

Wild Borders

"Can we get everything ready for tomorrow?"

Rick nodded and ruffled his son's hair. "Sure, Trev."

A lump formed in Lani's throat as she observed the affection between father and son.

"We're going fishing for my birthday." Trevor jumped up and down like a jack-in-the-box on an overdose of caffeine. "Wanna come? It'd be so cool if you'd go with us. Please?"

She glanced at Rick and then back to Trevor. "Sure, if it's okay with everyone else."

"Fine by me," Rick said.

"All right!" Trevor spun in circles, and Lani wondered how he managed to maintain his balance. "That's so cool. I'm gonna go tell Grandma to pack a lunch for three."

As the boy dashed away, Lani's stomach flipped. "Sadie and Chuck aren't going?"

Rick gave her his slow, sensual smile that sent tingles from her head to her toes. "Mom and Chuck have friends from out of town visiting for the day, so it'll just be the three of us."

"Oh." She tried to sound casual, to not let on that the prospect of spending the day with Rick, without Sadie and Chuck around, made her more than a little nervous.

"We'll have Trevor to chaperone, if you're worried about us being alone," he said as he studied her.

"I'm not worried." She shook her head. "But will I be interfering? Did you intend for tomorrow to be a father/son day?"

He smiled, his eyes warm and welcoming. "You're not interfering. Trevor wants you to come and so do I."

"Thanks." She took a deep breath and smiled in return. "It sounds like fun."

Rick stood and looked down at her. "It's about time for dinner. You coming?"

"Sadie made lasagna." Lani shut off her recorder, grabbed her notepad and got to her feet. "Can your mother ever cook."

109

"You've got that right." Rick patted his stomach. "I might have to start counting calories like my sister."

"Ha. You don't have an ounce of fat anywhere on your body," Lani retorted.

He chuckled. "I guess you'd know that now, wouldn't you?"

"Oh, god." She hid her face with her notepad, trying to cover her furious blush. "That wasn't what I meant, and you know it."

But yes, she knew for a fact that Rick was solid muscle. Everywhere.

"Great dinner, Mom," Rick said after he took the last bite of his third helping of lasagna.

He couldn't help watching Lani's lips as she wiped her mouth with a cloth napkin. "It was wonderful," she agreed. "And I loved the spicy dressing you made for the tossed salad."

"Glad you liked it," Sadie replied just as the telephone rang. "I'll get the phone." She pushed back her chair, and left the room.

"How long will you be staying here, Lani?" Trevor asked.

She gave Rick's son a warm smile. "My flight is scheduled to leave the eighteenth."

Trevor took a drink of his apple juice, slurping it through a straw. Then he asked, "How many days is that?"

"A little over two weeks away," Lani replied.

"Oh." The boy cocked his head. "That's not very long, is it?"

She stood and started gathering dirty dishes to take to the sink. "Fifteen days."

"Rick." His mother appeared in the doorway holding the phone. "It's your sister."

"All right." Rick stood, took the phone from Sadie, and headed into the study. "Hi, Sis."

"Hey there, big bro," Callie replied. "So, Mom tells me there's a woman staying with you all at the ranch."

Knowing what was coming next, he stared at the ceiling. "Yeah."

"Mom says Lani is intelligent, attractive and nice, and Trevor really likes her."

He rolled his eyes. "Uh-huh."

"And Mom says you have the hots for this woman."

Well, hell. Rick shook his head. "Can't believe everything you hear."

Callie giggled and he could picture her impish grin. "Mr. Confirmed Bachelor is having second thoughts, isn't he?"

Rick glanced through the door and saw Lani talking with Trevor. He liked how she crouched down to his son's level so that they were eye-to-eye when they talked, and she focused on him like he was the only person in the room.

"Don't get carried away," he said.

"Ha!" Callie laughed, and then lowered her voice as if someone might overhear. "So, tell me, have you laid one on her yet? A big ol' smack?"

"Never kiss and tell," Rick said, still watching Lani talking with Trevor. "Did you just want to bug me or do you have anything else to say?"

"Nah, just wanted to gloat." Callie chuckled. "Gotta get the twins to bed. Give Trevor a kiss for me, and love to Dad."

After he said his goodbyes and sent his love to his niece and nephew, Rick punched the off button and set the phone into its cradle. He sauntered into the kitchen to where Lani was chatting with Trevor. She was sitting in a chair now, her back to Rick.

"Yeah, Dad takes me fishing lots," Trevor was saying. "He always does stuff with me, like playing catch, and games and trucks."

Rick stood behind Lani, breathing in her intoxicating scent. He wanted to run his hands in her honey-blonde hair, to feel the silken strands sliding through his fingers.

She stiffened and turned to look up at him. "Rick."

"Don't let me interrupt." He grabbed the back of Lani's chair and leaned forward. He sensed the tension in her as if his presence unnerved her.

Trevor flipped his hair out of his eyes. "I was telling Lani what a cool dad you are and how you're always doing stuff with me. You're lots cooler than Bobbie's dad."

"Is that so?" Rick released the chair and walked around Lani to ruffle his son's hair. He could feel the difference in Lani as soon as he moved, as audible as a sigh.

"Yup." Trevor gave an enthusiastic nod.

Rick crouched beside his son. "I was just on the phone with your Aunt Callie. She said to give you a big ol' smack on the cheek for her."

Trevor screwed up his face. "Ewwwww!"

Rick laughed. "How about a bear hug? And we'll just tell her that I gave you a kiss."

"Okay." Trevor threw his arms around his dad and squeezed him tight.

God, being hugged by his son was one of the greatest feelings on earth. Trevor smelled of dirt, sweat and dog, and Rick couldn't imagine anything better.

When Trevor pulled away, Rick said, "It's bedtime and we need to get up early to go fishing. You'd better take your bath and brush your teeth. And don't forget to wash your face."

Trevor groaned and pouted. "Ah, Daaaaaaad. I wanna play a video game."

"No." Rick stood and forced himself to look stern. "In the bathroom. Pronto."

"But—"

"Now."

Trevor glared at Rick and stomped off to the bathroom, and shut the door. Hard.

Smiling, Lani got to her feet. "I'd better get to bed before I get into trouble."

He caught her wrist and pulled her close to him. "If you're not good, I might have to turn you over my knee."

"Just try it, cowboy," Lani murmured, but her cheeks turned red and he was sure she was imagining him following through with his threat.

Damn, she's cute.

He chuckled as she dodged past him and escaped into her room.

* * * * *

"Dad Dad Dad Dad!" Trevor's voice shattered Rick's sleep. "Wake up, Dad. It's my birthday. Wake uuuuup!"

Rick pretended to remain asleep as Trevor shook him. Finally, he opened one eye. "Son, are you sure today's your birthday? I could swear—"

"Daaaad. It's July fourth, my birthday, and you promised to take me to the lake today, remember?" Trevor jumped on the bed and bounced on Rick's chest, the boy's brown hair flying in all directions. "Come onnnn, Dad. Get uuuuup!"

Rick glanced at the clock. "It's barely five. Don't you think that's a little early? Why don't we just go back to bed?"

Trevor rolled his eyes and bounced on his dad. "Come on, come on, come on. You promised to take me fishing. You promised."

"Oh, yeah?" Rick tickled Trevor in his most ticklish spots until the boy squealed with laughter, flopping around like a fish out of water.

Trevor squirmed out of Rick's reach, tumbled off the bed and shot out the door. "Lani Lani Lani Laaaaiiiiinnnnneeeee! It's time to go fishing." He opened her door and darted in.

Rick raised an eyebrow. After the first night, he figured she'd kept her door locked to keep him out. Not that he'd invite himself in. She'd have to do the inviting.

"Happy Birthday." Lani's sleepy voice came from her room, and then Trevor was pulling her through the door. Rick saw she wore the same pink T-shirt and boxers he'd seen her in at the hotel.

"'Mornin'," Rick said, noting all her sensual curves that the clothes couldn't hide.

"Too early to tell." She ruffled Trevor's hair. "Hey, Taz, how about a shower first?"

"You look great. Just go like that. Come on!"

Rick caressed her with his gaze. "You look beautiful."

Lani blushed, and Trevor said, "How come you're turning all red?"

"Never mind. Give me ten minutes to shower." Lani ducked back into her room.

Once everyone was ready and the truck loaded, the trio headed to Parker Lake in the Huachuca Mountains, the sun barely rising over the horizon. The night before, Sadie had packed a picnic basket brimming with ham and cheese sandwiches for Lani and Rick, peanut butter and jelly for Trevor, and thick slices of her Polish coffee cake. Rick had loaded the fishing poles and tackle. They made good time, and when they arrived, found they had the lake to themselves for a while.

After they'd caught a stringer full of fish, and Trevor had broken his line for the third time, Rick sat down to re-string the line. Lani settled next to him on the picnic blanket and wrapped her arms around her bare knees.

Pink. She always wears pink, and it suits her, he thought. She wore a button-up shirt and blue shorts, showing off her long legs. A thick scar ran along her upper thigh, partially hidden by her shorts.

She inhaled and turned her face to the sky. "Mmmm, it smells wonderful out here. I love the fragrance of pine and fresh mountain air."

He forced himself to look away to check on his son, who was busy skipping stones across the lake, surely scaring all the fish away. But what the heck. The kid was having fun and it was his birthday.

Trevor was a strong swimmer, and he knew the rules about not entering the lake without an adult, but Rick didn't want to take chances. He started re-stringing Trevor's line, glancing at the boy every now and then as he and Lani talked.

"You've done a wonderful job as a single dad," Lani said as she watched his son.

"He's one hell of a kid." Rick smiled. "I've always worried about him not having a mom around, but he seems to be doing great."

"That must have been difficult, to lose somebody you loved when you were so young." Her voice was soft and thoughtful.

Rick didn't know what possessed him. He never discussed Lorraine, but talking with Lani was easy. Natural.

He shrugged and said, "It was sad, but sadder yet that it was her own damn fault. She was drunk and almost took other lives along with her."

Lani put her hand on his arm, concern in her eyes. "You don't have to tell me this."

"It's all right." Rick took a deep breath and rubbed at his neck, releasing tension in his muscles. "Thank god, Trevor and those other folks lived. It's a real shame Lorraine died, but what's done is done."

"I'm so sorry." Lani squeezed Rick's arm, and to his

surprise, he could see tears glittering in her eyes. His throat tightened, and he regretted spilling his guts.

"There's nothing to be sorry for," he said softly. "I have Trevor, and he means the world to me."

He decided he'd better change the subject. "Have you gone fishing before?"

"Years and years ago."

Rick glanced from Trevor to Lani and saw a haunted look in her eyes.

"With my sister, mother and even my father." Her voice was as distant as her gaze. "We loved to go."

"Where do your folks live now?"

Lani was silent, and then she said, "They all died six years ago." Her voice caught. "I keep thinking I'll get over it, but not a day goes by that I don't miss Mother and Naya. That I…that I don't wonder why I survived the plane crash, and they didn't. Why wasn't it me instead of them?"

"I'm sorry, honey." Rick set the fishing pole down, put his arm around Lani and brought her close, holding her head against his chest. Ice chilled his veins at the thought of her being in such a tragic accident, and the knowledge that she could've died.

As he stroked her hair, he breathed in her scent of honeysuckle and sunshine, and felt her tears through his shirt. He watched Trevor as he rocked Lani, thankful that his son had survived the collision that had taken Lorraine, but wishing Lani's family had been as fortunate as his son.

"Oh, Rick. I'm sorry for crying all over you." She tried to pull away, but he held onto her, and she relaxed against him again.

It all made sense. "That's why you're afraid to fly."

Words spilled from her lips in a rush, like she was exorcising her demons. "Especially small planes. I'll never go in one again. The charter we'd taken on a sightseeing tour lost power and slammed onto the runway. I—I can still smell the smoke...and feel the flames...and hear the screams."

She turned her tear-streaked face to Rick. "I still don't understand why they died, and I lived. Why I walked away with only this scar." She rubbed her leg as if trying to scrub away the memories of the accident.

He kissed her forehead and glanced at his son playing at the water's edge. "You were meant to survive. Like Trevor. I'm sure your family would want you to live. To get on with your life."

"I know you're right, but it's so hard." She was quiet, as if searching through her feelings, trying to understand the reality she had to face when everything was over.

When she finally spoke, her voice was soft and full of regret. "That's why I fell into a relationship with James. Why he fooled me so well." She sighed and shook her head. "I put up with his abuse for so long because I was too devastated to lose again. In truth I was stupid not to realize that leaving James would the best thing I could do to get on with living."

Rick hooked a finger under her chin, and wiped away her tears with the heel of one hand. "You're not stupid, Lani. You're intelligent and beautiful. It sounds like this bastard took advantage of you at a fragile time in your life. And if I meet the SOB, I'd like to make him pay."

The corner of her mouth twitched. "I can just picture you, dressed in white and riding to my rescue."

"I wear mostly black." Rick gave a gentle smile. But that smile faded as he searched her eyes and the next question came to his lips. "Did he hit you?"

Lani stiffened and looked away. "James punched with words. He knew exactly how to rip me to shreds without laying a finger on me." A shuddering sigh rolled over her. "He attempted to control every aspect of my life. I was an idiot to not come to my senses sooner."

It was an effort for Rick to control the anger burning him.

He swore under his breath and pulled her closer. "So help me, that bastard better never stray across my path."

"Why did I just tell you my life story?" She drew away and met his gaze. "Why do I trust you?"

He brushed his lips across her hair, breathing her scent. So beautiful, so sensual, so sweet.

"What do you want from me?" Lani's voice trembled, saying more than her words, telling him of her fear of loss and betrayal. Her fear of repeating past mistakes.

Rick ran his thumb over her forearm, to the inside of her elbow and back, feeling the softness of her skin against his calluses. "What do I want from you? Nothing. Everything. Whatever you'll give me."

Chapter Eight

ᔓ

Lani caught her breath as his words gripped her heart.

Nothing. Everything. Whatever you'll give me.

Trevor darted up from the lake. "Is my pole fixed, Dad? I want to catch more fish!"

Rick squeezed her hand, sending dangerous sensations through her belly. With movements as fluid and graceful as a mountain lion, he scooped up Trevor's fishing pole and stood. "Hold your horses, kiddo."

The moment Rick left, Lani felt alone. Like a part of her was missing. His scent had been so intoxicating, his touch so sensual, surrounding her with his masculinity. She'd bared her soul, and just by telling him, felt lighter, as though she truly were alive again.

But did she dare trust him with her heart?

As she watched Rick with Trevor, she couldn't believe that voice inside her that said all men were like James and her father. She couldn't believe Rick would intentionally hurt anyone.

She watched as Rick cast Trevor's line then worked with his son with such patience. Why did she feel like she could talk to him so easily? Perhaps it was the day. The intimacy of spending time together with just the three of them. Yet they'd probably spent a good hour chatting yesterday, long after the interview had ended.

While he settled Trevor on a log to wait for fish to nibble, she took the opportunity to study Rick. His denim shirt accented his vivid blue eyes, and when he laughed at something his son said, that adorable dimple appeared in his cheek. Jeans molded his muscular thighs, and even though he was a big man, tall and muscled, his movements were as fluid as a mountain lion.

And those hands. Strong, large. She thought of the texture of his skin against hers, how it felt when he'd held her face in his hands and kissed her, his calluses rough against her cheeks.

Lani glanced from Rick's hands to his face and froze. He was watching her with the same hunger in his eyes that must have been apparent in hers. Yearning curled in her abdomen like molten fire, and for endless seconds, she couldn't tear her gaze from his. Then a fish tugged on Trevor's line, and Rick turned back to his son.

God help her, but she wanted him. Needed him.

It took all her effort to stop staring at Rick. She fought to compose herself, gazing out at the midnight blue of the lake, listening to the soft lap of the water against the shore. His husky voice washed over her as he spoke to Trevor in a low, even tone. The boy's answering voice, so high and sweet, took hold of her heart, never to let go.

With her eyes closed, she focused on the wind whispering through pine and juniper trees, and drank deep of the scents of rich loam and pine. The breeze caressed her face, as soft as Rick's touch, and she ached for him, wanting his fingers sliding over her skin.

Lani opened her eyes, forced the thoughts away, and scooted to her feet in an abrupt movement. After brushing stray pine needles from the seat of her shorts, she strolled to the edge of the lake just as Rick helped Trevor reel in a fish.

"It's a big one, Lani!" The boy hopped along the water's edge while Rick added the fish to the stringer. "It's really, really big. It almost pulled me in! It's a catfish. Do you like catfish?"

"Love 'em." Lani put her hand on Trevor's shoulder.

"I think that's enough." Rick pulled the stringer out of the lake and tossed it into the ice chest they'd brought for that purpose. "We need to get back for cake, ice cream and fireworks."

"Okay. But first I wanna show Lani how to make a wish in the lake." Trevor scooped up a small rock and held it up to her. "You take a rock and squeeze it real tight." The boy wrapped his fist around the stone. "Close your eyes, make a wish, and throw the rock into the lake. But you can't tell nobody what you wished for or it won't come true."

Lani laughed, delighted in the boy's enthusiastic instructions.

Trevor gripped the rock in his hand and shut his eyes even tighter. His lips moved then he leaned back and threw the rock into the water. He opened his eyes and pointed to the ripples. "I threw it really, really far, and I made a great wish. Your turn."

She knelt and selected a flat round stone, then stood. Trevor bounced up and down on the shore with unbridled energy. "Come on, Lani. Close your eyes and make a wish!"

What did she wish for? She shut her eyes, feeling the smoothness of the stone against her palm.

Rick. His name popped unbidden into her mind, and a flush heated her body. But then the thought of James chased away the warmth, leaving only cold. Reminding her that she shouldn't make herself vulnerable again.

"Lani!" came Trevor's sweet voice. "Are you going to make a wish?"

"Yes," she replied, her voice too hoarse, filled with the pain of longing and the emptiness of regret.

And then it came to her, as clear as that July summer sky. She wanted a child as wonderful as Trevor to call her own. With her eyes still squeezed tight, she brought the stone to her mouth and kissed it, feeling its smooth contours with her lips, then pitched the rock into the lake.

"Wow, you can throw far!" Trevor shouted.

Lani opened her eyes to see Rick beside her, his intense blue gaze boring into her as if he could see her dreams and know her thoughts. She shivered, longing to ease her arms around him and feel the comfort of his body next to hers.

Trevor bounded between them, and crinkled his freckled nose. "Why'd you kiss the rock? Do you think it'll make your wish come true?"

She shrugged and tried not to look at Rick. "With all my heart, I hope so."

Trevor tugged on his dad's sleeve. "Dad, your turn. Make a wish before we go."

Rick scooped up a rock and gazed at Lani. Her stomach somersaulted again, and she wanted to touch him, to be near him. He closed his eyes, brought the stone to his lips, and kissed it. For a moment, Lani wished she was the stone, and that he had his lips pressed against hers. He leaned back, the muscles in his arm rippling as he and flung the stone into the lake.

"Cool!" Trevor bounced up and down. "You threw it really far, even farther than Lani. How come you kissed your rock, like she did? You've never done that before. Do you think your wish will come true?"

Lani's gaze met Rick's and her throat grew dry.

Rick tousled Trevor's hair and smiled, but never took his eyes from Lani's. "I hope so, Trev. I hope so."

By the time they reached the ranch, it was late afternoon and Rick was starving. "We'll head on up to Bisbee for fireworks after dinner," he said as they piled out of the truck. "And of course, after birthday cake for the birthday boy."

"All right!" Trevor clutched pine cones in his hands that he'd gathered in the forest. "Grandma makes the best cakes in the whole world," he said to Lani. "She always bakes a red velvet cake for my birthday with blue and white frosting on account of it's the Fourth of July, and it's my favorite."

The boy dashed off, then stopped. "What about presents, Dad? Do I get presents, too?"

Rick rubbed his chin. "Hmmm, presents? I knew there was something I forgot."

"Daaaad!"

With a grin, Rick pointed toward the house. "Why don't you go inside and see."

Trevor whirled and tore off like a mini tornado.

Lani grabbed the picnic basket and thermos while Rick took the ice chest full of catfish, and they walked together in companionable silence. The house smelled wonderful when they walked in—like fried chicken and hot biscuits.

"No catfish for dinner tonight," Sadie was saying to Trevor when they walked in. "We'll have it tomorrow."

"Ahhh Grandma, why not?" Trevor pouted, his lower lip thrust out, and Lani almost laughed aloud.

"Not enough time to clean the fish and fry it up before the fireworks. That's why." Sadie turned back to the stove. "Besides, I made your favorite. Fried chicken."

"It looks awesome, Grandma." Trevor peeked under foil covering a plate mounded with fried chicken. "Mashed potatoes and gravy and corn on the cob, too?"

Sadie nodded. "That's right."

Trevor hugged her. "Thanks, Grandma."

She waved him off to the bathroom. "Go on and wash your hands."

Holding out his palms, Trevor said, "They're clean. I cleaned them in the lake."

Sadie planted her hands on her hips. "Get into that bathroom and wash with soap and clean water. Do it before I cloud up and rain all over you!"

"Yes, ma'am." Trevor spun and headed for the hall bathroom.

Rick chuckled and Lani snickered. Sadie brandished her spatula at the two of them, but with a smile. "That's enough out of you kids. Go clean up."

Before dinner Lani took a quick shower and put on a button-up pink blouse with a short jean skirt. After cake and presents, they headed to town.

They reached the park in Bisbee just before dark and crowds were gathering. Rick parked in their favorite spot near the old ballpark where years ago he used to play Little League, and they set up lawn chairs around the SUV. Trevor settled between Chuck and Sadie, so excited he could hardly sit still.

"When'll the fireworks start?" Trevor bounced in his chair like a Mexican jumping bean. "I can't wait!"

"As soon as it gets dark." Chuck patted Trevor's knee. "Can you hold your horses that long, Pardner?"

Trevor wiggled out from under his Grandpa's hand and stood. "I hope it hurries up and gets dark really soon."

"How about a walk in the park while we're waiting for the fireworks?" Rick asked Lani, hoping he would have some time alone with her.

She smiled and said, "Sure."

After Rick let everyone know what they were doing, he and Lani strolled across the street into the park, the way lit by an occasional streetlight. The night smelled of fresh cut grass, charcoal and barbeque and the air was filled with chatter and dogs barking.

As they walked past folks sitting on picnic blankets and lawn chairs, they dodged the occasional beer cooler and avoided being trampled as laughing children raced past them. Rick noticed how Lani's gaze followed the kids, a soft smile on her face. He remembered when Lani had told him how she'd always wanted children, but how her bastard of a husband had been so cruel in his response.

A mutt streaked by, almost tripping Lani. Rick caught her

hand, helping her balance, then laced her fingers with his. She stopped and studied him, emotions flickering across her features.

Fear? Longing?

Rick squeezed her hand. "I'm not going to hurt you."

She paused as if considering his response and then said, "I don't know about that, Rick McAllister."

They walked further into the park, as far away from the crowds as he could take her. Finally Rick pulled Lani under the shadows of a huge old oak tree and brought her close, resting his back against the tree, shifting so that his gun didn't press into his spine. She hesitated, then leaned closer and wrapped her arms around his neck.

Desire stirred in him as her warm body pressed to his. He brushed his lips over her hair, drinking in her womanly scent. His cock hardened even more, and he was afraid she would draw away if she felt how much he wanted her.

He'd just have to take that chance, because right now, he wasn't letting go.

The sound of voices and laughter in the distance dimmed as the world narrowed, focused, and Rick's only thoughts were of Lani. She stirred against him, and he sucked in his breath as her innocent movement hardened him even more.

"Lani," he said against her forehead. "Do you have any idea what you do to me?" She lifted her face, and he stroked a soft wave of hair away from her eyes.

She smiled. "Tell me."

He pressed her closer to him. "You can't feel it?" It was too dark to tell if she blushed, but he would've bet she did.

Lani bit her lip and then said, "Um, yes. Hard to miss."

"It certainly is." Rick raised his eyebrows at the double meaning of her words.

She groaned. "I didn't mean that. What am I going to do with you?"

"Whatever you want, darlin', I'm yours." He cupped her face with his hand, her skin soft and smooth against his palm. The thought of kissing her, holding her, loving her, stoked the fire that burned for her, that heat he knew could consume them both. "It's been too long since I've tasted you."

Her lips trembled against his thumb as he ran it over her mouth. "Not that long, cowboy."

"Definitely too long." Rick moved his thumb from her lips, trailing it over her chin, then along her jaw to her earlobe. She shivered and moved her mouth to his palm, the caress of her lips shooting liquid fire through his veins.

He moved his lips to her ear. "You're like honey on my tongue."

Lani made a sound that could've been an answer, or a groan.

There was no doubt she'd been hurt in the past, no doubt she was scared of becoming involved in any kind of relationship. Hell, it almost scared him, how badly he wanted her. But there was one thing he did know, one thing that was absolutely clear in his mind.

He wanted her for keeps.

Rick kissed the tip of her nose. "Tell me what you want," he murmured, his voice hoarse with all his pent up desire for this woman. *His* woman.

"Kiss me," she whispered. "Please."

In a slow tantalizing movement, he brushed her forehead with his mouth, then trailed kisses over the elegant arch of her eyebrow, down to the tip of her nose again. She trembled as Rick traced her lips with his tongue, teasing one corner until she moaned and parted her lips. His tongue darted into her mouth, lightly caressing the serrated edge of her teeth before slipping deeper into her mouth. Her tongue met his in a tentative movement, like she was afraid to show him how much she wanted him.

"You taste even better than I remembered," he rumbled

against her lips then pulled away so that he could look at her.

She moved her palm to his face, and for an endless moment she stroked his cheek and gazed into his eyes. "I lose my head with you. I can't afford that—I can't afford to lose myself again."

Rick kissed the corner of her mouth, and moved to her earlobe. "If you get lost, I'll help you find your way back." He nipped at her lobe. "I need you, Lani. I'm not whole without you."

"You don't really know me," she said, her voice husky. "I barely know you."

"Give it a chance. That's all I'm asking." Rick brought his mouth back to Lani's, kissing her with a fierceness that surprised even him.

This time when she pulled away, she said, "I'll only be here a short time. That's not long enough to give anything a chance."

"Pretend we have all the time in the world." He brought up one hand and slipped it into her silken blonde hair. "Just let go, darlin'."

"It's so hard." She lightly bit her lip and then added, "I've only been with one man. And he was the biggest mistake of my life."

"You were with the *wrong* man." Rick clenched his hand in her hair, lightly pulling on it as if that would draw her away from the bad memories and bring her into the present. "What I want you to think about is you and me. Right here, right at this moment in time."

The moon shone through the oak leaves, shadows and silver beams of light dancing across Lani's features. She gave a tentative smile and whispered. "All right."

He cupped the back of her head in a possessive move and brought her mouth to his. This time she readily took him, surprising him with how intensely she returned his kiss. Suddenly it was her demanding, her needing, her wanting.

And he wanted to give her everything.

His cock ached and he longed to bury himself deep within her core. To feel her naked body beneath him, to taste her silken skin.

When he drew away, Lani gasped for air, her eyes bright in the silvery light. He clenched his hand in her hair and lightly pulled. She moved with him, tilting her head back and exposing the pale flesh of her neck. With one hand still in her hair, he slipped his other hand below her ribcage, holding her as he nibbled a path down her neck to the V of her blouse to the gentle swell of her breasts and flicked his tongue along her cleavage until she moaned.

Every touch burned like fire, searing her with every stroke of his fingers and tongue.

Rick slipped his hand from her hair and with deft fingers he unbuttoned the top two buttons of her blouse and settled his fingers at the front clasp of her bra. He paused, waiting for her to tell him to stop, but instead she slid her fingers into his hair and whimpered.

When Lani didn't stop him, he unhooked it and freed her breasts, exposing them to the cool evening air and to his intent gaze.

"Damn but you're beautiful, woman," he said and then traced lazy trails with his tongue from her cleavage toward one nipple.

Lani didn't know what she was doing and why she was encouraging Rick to go as far as he was. She just knew that she needed a man's touch—no, *his* touch.

And god but he knew how to touch her. The fire he had started within her burned hotter and brighter. Her nipples tightened almost to the point of pain and her mons ached and flooded with moisture. She could think of nothing but wanting him and how it would feel to have nothing between them…his chest rubbing against her nipples, his hips between her thighs…

"What if someone sees us?" she asked, suddenly remembering they were in a park.

"We're alone, far from the crowd, in the dark," he murmured, his warm breath causing her nipple to ache even more.

When his tongue circled her nipple, she gripped his hair even tighter, holding onto him. She knew she shouldn't be allowing this, virtually in public, but it felt wonderful to turn loose and just experience, just enjoy the feel of his hot mouth teasing and suckling her nipple.

That deep thrill she had every time she was around Rick intensified and headed down below to her mons. Her panties dampened and she ached so badly that she felt herself on the edge of an orgasm. But she couldn't climax from him just sucking her nipples...could she?

"I want you so damn much," he said and moved to her other nipple lightly nipping at it and causing her to gasp and bringing her closer to that fine edge of losing control.

Her other nipple felt cool and moist from his mouth and achingly hard. Rick cupped both breasts in his big hands, and they were large enough that she filled his palms. He brought her breasts up high, pressed them together and flicked his tongue back and forth over both nipples.

"I don't know what you're doing to me," she started, "but I—I, oh god that feels good."

Lani moved her hands to his shoulders and gripped him tight as her body started trembling. "What are you doing to me?"

"Come on, baby," he murmured in between licks, "just let yourself go."

Let go, Lani. Just let go.

Still holding onto Rick's arms, she leaned back and focused entirely on his mouth and his tongue as he went back and forth from one nipple to the other. She lost herself in the sensation, giving herself up to it, and to him.

Her entire body vibrated. She whimpered, so on edge she could just scream.

And then he pinched one nipple at the same time he nipped the other and she did cry out. Her entire being shuddered and shook. A powerful orgasm stormed within as he kept his hold on her nipples. She heard booming and saw brilliant flashes of color and the moment he released her nipples, she collapsed against his chest.

"Oh. My. God." She was stunned at what had just happened and shocked that she'd allowed it to. "I can't believe I just—I just climaxed like that."

He gave a low chuckle. "Darlin', you have the most gorgeous and sensitive breasts. I could just eat you up."

She sighed and fully relaxed against Rick, her bare nipples pressing against the roughness of his shirt. "You make me feel fireworks. I can even hear them."

Rick gave a low chuckle. "I'd like to take credit for that, honey, but looks like it's the Fourth of July fireworks, you're hearing."

Lani opened her eyes as sparkling red and blue fireworks exploded above them, filling the dark sky with twinkling lights. They winked out one by one, like hundreds of fireflies blinking through leaves of the oak. Several more fireworks burst above them all at once in an even more brilliant display.

She shook her head and looked back at Rick. "Those aren't the fireworks I'm talking about."

He drew her closer. "Just say when, and I'll give you all the fireworks you need."

Lani shuddered with another sigh that mingled with the last sparks of her orgasm. "Rick, I—I don't know. I don't know that I could handle more fireworks with you."

Rick leaned back far enough to catch both sides of her bra and fastened them over her breasts while he said, "Honey, all I'm asking you to do is give things a chance to develop."

Her nipples tingled as he hooked her bra and it was all

she could do to keep her voice from trembling with desire. "This is too fast for me. I can't even believe I went this far with you." She searched his features as he buttoned her blouse, but it was too hard to read his expression the way his Stetson shadowed his face. "You gave me an orgasm from just touching my breasts for goodness sake."

When her blouse was buttoned, he raised his head and she could clearly see his purely male smile illuminated by the brilliant fireworks. "And I loved every minute of it." His expression grew serious as he continued, "Don't be afraid of what's happening between us, Lani."

She stepped back and smoothed down her blouse, just for something to do with her hands. "I need to slow down, okay?"

Rick gave a nod. "All right. We'll just take this one day at a time."

Lani sighed with relief mingled with regret that she couldn't just let herself go. "Thanks, Rick."

"Don't thank me." He moved so that his arm rested around her shoulders. He hugged her close as they started back across the park. "It's going to be hell keeping my hands off you, sweetheart."

Chapter Nine

ຄ

"Have lunch with me," Rick said to Lani at breakfast. "After your interview with Dee MacLeod, we could meet at the Monroe Café."

"Sounds like a wonderful idea." Sadie spooned scrambled eggs onto her plate. "If I didn't have to run errands in Tucson with Chuck and Trevor, I'd drive to Dee's with Lani and join you."

Lani tried to hide the leap of excitement at the thought of spending time alone with Rick. "I probably won't get back to Douglas until one."

"Perfect." Rick stood and grabbed his empty plate. "Need directions?"

"I'll draw a map." Sadie poured a glass of orange juice. "You get on to work."

Lani couldn't help watching Rick as he headed to the kitchen to slip his plate into the dishwasher and then leave for work. Was she making a huge mistake by agreeing to have lunch with him? Had she already made a mistake by what had happened last night?

For crying out loud, she actually came from a man suckling her breasts!

And not just any man. Rick McAllister, the sexiest cowboy on earth, the man who had already lassoed her libido.

Could she chance letting herself get involved with the man, even if it was short-term?

Especially since it would be short-term. She'd only be there a couple of weeks more.

She must be out of her mind. Lani rubbed her forehead

with her fingertips and tried to shove away memories of Rick's kisses and the way he'd brought her to orgasm. It was hopeless. She couldn't stop thinking about the way he'd held her, his earthy smell, his gentle touch, his sensual mouth.

After buttoning up her blouse last night, Rick had kept her close as they strolled back toward his family. But before they crossed the street Lani had pulled away, not ready for his family to see them together.

He'd simply given an earth-shattering, sexy smile that made her knees quiver, and she almost grabbed his hand to steady herself. She wasn't sure if she was disappointed or glad that he hadn't pressured her for more.

Who was she kidding? She could do nothing but think about the man. How did he manage to get so completely under her skin?

As Lani drove Sadie's SUV to the MacLeod Ranch, the twenty-five miles to Douglas scrolled by, the sky overcast with the threat of a monsoon storm. She glanced at the hand-drawn map on the seat beside her, and checked to make sure she'd taken the right exit.

Every few miles she passed a white and green Border Patrol vehicle. When she drove through Douglas, it seemed like it increased to about once every minute. Her heart beat a little faster as she thought about Rick, knowing that he was somewhere in that town.

"Get your head back to business, Lani," she muttered.

Another fifteen miles east of Douglas, Lani turned off on a dirt road leading to the ranch. She drove past the well-kept barbwire fence, over a cattle guard, and down the primitive dirt road that caused the SUV to rattle and shimmy every inch of the way.

Chuck had taught her some ranch terms the day before, so she actually knew what a cattle guard was. She even recognized the breed of cattle grazing on the northern pasture of the MacLeod's ranch as Black Angus, the same breed as the few head Chuck still kept on the JL Star.

Unlike the JL Star, only a few mesquite bushes dotted the Flying M's expansive rangelands. Tawny mountains rose like earthbound sentinels behind the sprawling ranch house, a stark contrast to the endless yellow field of grass at its feet.

After Lani parked, she jogged up the steps to a porch crowded with beautiful green houseplants. Before she could knock, a willowy redhead opened the front door, a Border collie at her side. "You must be Lani, Trace's friend." She held out her hand. "I'm Dee Reynolds."

"It's great to meet you." Lani smiled and shook Dee's hand, noticing her strong grip. "Trace shared a lot with me about growing up here on your ranch."

The woman gave a brilliant smile, and with her classic beauty, Lani could see that Dee must turn more than her fair share of heads. "Trace is in Texas with her husband Jess, but she hopes to make it here before you head back to San Francisco."

Lani nodded as the dog nuzzled her hand. "It would be great to see her before I leave, and to meet her husband."

"Well Blue certainly approves of you," Dee said with a laugh as she looked at the dog.

"You're beautiful, Blue." Lani allowed the Border collie to sniff her hand then rubbed his head.

A man stepped through the front door, and Lani almost stumbled over Blue in surprise.

"Pardon," John Stevens said around the toothpick in his mouth, touching the brim of his cowboy hat as he paused in front of her.

"No problem." Lani smiled. "Are we still on for our interview?"

"Uh, yeah." He turned to Dee. "Gotta be on my way, Dee. Thanks for letting me use the john."

Dee smiled. "We'll talk later, Bull," she said as he headed down the steps, and he turned back just long enough to give a quick nod in acknowledgment.

"Hope I wasn't interrupting anything," Lani said as John Stevens climbed into his truck.

"Nah." Dee winked at Lani. "Bull only stopped by for a minute. He's off to the cattle auction, trying to rebuild his herd. Wanted to know if I'd like him to buy a few more cattle for our herd. Rustlers made away with a good number of them last fall."

Lani raised her eyebrows. "Rustlers?"

Dee gave a dismissive wave of her hand. "The bastards are in jail now, so it's old news."

Blue followed at Lani's heels as Dee led her into the sunny interior of the home and offered Lani a glass of ice water. She gladly accepted, taking a long draught to quench her thirst. She opened her laptop and booted it up at the kitchen table, set her recorder out, and turned it on.

"So." Dee folded her arms on the table and leaned toward Lani as if sharing a secret, her peridot green eyes sparkling. "Tell me how you're enjoying your stay with one of the most gorgeous eligible bachelors in these parts? In any parts, for that matter."

The question came just as Lani took another drink of water. She choked and came close to spraying a mouthful of that water all over her laptop and the lovely Mrs. Reynolds. For at least the millionth time, Lani cursed the flood of red rushing to her face.

"Ah. Rick has charmed you, too." Dee grinned and sighed like a schoolgirl. "I had a crush on him from the time I was fourteen until I met Jake eleven years ago. No one would ever do for me again once I met Jake."

Lani managed to keep her tone casual. "So, Rick turns on the charm for all women?"

"Nah." Dee shook her head. "He was born with it. He

doesn't have to do anything but walk into a room and you can just see the women drool. Part of his charm is that he doesn't even realize the effect he has on females."

A perverse desire to know more about him rose up in Lani, even if it shattered her illusions. "A lot of guys would take advantage of that."

With a little snort, Dee said, "Not Rick. I don't think he's dated more than a couple of women in the five years since his wife died."

Dee smiled and twirled a diamond and peridot wedding ring around her finger, and Lani noticed the rancher was also wearing a peridot heart necklace. "Sadie keeps thinking Rick will eventually find his soul mate," Dee said. "He may be a grown man, but his mama can't help but worry about him. She's hoping Rick might be more than a little interested in you."

"Yes. Well." Lani's face burned as she turned to her laptop and brought up the list of questions she'd prepared for the interview. "We'd better get started so that I don't take up too much of your day."

"Take your time." Dee leaned over and scratched her dog behind his ears. "It's another hour or so before Blue and I have to head off to feed the horses and check the stock tanks."

"Thanks." Lani glanced at the first question on her list. "Can you tell me how the traffic of illegal aliens affects ranchers?"

Dee ran a careless hand through her auburn hair and settled back in her chair. "In more ways than you might realize. Take Bull Stevens for example. Illegals cut his fence and he lost thousands of dollars when his herd strayed through the fence and got into some bad feed and died."

Frowning, Lani said, "No wonder he hasn't looked pleased when I've mentioned talking to him about illegal immigrants."

The rancher gave Lani a wry smile. "That's putting it

mildly." Dee jerked her thumb toward the window. "Then there's Kev Grand, who lives across the way from us. His loss has also been in the thousands."

Lani cocked her head as she remembered the name. "It's been some time, but I read an article in the New York Times that Mr. Grand is one of the vigilantes who took matters into his own hands."

Dee nodded. "You might say that, though he's really not the vigilante the papers have made him out to be. He just got tired of all the destruction to his property, as well as the drug traffic. So he set up sensors, started patrolling his own property, taking illegals into custody and calling the Border Patrol to escort them off his land."

Lani asked a few more questions about Kev and then asked, "Do you know how many agents work this area?"

"Up until a couple of years ago, there were only fifty Border Patrol Agents in this sector, rotating in three shifts. And yet thousands of illegal immigrants crossed the border every day. They've increased the number of agents from fifty to something like five hundred."

Lani raised her brows. "What a difference."

Dee nodded. "Yes, and believe it or not, it's still not enough."

"You mentioned destruction," Lani said. "What kind?"

"Like most ranchers around these parts, including the Flying M, Kev has had a lot of damage, with fences being cut in places the illegals passed through." Dee sighed. "This is a bigger problem than you'd think. Not only will cattle cross from one rancher's property to another, they could also end up in Mexico."

Lani's fingers flew over the laptop's keyboard as she took notes, questions flying even faster through her mind. "What other damage has been done?"

"Kev and other ranchers have had problems with *coyotes* shooting holes in fifty-thousand-dollar water tanks, as well as cutting water lines, just for the sake of getting drinking water." Dee clenched her jaw and shook her head. "What makes this even more frustrating, is that they could find open stock tanks anywhere around here, every mile or so, where these people can drink without the *coyotes* destroying property."

Lani checked the next question on her list. "Do you have illegals cross your property or come up to your home?"

"Dozens of them cross our rangeland every night, and we've had groups of thirty to forty camp out in the pasture."

"Do you ever feel like you're in danger?"

Dee tilted her head in consideration. "Well, for the most part, no. These tend to be people coming to the U.S. to make a better life, and earning more money than they could in Mexico. But I've heard a few stories that have made me uncomfortable."

The rancher drummed her slender fingers on the table. "Now those *coyotes* are nasty. Real bad news. There's one in particular whose name keeps coming up. His name is Gordo, and from what little I've heard, he's a real SOB."

"Gordo? That means 'fat' in Spanish, correct?"

"Yes."

After Lani had interviewed Dee for a while longer, Blue bounded to the front door and back. He gave a low 'woof,' nuzzled Dee's hand again, then trotted back to the door with an expectant look on his expressive face.

Dee laughed. "Time to feed the horses. Any more questions?"

"I'm set." Lani shut down her laptop. "You've been terrific."

"No problem. Call me if you have more questions, or send me an e-mail." Dee gave Lani a business card then walked her to the front door with Blue dancing at their heels.

As Lani turned to leave, Dee placed her hand on her arm. "I know it's none of my business, but if Rick is interested in you, don't let him slip through your fingers. He's a good man. One in a million."

Lani swallowed and attempted a smile. "Ah. Thanks."

Butterflies invaded Lani's stomach while she drove down G Avenue, Douglas's main street, to the Monroe Café. She parked the SUV in front of the row of buildings crammed side-by-side along the street. Gold letters announced the café's name, along with the proclamation that it was the oldest restaurant in Douglas.

Wiping her sweaty palms on her jeans, Lani took a deep breath. It was only lunch with Rick, for goodness sake. Not a date.

Sheesh. She'd let the man give her an orgasm last night by sucking her nipples!

Then she saw him walking toward her on the sidewalk. His sexy smile. His walk, so fluid and powerful. No man should be allowed to be that gorgeous.

Lust. Pure and simple. She lusted after the man.

Another deep breath and then she grabbed her purse, got out of the SUV, and joined Rick where he waited in front of the café.

"Hello, darlin'." Rick smiled down at her, his azure eyes caressing her with a glance. He didn't even have to touch her, and she felt like she'd been kissed.

"Hi." Her voice was breathless and she couldn't think of anything else to say.

He opened the door to the café and motioned her in, his hand at her elbow. Delicious smells of barbeque and hot biscuits enveloped Lani as soon as she entered. It was a narrow room, one wall lined with floor-to-ceiling photos, posters and playbills of Marilyn Monroe. The other wall was complete with a bar and glass fronted display cases filled with pies and cakes.

They were silent as they waited for the host to seat them, but Rick's nearness about drove Lani wild. All she could think about was last night, his kisses, his body pressed against hers, the way his mouth felt on her, and his promise of fireworks. No doubt in her mind, that he could give her that and more.

She was so deep in thought about him that she almost jumped out of her skin when the host spoke, asking where they would like to sit. Warmth crept up her neck as she realized Rick was watching her, and she wondered how obvious her expression had been.

When they were seated in a booth, they took a few moments to examine the menu. Lani chose grilled chicken, and Rick ordered barbequed spareribs.

"How was your interview with Dee?" Rick asked when the waiter left.

Lani turned away from the picture of Marilyn that she'd been studying. "Dee's terrific."

"I've known her since I was a kid. We saw each other off and on at events around the county. She was into barrel racing and I was into calf-roping."

"You were into rodeo?"

He smiled. "I owe a lot to the junior rodeo circuit for helping me get through my shyness when I was a boy."

"You? Shy?" Lani raised her eyebrows. "Never."

With a shrug, Rick said, "Let's just say that I could hardly look a person in the eye, but that club helped me to gain some confidence and believe in myself."

Lani rested her elbow on the table, her chin on her palm. "You surprise me."

"I'm full of 'em." He folded his arms and leaned forward. "Just try me."

The waiter arrived with their drinks, saving Lani from yet another blush. She squeezed lemon into her iced tea, and added a packet of artificial sweetener.

"That stuff'll—"

"Kill me. I know." Lani smiled and met his gaze. "You told me the same thing on the plane about my diet soda."

By the look in his eyes, she was sure he was thinking about that first night they'd kissed. She still couldn't believe she'd kissed a man the same night she met him. But, well, it had been Rick. In her heart, she knew that dinner and kiss would never have happened with any other man.

Lani rested her chin on her hand again, studying Rick's handsome face and his brilliant blue eyes. "What was your childhood like?"

He shrugged. "Not much to tell. I grew up around here and had a pretty good time. My biological father took off when I was younger than Trevor, so there were some tough years."

Lani's soul twisted at the thought of Rick, young and fatherless. "I'm sorry."

"Don't be." Rick smiled and squeezed her free hand. "He wasn't much of a father. Mom met Chuck a couple of years later, and when I saw how happy he made her, I was all right with it. As far as I'm concerned, Chuck is my dad."

"Did you play sports in school, other than calf-roping?"

"In high school I was a decent linebacker for our football team, and did pretty well in right field on our baseball team."

"I bet you were more than pretty good." Lani could just imagine him in those tight pants that football players wore. "After high school?"

"I headed off to the University of Arizona. I wanted to go into law enforcement, and while I was in college I decided to get on with the Border Patrol. I went into the academy after graduation, and later was stationed along the Texas border. That's where I met Trevor's mother."

"Your son is precious," Lani said. "You're fortunate to have such a great kid."

He smiled. "Yeah, I am."

Lani returned his smile. "And he's lucky to have you as a father."

The waiter served their lunch, and they ate while they talked. Lani told Rick what information she'd gathered so far on the problems with illegal immigration, and he ventured his opinion on a few issues.

As far as Lani was concerned, their lunch was over too soon and Rick had to get back to work. He walked her to the SUV, and as she opened the door he said, "Thanks for having lunch with me."

"Thanks for asking." Then surprising even herself, Lani reached up and brushed her lips over his. "Later, cowboy."

Before he could react, she turned away, climbed into the vehicle and shut the door, her lips tingling from the brief caress. He just smiled and watched her drive away.

Late afternoon sun peeked through the monsoon-darkened sky as Rick reached the offices of the Douglas Herald. The newsroom occupied the bottom floor of one of the town's oldest buildings. Smells of ink, newspaper, and stale coffee overpowered the dingy lobby.

"Rick! Long-time-no-see," said Patti Duarte, the paper's combination office manager/columnist. She stood up, her blonde ponytail bobbing as she bounced toward the front counter. "Where ya been hiding out?"

He leaned against the counter. "Looks like you've been keeping this place above water. And looks like you're about to pop. I didn't even know you're expecting. Congratulations."

Patti, who had always reminded him of a pixie until that moment, patted her enormous belly. "Thanks. Twins, can ya believe it? I look like I'm about to explode, but we've got another two months."

Her blue eyes sparkled, and her cheeks seemed full and shiny. Rick finally understood that old saying about pregnant women. They did glow. For one strange minute, he pictured

Lani, her belly large with his child, her face as radiant as Patti's.

He shook his head, pushing the vision to the back of his mind. "Twins. Bet Paul's as proud as a rooster at the crack of dawn."

Patti snorted. "He's scared shitless."

"Can't say that I blame the guy." With a chuckle, Rick nodded to the back room. "That new reporter here? David Connor?"

"You mean you're not here to see little ol' me? Hold on, let me get him." She smiled, then disappeared through the doorway. Within a minute, she returned. "Come on back and meet god's Gift to the newspaper business."

Rick raised his brows. "God's Gift, huh?"

Patti rolled her eyes. "Thinks he is. Every time AP picks up one of his stories you'd think he won the Pulitzer."

"Miss working with Gerardo?"

"You betcha." Patti led Rick into the back room, past ancient printing press to a man sitting behind a computer at one of three metal desks. "David, this is Border Patrol Agent Rick McAllister. Rick, this is David Connor, Editor-in-Chief and reporter extraordinaire."

Patti winked at Rick as she left the room, and he held back a grin.

"Pleased to meet you, Agent McAllister." Connor didn't offer his hand. Instead, he made a show of tossing his head, flipping his dark hair from his face.

"Uh, yeah. My pleasure." Right off, Rick didn't like the guy. Something about the arrogant look in Connor's brown eyes made him wary. Still, he had to get what he came for, so he stuck out his hand and forced a smile.

Connor gave Rick a limp handshake. Soft and damp. No calluses, no weathering.

"Have a seat." Connor pointed to one of two vinyl chairs

in front of his desk. What can I do for you?"

"Thanks." Rick settled into the chair. "Gerardo was a good friend of mine. Thought I'd come in and get acquainted with you."

Connor gave Rick what amounted to a patient father-speaking-to-child smile. "But you have another reason for being here as well."

Might as well lay it on the table.

"No wonder you're such a good reporter, Connor." Rick smiled. "Let's get to it. One of your sources gave you a big story on the life of an undocumented alien, and he mentioned a *coyote* named Gordo."

Connor tossed his hair back and smirked. "I don't reveal my sources, Agent McAllister."

Rick nodded, trying to maintain his cool. "I understand what you're saying. Any source of yours that I might talk to would never be connected with you."

"I don't reveal my sources."

"Hold that thought, partner." Rick leaned forward in his chair. "While it's real good of you to stand up to your journalistic ethics, I want you to sit back and think for a moment. Think about all those good people crossing the border and dying. Dying 'cause some bastard *coyote* doesn't give a damn about them. Some bastard that's stealing from, beating, raping, and murdering these folks."

Connor shifted in his chair. "I have my integrity to consider."

"It'll remain intact. Give me a name and no one'll be the wiser."

"Like I said my integrity is on the line." Connor's eyes shifted to the doorway and back to Rick.

Patience rapidly dwindling, Rick spread his hands on Connor's desk. "Consider this. How can a man look in the mirror and know he could've saved lives, but left them dangling for his own gain?"

Connor's eyes narrowed, and his lips thinned. "Why do you give a rat's ass?"

Rick gave the reporter a level stare. "Tell you what, Connor. I don't give a damn what you think of me. What does concern me is day after day these *coyotes* get away with murder. But my conscience is clear, and I don't lie awake at night, because I know I'm doing all I can to save lives. It's not enough, but I'm trying."

Rick got to his feet. "How well do you sleep at night?"

Connor didn't move. "I sleep fine."

"Uh-huh. The next time you get to write a story about some poor man, woman or child, dead at the hands of a *coyote*, you think real hard if something you can tell me might have saved their lives. Or many lives. And ask yourself if you're not just as bad as the man who killed them." He pulled his business card out of his wallet and tossed it on the reporter's desk. "Call me if your conscience gets the better of you. I can find my way out."

Chapter Ten

℘

A couple of hours later, after stopping at the station to shower in the locker room, Rick reached the ranch and his temper had cooled. He noticed Chuck's truck was gone, but Sadie's SUV was parked in the driveway.

When Rick walked in the door and kicked off his boots, he smelled something great, like Italian food. Tomatoes, basil and oregano. He headed to the kitchen and smiled when he saw Lani. Her back was to him and she was wearing a pink blouse, a short little skirt and was barefoot. She stood at the range lifting the lid off a pot, then turned off the flame beneath it. She looked good there, like she belonged.

He walked up behind her and slipped his hands around her waist. She gave a little yelp and whirled around, brandishing the pot lid.

She held her other hand to her heart. "Don't *do* that!"

He took the lid from her and set it on the counter. "I should've learned by now that you're pretty dangerous to startle."

"You'd better watch yourself, cowboy." Her voice was low and breathless, her eyes wide.

"I'd rather watch you." Rick studied Lani's lips and braced his hands on either side of her, pinning her against the counter. "Where is everyone?"

"I think they'll be back from Tucson in an hour or so." She glanced at the stove, then back to him. "I'm making angel hair pasta for dinner. With garlic bread and steamed broccoli. The sauce is done, and I've got everything else ready to throw together once they get here."

He didn't take his eyes off her lips. "I'm hungry."

She waved one hand, shooing him away. "Don't you have to take your shower or something?"

"Didn't do any field work," he murmured. "But I took a shower in the locker room."

"Oh." She would have been happy to volunteer to soap his body all over...

"Let's start with dessert." He said, his lips a breadth from hers.

Lani smiled. "Dessert sounds good."

She gave a surprised yelp as Rick grabbed her around the waist and set her on the countertop, away from the range top.

Her pulse raced as he pushed her skirt up around her waist. Thank goodness she was wearing her nice silky pink underwear and not her cotton grannies. "What are you doing?" she asked, even though she had a good idea what he had in mind.

"Sampling dessert." He hooked his fingers onto the sides of her panties and looked at her, waiting for her to tell him to stop.

She worried her lower lip as she stared at him and her panties grew damper. *Why not? Why not enjoy what he's offering?*

Right then and there she knew she was a goner when it came to this man.

Instead of answering aloud, Lani braced her hands on the countertop and lifted her hips.

Rick gave her that slow sexy smile that made her insides melt. He pulled her underwear down her thighs, then gradually eased them over her legs and ankles, teasing her with every deliberate movement. Just the way his fingers caressed her legs as he brought the panties down was enough to make her mons flood with moisture and her nipples ache.

He stuffed the pair of pink panties into his back pocket

then pushed her thighs apart with his hands, totally exposing her to his gaze. The countertop was cool beneath her ass but her body was already burning up. She was faintly aware of the pot of sauce boiling on the range and the smell of pasta and garlic bread. But everything faded as her world came to a pinpoint on the man between her thighs.

"You have a beautiful pussy, darlin'," he murmured as he lightly brushed his fingers over the blonde curls of her mons.

She trembled at the contact and her cheeks heated at the word *pussy*. It was a soft sexy word and just as erotic as the word *fuck*, but both were words she couldn't say out loud.

Rick set his Stetson on the counter beside Lani then knelt on the tile floor between her legs. He gripped her thighs with his large hands as he brought his face to her folds. He paused and inhaled, "You smell like heaven."

Lani shivered and bit back a moan. What was she doing?

Feeling and experiencing what life has to offer. What this man has to offer. Go for it, Lani. Live!

But she couldn't hold back that inner voice that worried about the consequences. "What if everyone comes home early?" *What if I can never say no to you?*

He gave her a wicked grin. "Then I'll throw you over my shoulder and cart you off to my room and finish the job."

Before she could think of a suitable reply, Rick parted her folds with his callused fingers and licked her slit with a long slow swipe of his tongue.

Lani moaned from the exquisite sensation and watched him sliding his tongue over her clit. She clenched the edge of the countertop as he pressed her thighs wider apart and licked and sucked her swollen nub. His tongue swirled and tasted her as he slipped two fingers into her channel. Blood pounded in her veins and in her ears, so loud she could hear nothing else.

She'd never had a man do this to her before, and the feeling was incredible. No vibrator on earth could replace the feel of a man's mouth on her folds, licking her slit, and his fingers thrusting inside her. She could just imagine his cock sliding into her channel, his rock-hard body pressed against hers.

She tilted her head back and felt her nipples hard as stones against her blouse. Rick's stubble was rough against her folds and the insides of her thighs, driving her closer to that place inside her that was growing, budding and blooming. She'd never felt anything like this and she was sailing so fast toward her climax that it fully blossomed inside her in a rush. She gave a little cry as heat burned her from head to toe and back again.

Rick slowed his movements but continued licking her clit until Lani's hips finally stopped rocking against his face. "No more," she begged and shuddered with another aftershock.

He stood and moved between her thighs. Slowly he brought his face to hers and kissed her long and deep. For the first time ever she tasted herself, and it was a different and tantalizing experience. It made another tremor go through her just knowing that mouth had been on her mons.

With a smile he moved back and caught her around the waist. He lifted her off the countertop and set her on her feet.

Rick tugged her skirt down over her hips while Lani tucked in her shirt. "I can't believe we just did that," she said.

His lips quirked as he dragged his hand over his mouth and chin, wiping her juices from his face. "I've been dying to taste you since I met you."

At that moment the front door crashed open and Trevor's yell shattered the moment.

"Dad! We're home!"

Lani bolted out of his arms before Trevor made it into the kitchen. Rick winked at her and then smiled at his son. "How's my favorite guy?"

After Trevor had run off to his room and Rick greeted his mom and dad he excused himself and headed down the hallway.

Lani's gaze widened as she watched him walk away and she prayed that no one else had noticed.

Her bright pink silky panties were peeking out of his back pocket.

* * * * *

"Eduardo Montaño, please," Lani said to the courthouse's elegant receptionist. The nameplate on the woman's desk read *Portia Zapata*.

"Do you have an appointment with the mayor?" The receptionist wore a sleek black business suit, her voice smooth and professional. She seemed accustomed to heading off unwanted visitors.

"Yes. I'm Lane E. Stanton with *City by the Bay* Magazine," Lani replied.

While the receptionist buzzed the mayor's office, Lani ignored the urge to fuss with her skirt and her press badge, doing her best to appear calm, cool, and collected despite the humidity. She'd spent the past week in casual clothing, and for the first time she could remember she felt confined wearing a silk suit and nylons. On top of that, the leather pumps pinched her toes and she longed to be in her casual sandals or tennies. She'd arranged her hair in an elegant chignon at the nape of her neck, applied her makeup with a subtle hand, and wore diamond studs in her ears.

One of the most important things she'd learned early in her career was to dress as the natives do. When interviewing a rancher, dress comfortably in jeans and a blouse. When speaking with an office clerk, wear nice slacks or a pant outfit. When meeting with a politician, dress to kill.

A few moments later, the receptionist escorted Lani into the mayor's office. The news reports she'd seen of the mayor hadn't done him justice. He was almost beautiful with his long black eyelashes and aristocratic features. Not a speck of gray marred his ebony hair or his full mustache.

"*Buenas días*, Ms. Stanton," the mayor said with a small bow. "With the name Lane, I expected a man, and instead I find myself in the company of a most beautiful *Señorita*. Or is it *Señora*?" His voice was well modulated, his manner that of a true politician.

She smiled. "Thank you, Mayor Montaño. I appreciate you taking the time to meet with me. Is there a Spanish word that translates to Ms.?"

He took Lani's fingers lightly in his, lifted them to his mouth and brushed his lips across her knuckles. His cologne was heavy, a cloying smell that reminded Lani of her ex-husband's cologne. "I'm afraid not. Call me Eduardo, please. May I call you Lane?"

As she withdrew from his grasp, Lani replied, "Of course."

"Have a seat, Lane." With a sweep of his arm, he gestured to one of two leather chairs in front of his desk. After Lani sat, the mayor hitched up his slacks and settled into the chair next to her.

"Mr. Montaño—"

"Eduardo, please."

"Ah, yes." Lani swallowed. "Eduardo. May I record our interview so that I can ensure my notes are accurate?"

He nodded and crossed his legs at his knees. "By all means."

After Lani pulled the recorder out of her purse, she turned it on then withdrew her notepad of questions. She glanced at the rich furnishings, trying to get a sense of the man she was about to interview.

Behind the desk was a large window, but the wooden blinds were drawn shut. Bookshelves lined one wall, filled with brass sculptures of bullfighters and bulls, as well as a few thick volumes. Oil paintings of matadors in vivid hues of reds, greens, blues and yellows dominated the other two walls, the fighters waving traditional red capes before powerful black bulls.

"You have a lovely office," she said. "I see you have a penchant for bull fighting."

"*Sí.*" Montaño's mustache twitched and he gave a ruthless smile. "The greatest of all sports."

Lani turned from looking at the sculptures and gave him her let's-get-down-to-business smile. "I understand you're running for United States Congress in this fall's election, and your campaign is on an immigration reform platform."

"Yes, that is correct." He placed his elbows on the arms of his chair and steepled his fingers. "I feel very strongly that something must be done to alleviate this ongoing problem."

"Will you explain?"

He nodded. "But of course. First, I believe we should grant amnesty to all Mexican nationals now living in the U.S." He ticked off the points on his fingers. "Second, I advocate free schooling for children of undocumented aliens in all states, and that we should not require these children to prove citizenship in order to go to school. Third, I believe that no one in any state should have to provide a social security number or proof of residency to obtain a driver's license."

Montaño continued in the manner of a politician practiced in outlining his views. "Fourth, I oppose mandatory reporting by employers of their employees' nationalities. Fifth, I do not believe we should fine employers who hire undocumented workers. And sixth, I do not agree with dragnets that round up immigrants from their homes or workplaces."

Lani made a note to herself on her notepad. "How do you feel this will help the problem with the numbers of people attempting to cross the border illegally every day?"

"I believe that we must ease the hardship of the suffering souls living in fear and despair on our side of the border," he replied. "Those poor people on the other side are in my thoughts and prayers. However, they must wait and cross into this country legally, as did my father, many years ago."

Typical politician. Talking in circles around her questions.

"I see. Now regarding the number of aliens crossing the border illegally, do you feel that going after the smugglers and *coyotes* would get to the root of the problem?"

"Of course we wish to find and prosecute these reprehensible beings." Montaño shrugged. "Let me express how much it saddens me that these smugglers of humans, these so called *coyotes*, continue to cause the loss of so many lives. It's a terrible problem and something must be done about it."

She met his gaze head on. "What do you propose?"

"First we must address the most important issues on immigrants already living in this country, before we can tackle that obstacle."

Not going to get a straight answer.

Lani checked her list of questions and looked back to Montaño. "What do you know of a *coyote* named Gordo?"

For a fraction of a second, Lani thought she saw unease in the mayor's eyes, but a questioning look replaced it almost at once. "Gordo? I do not recall a *coyote* by that name. Where did you hear it?"

Was there something in his look? "Someone must have mentioned it to me," Lani said and went to the next item on her list.

Montaño answered more of her questions in his carefully rehearsed manner, then glanced at his watch. "As much as I enjoy your company, *Señorita*, I have another appointment I must attend to."

She gathered her belongings and thanked the mayor. He seemed like he was a nice enough man for politician. As she left she wondered why the interview with him had made her feel so uneasy.

That evening when Sadie answered the phone, it was Rick. He let them know that he would be getting home late into the night due to work, and not to hold up dinner or wait up for him.

After dinner, Lani helped clean the dishes, and said goodnight to everyone, explaining that she had a headache and needed to get to sleep early. Once in bed she tossed and turned, and when she finally did fall asleep, it was less than peaceful.

It was going too fast! They would crash!

Screams filled the cramped cabin. Naya squeezed Lani's hand, crushing her fingers. "OhGodohGodohGodohGod," Naya cried over and over and over again.

"Head between your knees," Father yelled. Mother sobbed beside him.

Lani pushed Naya down. Naya was still praying. Lani's head filled with the chant, her heart pounding in desperate rhythm. "OhGodohGodohGodohGod, please! Let us live!"

The plane slammed forward, nose down. Impact! The seatbelt dug deep. Lani's head smashed into a seatback.

Spinning. They were spinning. Luggage burst from overhead compartments. Around and around they whipped. Back and forth. Suitcases battered her arms. Screams. Shrieks. The sound of metal grinding, tearing, as the plane ripped in half.

The caustic smell of electrical smoke filled the cabin. Sparks, then fire!

Whirling. They were spinning, screaming.

Slower, it moved slower, but Lani's head still reeled. The screech of metal against asphalt raked across her spine, like a giant hand scraping down an immense chalkboard. Finally, finally, the plane shuddered to a stop.

Were they really alive? Did they make it?

Fire. Smoke. Screams. Sirens. The stench of burning flesh. Pain seared Lani's thigh and she saw torn cloth, her flesh flayed open, blood covering her lap.

Naya's hand still clutched Lani's in a death grip. Lani lifted her head and looked at her sister. Blood shrouded Naya, and her mouth and eyes were wide open, frozen with fear.

"*No!*" Lani bolted upright in bed. Tears streamed down her face, her clothes soaked with sweat, every inch of her body trembling.

The door burst open. Light from the hall silhouetted Rick's big form, his hair rumpled. Through her tears she saw concern stamped across his features.

"What happened?" He shut the door and in two long strides, he reached her. One look at her face and he slid onto the edge of the bed and pulled her into his lap. "Are you all right?"

She sobbed against his strong shoulder. She couldn't speak. Couldn't force the images from her mind of smoke, flames, twisted metal, and her dead sister's face. Lani's leg throbbed, as if her skin was still shredded, blood still pouring from the wound.

"A nightmare?" Rick's voice was soft and soothing.

She shuddered and nodded against his chest. "I—I dreamt about the plane crash. Naya. Her face. It was so—so real."

For a long while, he held her, gently rocking her, trying to soothe the horror of her nightmare. Terror and grief raged within Lani. She could barely think. Barely hold the screams trapped in her throat.

"Easy," came Rick's low murmur through the chaos. "I've got you. You're safe."

Safe? How could anywhere be safe? Her swallowed screams turned to sobs. Nowhere on Earth would ever be safe again. Father. Mother. Naya.

Dear god. Naya!

Hot tears streamed down Lani's cheeks, but Rick's embrace didn't falter. "Let it go. Let it out. I'll be here. Right here."

She let herself believe him, let herself relax in his powerful arms. The easy sigh of his breathing lulled her, and she smelled his earthy, grounding scent. So strong. He felt so strong. Her hand slid across his naked chest, through the patch of curling hair and the dampness of her tears against his flesh. Slowly, ever so slowly, the room returned to proper focus.

Rick. He was holding her still, his protective arms cradling her with more gentleness, more caring than she'd known from any man. Her heartbeat quickened, and once more, intense emotions stirred—but not fear. Not grief.

The antidote. Passion. Tenderness.

She turned her face to look into his eyes. Fathomless pools, midnight blue in the faint light. "You're always comforting me."

He brushed his lips across her forehead. "Do you need me to stay awhile longer?"

Closer. She wanted closer. She wanted his lips, wanted him to kiss her until there was no turning back. His body pressed to hers, nothing between them but a fine layer of perspiration. The intensity of her desire shocked her, but all she could think about was how much she wanted him. Now.

She turned her mouth to his chest, kissing the salty flesh, moving her lips to his collarbone and trailing her tongue along his skin. His breath hissed out, stirring hair at her temple. She wanted him to kiss her the way he had at the park. So thorough, so exquisite that time meant nothing. Only the sound of his heartbeat against hers, the feel of his hands and lips on her body.

As Lani lifted her head, Rick pressed his fingertips to her mouth, stopping her from reaching his lips. She kissed his hand instead, moving her lips over each finger.

He groaned and shuddered. "Not now, not when your

heart aches like this."

"But…" Disappointment swelled within Lani. He didn't want her.

"Yes, I do want you," he replied as if she'd spoken the words aloud. "More than you can imagine." His cock pressed against her hip like a rod made of steel, and she knew it was true.

"But let me be your friend tonight." He stroked her hair behind her ear. "Let your head clear, and if tomorrow, you still want that kiss…"

With a reluctant sigh, she snuggled closer, enjoying the feel of his chiseled body, his muscular arms wrapped around her. How different he was from James. James, who took advantage of her vulnerability.

As she shifted in his lap, Rick tensed. He gave a muffled oath, moved Lani to the bed and stood. "You ought to sleep."

She could barely see him in what little light poured in from the hall, but it was enough to see the powerful muscles in his chest, the hard line of his body, the thrust of his cock outlined against the white of his briefs.

A moan caught in her throat. He was so beautiful.

He took a ragged breath. "Don't look at me like that, honey. Like you want to eat me whole. I can hardly think straight as it is."

She slid down her pillow and pulled the covers to her waist. "Okay."

"'Night." He smiled, rakish yet wistful, and turned toward the door.

Lani sat up again. "Wait."

Rick stopped and looked back with hooded eyes.

Longing swelled within her, and something else. Something that made her want to tell him what his thoughtfulness did to her, how it made her desire him more than ever. But she only said, "Thanks."

"Get some sleep, honey." And then he was gone, closing the door behind him.

For a long time, Lani remained awake, but the nightmare didn't haunt her as she feared it would. All she could think about was Rick.

Chapter Eleven

ℰℓ

Rick spent a frustrating day chasing dead-end leads, finding himself no closer to learning the identity of either Gordo or *El Torero*. By the time he'd exhausted his last resource, orange and pink streaked the western sky, the sun sinking behind the Mule Mountains.

And he was late. Marnie and Stan Torres had invited Rick's family and Lani to dinner. Marnie had promised to make her wicked chili con carne, homemade flour tortillas, and flan, a Mexican custard, for dessert. But Rick just wasn't up to socializing, even though he hated to miss the chance of being around Lani.

Dead tired, Rick stopped by the Torres's ranch to make his appearance and his excuses. Sadie and Chuck were there when he arrived, but he didn't see Lani or Trevor. Sadie let him know that Trevor had come down with a stomach bug that afternoon, and Lani had volunteered to stay with him.

Only the porch light was on when Rick finally made it home, and the house was quiet, save for crickets chirping and Roxie sniffing her greeting. Absently, he scratched the dog behind her ears, feeling a surge of disappointment that Lani had apparently gone to bed. He'd hoped to spend a few moments with her — hell, more than a few moments.

Not that he was able to get to sleep right away after being near her. Warmth seeped into his blood when he remembered last night. He'd gone to Lani to comfort her, and when she'd calmed down, she'd reached for him with desire in her eyes and passion in her soul. Had he been a fool for turning away from her?

No, as much as he wanted her, he could never do that.

When she came to him for more than petting and sexual play, it would be with a clear head. It would be because she wanted him. Last night could've just been a reaction to the adrenalin pumping through her body after her nightmare. No greater aphrodisiac than adrenalin.

Rick kicked off his dusty boots by the front door and tore off his socks, then put his gun in the cabinet. He'd spent the day researching files, watching surveillance tapes and talking on the phone, and hadn't come in contact with any UDAs, but he still wanted a shower.

In the kitchen, he washed his face and hands in the sink, before giving Roxie a bowl of dog food and water. He made himself a sandwich with Sadie's homemade bread and leftover ham, and scarfed it down along with a glass of orange juice.

When he finished eating, he went to the bathroom but found the door locked and heard water running in the tub. So, Lani wasn't asleep after all. What would she think if he slid into the bathroom and offered to join her? Would she welcome him? He shook his head and smiled. Just maybe.

He checked on Trevor and found the boy fast asleep, then went to the laundry room and stripped off his clothes, then headed to Chuck and Sadie's bathroom to take his shower.

After a nice hot shower, Rick felt more than refreshed. His blood boiled and his cock made the thick terrycloth towel around his waist stand at attention. The tile felt cool under his bare feet as he headed toward his room, wondering if he should knock on Lani's door.

But when he reached the hallway, Lani was there. His pulse picked up and his gut tightened. She stood in the doorway of Trevor's room, a soft smile on her face. Only light pouring from her bedroom lit the hall, but it was enough that he could study her.

Heat pooled in Rick's groin as he watched Lani, his arms aching to draw her close, aching to touch her face, aching to stroke her body. She was beautiful. Her skin pink, the ends of her hair damp. And of all things, she wore his faded bathrobe.

She turned away from Trevor's room and froze.

"Hello, Lani," Rick said softly.

"Rick." She hugged the robe tighter. "I thought you'd be going to the Torres's."

"Too tired." He smiled and leaned against the doorframe of her room. "At least I was."

Lani wiped a tendril of damp hair from her face, her chocolate eyes drawing him closer. "I was just checking on Trevor."

Rick struggled to stay put, to keep his hands away from her. "How's he doing?"

"His fever's down." She glanced in the boy's room, then back to Rick. In the background, he heard country western music playing on Trevor's radio.

Her gaze darted to Rick's bare chest, as if she'd just noticed he wore only a towel. She blushed as she looked back to his face. "I'd better let you get to bed."

She brushed past him, into her room. Her soft body slid by him as silken as a caress, the fragrance of her warming him like whiskey in his veins. And god help him, he followed her.

"Lani."

The Victorian lamp bathed her in a rose glow, her hair glittering in the gentle light like strands of finest gold. As she turned back to him, she made a soft sound and bit her lip.

"Are you all right?" Rick reached for Lani and pulled her to him. She buried her face against his bare chest and slid her arms around his waist. She fit against him perfectly, the top of her head just reaching his chin. He stroked her hair down to the damp ends, and then again.

A deep breath, and then she shuddered. "You smell so good." His chest muffled her voice.

"No, darlin' it's you. Honeysuckle and soap." He smiled. "You look sexy as hell in my robe."

Lani lifted her head and the sensual glitter in her eyes made him want to take her right then and there. "When I took a bubble bath, I forgot to bring my clothes into the bathroom. So I borrowed your robe from off the door hook. Do you mind?"

"Never." He gave a wicked grin. "But I envy all those bubbles, touching you, covering every inch of your body. And right now I envy my bathrobe even more."

She caught her breath, her eyes growing wide and her lips parting.

Her mouth looked so inviting, so delectable. He lowered his head and brushed her lips with his. Lani wrapped her arms around his neck and kissed him. Long and tender, her tongue teasing him with cat-like strokes. He answered by deepening the kiss, delving into her until his head spun and she had completely intoxicated him. He was drunk with the taste of her, the smell of her, the feel of her.

Rick gritted his teeth, his body rock hard against her feminine softness. She trembled in his arms and he pulled away. "I'm finding it tough to control myself around you."

She drew him back and melded her body to his. "You taste like orange juice, and something more." She kissed him again, and trailed her lips over the stubble on his chin, down to the hollow of his throat. "Man. You're all man."

Fire burned within Rick, desire so fierce it shook him to the soles of his feet, nearly knocking him on his ass with its intensity.

His breathing grew ragged as he captured her mouth with his. God, but she tasted good. Her lips, so soft and sweet, tore away at his resolve. "Lani. Honey. I don't know if I can take much more of this. I'm about to throw you on that bed and take all of you."

"Please," she whispered, nuzzling at his ear. "I want those fireworks you promised me."

Rick squeezed Lani to him. "Are you sure? Very sure?"

His words made her even more confident in her decision. Like a light shining into a darkened room, she realized it was what she'd wanted all along. She didn't just want kisses and almost-sex. She wanted all of him. She wanted him so deep inside her that she could feel him everywhere.

He wasn't James. Rick would never hurt her. And even if it didn't last, she needed Rick with a desperation that almost frightened her.

She nodded, her heart pounding, her throat tight. "I want to be with you more than anything."

"You're trembling." He stroked her cheek, then slid his fingers into her hair. "Are you afraid?"

"No. It's just that I...I've never been with anyone other than...him." She brushed her lips against Rick's neck. "He never made me feel the way you do. Never."

"Lani," he whispered. "There's never been a woman I've cared more about than you."

"Please." She stroked his face, his stubble coarse against her palm. "Be with me."

"Don't move."

Rick pulled away and left the room, and she felt alone. Naked. Like a part of her was missing. In moments, he was back. With a flick of his wrist, he tossed a box onto the nightstand, and shut and locked the door.

"Condoms," she murmured as he brought her into his arms. Embarrassment burned her cheeks for never having thought of needing them. But at the same time she marveled at the man in her arms. After leaving James, she'd stopped taking the pill, not planning to have sex with any man. And there she was, wanting Rick so much she could hardly think straight.

He pressed his lips to he forehead. "Second thoughts?"

"No." She shook her head. "I want you so bad I'm shaking."

"Same here." He laughed, low and sensual. "And that's

never happened to me before."

She melted against him, breathing in his utterly male scent and running her hands through the hairs curling on his chest. He felt so solid, so good beneath her palms.

A flash of reality struck Lani and she tried to step away. "Oh, my god. What am I thinking? Trevor is down the hall."

He kept her caged in his arms, nuzzled her hair and chuckled. "Why? Do you make a lot of noise?"

She flushed. "No — I — "

Rick trapped her mouth in a slow, sensual kiss that burned Lani to her soul. Her knees gave out, but he was holding her tight to him.

After devouring her lips, he lifted his head and gave her a lazy smile that sent heat flushing over her anew. "You're warm, sweet, passionate and sexy as hell."

Pleasure tingled within every nerve in her body. He made her feel so alive, so wanted, beautiful even. She glanced at the door. "What about Trevor?"

"The kid sleeps like a rock. His radio is on, and his room is all the way down the hallway." Rick caressed her shoulders through the robe, the heat of his hands warming her. "As long as we're discreet and keep the door locked, I don't see a problem."

He hooked a finger under her chin and smiled. "Have you changed your mind?"

She shook her head. "No. I want you."

"Good, 'cause I sure wasn't looking forward to a cold shower." He wrapped his arms around her waist and lowered his head. "I've never tasted anything as good as you."

He traced his tongue along her bottom lip, and then the top, a slow, sensual tease. A wave of dizziness swept over her, and she felt like she would never breathe again. Their tongues met, flicking, dancing, and she wanted more of him.

With a groan, he lifted his head and pulled at the neckline

of her robe, baring her shoulder. He caressed the naked skin. "What're you wearing under there?"

His feather kisses continued from her neck down to the rounded softness of her shoulder, bringing another moan to her lips. She found it almost impossible to speak. "Absolutely...nothing."

"Show me." Rick's voice was so husky, as he nuzzled her neck, it sent thrills skittering in her belly.

"Wait." She put her hands on his chest and glanced at the Victorian lamp. "We need to turn off the light."

"No. I want to see you." His gaze searched her face. "Every last bit of you."

Lani's cheeks heated and she tried to push away. "But I–" She dropped her eyes. "I'm not thin and beautiful."

"How could you think that?" Puzzlement and wonder crossed Rick's features when he lifted her chin with his finger and forced her to look at him. "You're perfect."

He slid his hands down her, alongside the curve of her breasts to her waist, and over the flare of her hips. She gasped as he cupped her rear, his hands warm through the robe. "I love to look at you and your curvy body. You're so sensual. So gorgeous. I've been dying to touch you everywhere. Every inch of you."

When she opened her mouth to protest, he put a finger to her lips. That simple touch, the way he traced her lips, undid her. Senses reeling, she shivered as Rick ran his finger over her chin down her neck, then between the swell of her breasts until he reached the tie.

One tug, and the robe fell open. Lani's nipples tightened, the air cool, but her body burning hot for him. She wanted to pull the robe around her, to cover her body, but he pushed it down her arms to land in a puddle at her feet.

"Beautiful. So incredibly beautiful." He caressed her with his gaze, taking in all of her from her swollen lips to her bare toes. She trembled, then caught her breath as he cupped her breasts and ran his thumbs over her nipples. "Tell me, Lani. Do you blush everywhere?"

She flushed with heat and he gave a soft chuckle. "I knew it. Your entire body turns that pretty shade of pink."

Lani wrapped her arms around his neck. "Shut up and kiss me, cowboy."

Rick pulled her to him, his chest hair tickling her sensitive breasts. They kissed with such urgency and fervor that she was drunk with the taste of him, the smell of him, and she wanted more. But he teased her, slowly relishing her body. He trailed his tongue down her neck, settling in along her collarbone, before beginning the leisurely descent to her breasts. She had to fight from crying out as he circled first one nipple, then the other. He took one in his mouth and tugged on it, driving Lani out of her mind with wanting him.

When he lifted his head, he gripped her buttocks with his hands, pressing his cock hard against her belly.

"Damn. What you do to me," he groaned as she moved her lips to his chest. She licked his flat nipples as he'd done to hers, then nipped at him, while running her hands over the soft hair of his muscled chest to his hard abs. She couldn't help herself—she wanted to eat him whole, to touch every inch of his body. He caught his breath as her hands neared his hips, where the hair disappeared in a V into the towel.

"Let me feel you." Her hands shaking, she pulled the towel away and let it drop to the floor. His breathing grew more ragged as she stroked his rigid cock, awed by the sight of him. "There's so much of you."

Lani knelt before him, running her hand from balls to tip, amazed at how big he was. She'd only seen one before and it wasn't half the size of Rick's.

She cupped his balls as she slid her mouth over his erection. With her free hand she stroked him at the same time she swirled her tongue around the head of his cock, just feeling and getting lost in the moment. It was not something she'd enjoyed doing before now, but with Rick she wanted to experience everything. Wanted to do everything she could to give him pleasure.

And she loved it.

Rick groaned and slid one hand into her hair, clenching his fingers in the strands that were still damp from her bath. He wanted to thrust his hips, to slide himself in and out of Lani's hot mouth, but he let her control her motions.

Gritting his teeth he kept a tight hold on her hair as she licked the length of his cock while stroking him at the same time. Her other hand caressed his balls, and he had the feeling she was enjoying getting to know him so intimately.

His climax built up within him, his gut tightening and his balls drawing up. "I'm gonna come, Lani, if you don't stop."

Her answer was a sigh that heated him, and then she took him deep, to the back of her throat. He tried to pull away, but she held onto him and sucked.

Rick came so hard he literally saw stars. Lani kept sucking on him even as she swallowed his fluid, drinking it down until he was spent.

When she slipped his cock out of her mouth, he couldn't believe that he was still semi-erect after what she'd just done to him. He brought her up, sliding her body against his. "You sexy little thing," he murmured as he bent down to kiss her.

Lani felt the heat of him, the hardness of his wet cock against her belly, and it amazed her that he was clearly ready and able even after he had just climaxed. His hands roamed over her as he kissed her, paying close attention to her breasts then moving down to cup her butt cheeks. He moved one hand between them and slipped his fingers into her folds.

"Your pussy is so wet for me," he murmured when he lifted his lips away from hers. "Tell me what you want, darlin'."

Now wasn't the time to be coy. It was time to admit what she had wanted ever since she'd met him. How could she say it without using the "f" word and definitely not using "making love" because this was just sex?

"Tell me," he said as his lips brushed over her forehead. "You can say it."

Lani bit her lip then took a deep breath. "I want you to... I want you."

Rick's gaze was entirely focused as he stroked her clit. "I want to fuck you, Lani." He plunged two fingers into her channel and she gave a soft cry. "I want you to tell me what you want, too."

She couldn't believe how much it excited her to hear him say it out loud like that. "I—I want your cock inside me, Rick."

With almost ferocious intensity, Rick kissed Lani, plunging into the satin of her mouth. He nearly growled as he lifted his head and took in Lani's dazed expression, her moist lips and the way her chest rose and fell with every breath.

Rick took her hand and led her to the bed, then pulled her onto it beside him. He twined his long legs with hers, and moved his thigh close to her slit. "I've wanted to make love to you since the moment I saw you in the Chinese restaurant," he said and then traced her nipples with his tongue. She gasped as he slid his hand down her belly to the apex of her thighs and cupped her mons.

"I—I—Rick." Lani choked back a cry as his finger teased her clit and wild vibrations rocked her. She clenched her hands in his hair and arched her back as he slid his fingers inside her satin warmth.

"You're so perfect," he murmured as he moved his fingers in and out of her channel.

Slow, agonizingly slow, he moved his mouth from one nipple to the other, licking and sucking each one until they were so hard they ached. Continuing his tease, he worked his way between her breasts, down her belly then licked her navel before moving on, but bypassed her mons and went instead to her leg. With his lips, he caressed the scar on her thigh, softly kissing the length of it.

Lani brought her hands to her nipples and pinched them, needing to assuage the ache as Rick took his time exploring her body. He kissed a trail down her leg to her foot then flicked his tongue against the sensitive spot at the arch. When he finished, he gently released her leg and moved to the other. He started the slow ascent, paying attention to her foot, the inside of her knee and the soft skin of her thigh at the juncture of her legs.

She trembled as he nuzzled the soft curls of her mound. He ran his tongue over the tops of her folds. He drove her wild when he again tasted that most intimate part of her, licking and sucking her swollen lower lips. Streamers of pure pleasure rippled through her as he flicked his tongue against her clit. She bit her lower lip to keep from screaming.

This time his tongue worked its magic at a much slower pace, as if he was attempting to drive her out of her mind. He slipped two fingers into her and drove them in and out the way she wanted his cock inside her. At the same time he pressed his face tight against her folds licking her hard. Her thighs trembled and her breathing grew more ragged. "I'm going to come," she said, barely able to speak.

He only licked her harder until she came with a jerk and a barely suppressed cry. Her body was still trembling, the muscles at her core still contracting so hard she could feel it from her mons to her ass.

Rick worked his way back up as her body shuddered, slowly circling her navel and licking a path up to her breasts where he licked and sucked them. When his mouth met with Lani's, his tongue made love to her, and she could taste herself on his lips. She enjoyed the feel of his weight on top of her, his hips between her thighs. She arched her back, wanting to be closer to him, wanting his cock inside her.

"Are you ready for me?" he murmured.

"Yes." She raked her nails softly across his back. "Definitely yes."

He leaned over to the nightstand and took a condom from the box, then knelt between her thighs as he tore open the package. She gazed into his gorgeous eyes and she wanted to lose herself in them.

No. With Rick, she wasn't losing herself. She was finding herself.

He sheathed his cock and tossed aside the wrapper. And then he braced himself above her, his weight partially against her. "I want to be a part of you."

"Now," she moaned. "Please, Rick. I want you inside of me."

He brought the head of his cock to the entrance of her channel and just stared down at her for a moment. "Lani," he murmured, the sound of his voice giving her raw pleasure.

She caught her breath, waiting for that moment when he would be inside her. Then he thrust his cock inside her. She gasped as he filled her so completely that she couldn't imagine ever being apart from him. It was like he belonged inside her. He remained motionless for a moment and she squirmed beneath him, wanting more.

Rick lowered his head and captured one of her nipples with his mouth and she bit back a cry of pleasure. She pushed her hips tight against his, wanting to feel him thrust inside her, so deep she could feel it throughout her body.

"You feel so good wrapped around me, so snug and tight," he said as he stared down at her. In the faint light his blue eyes glittered with desire. "I'm going to fuck you now."

"Yes." Lani scraped her nails down his back to his ass and gripped his muscled buttocks. "Don't make me wait any more."

"Damn." His strokes were slow and deliberate but his jaw was clenched and his eyes wild. Sweat dripped down the side of his face and a droplet landed on her chest. "I want to take you hard and fast, honey."

"Then do it," she urged. "I want it. I want it all."

Rick began thrusting harder into her, his hips firm against the cradle of her thighs, his balls slapping against her mons. Lani matched his rhythm, giving him everything she had and wanting to take more. She whimpered, needing as much of him as he could give.

He paused and hooked his arms around her knees, drawing her up and opened her wide. He plunged himself as deep as he could go and Lani felt his cock against her G-spot, that place she'd found only with her vibrator before. But oh, this was so much better, so incredible she could almost cry with the pleasure of it.

Rick plunged in and out of her, hitting that exquisite spot again and again. Ecstasy built within Lani—so great, so intense that she wanted to scream. Just as a scream was about to break loose, he kissed her hard, swallowing her cries before they could escape.

She wanted him harder and deeper, wanted all of him, until it built up to a crescendo, higher and higher, until she saw only colors and light, and felt a release unlike anything she'd known before.

Every thrust of his hips drove her beyond that pinnacle, taking her beyond this world and into a place filled with exquisite sensation. She climaxed yet again, and this time the pleasure was almost more than she could bear.

Rick's body grew tense and he gave a low growl as his cock throbbed within her. His thrusts slowed and her body rippled again and again. With one last thrust he held himself still, looking down at her with amazement in his eyes.

"You are beautiful, Lani," he murmured before kissing her, a soft slow kiss. "So beautiful."

Chapter Twelve

ɚ

Rick awoke before dawn, his arm numb, but he wouldn't move to shift Lani. He didn't want to wake her, not yet. He watched the gentle rise and fall of her naked breasts, her contented expression as she slept.

Last night amazement had filled him as he'd thought about what they'd shared. He'd never so thoroughly enjoyed a woman before, never in his life had wanted anyone like he wanted Lani. The realization of how deep that desire went hit him hard.

Too astonished to say anything, he'd drawn Lani into the circle of his arms, and she'd cuddled next to him, looking like a princess who had enchanted him completely. Just being near her hardened his cock, and if she hadn't fallen asleep, he would've made love to her again in a heartbeat.

His cock was hard as granite this morning. Every time he was near Lani, he felt such a desire to be with her in every way. And now that he'd tasted her and enjoyed her so thoroughly, he knew he'd never get enough.

It was still dark outside, but they'd fallen asleep with the lamp on, and he could see her clearly in its soft light. The sheet had settled around her waist, and her creamy peaks tempted him. Lani's breasts were full and high, her nipples a deep rose color and petal soft. Rick shifted so that he could lean closer to the tantalizing blooms. He kissed one and smiled as it grew taut beneath his lips.

"Mmmm," she murmured, and stirred.

He traced his tongue around the base of her hardened nub, then captured it in his mouth, gently nipping it. While he seduced her nipple, he watched her face.

Her eyes opened a slit and she smiled. "What a wonderful way to wake up." She stretched, then slid her hands into his hair, holding him close to her breast.

"Good morning, darlin'." He moved to her other nipple, gently raking his teeth over it. She gasped and arched her back. "I'm hungry. How 'bout you?" He scooted down, his tongue trailing to the hollow at her navel. He savored the taste of the salt on her skin, the smell of their sex.

"I—Yes," she moaned as his lips neared the fine curls between her thighs.

Rick wanted to slide into her velvet softness, but fought for control. The thought of pleasuring Lani again filled him with intense desire. He watched her face as his tongue found her folds and he reveled in her soft moans. When his tongue met her clit, she covered her mouth with her arm, obviously holding back a cry.

He thrust three fingers inside her while he licked and sucked her pussy. She squirmed and bucked her hips against his face. He drove her mercilessly toward completion and on, until she finally moved her arm from her mouth and said, "Stop, Rick. I can't take anymore."

With a smile he moved up and braced himself over her. He watched her face, wanting to see the wildness in her eyes. She slid her hand between their bodies, and grabbed his cock. "I want you inside me, now."

In a quick movement he flipped her onto her belly and Lani gasped. "Rick!"

He positioned a pillow beneath her hips, raising her up so that he could penetrate her more deeply from behind. He paused to sheathe his erection with a condom. "God, you're beautiful," he whispered as he slid his cock into her.

Rick loved the way her ass looked and the feel of her soft flesh beneath his palms. He watched his cock moving in and out of her pussy and he reveled in the soft cries she made against the bed sheets.

She fit perfectly. Everything about her did. She raised her hips back to meet him as he drove into her, the silky heat surrounding his cock. He plunged in an out, harder and faster than he had last night, and she took his every thrust.

Her body began to tremble and then she gave a broken cry and he felt her pulsating release gripping and releasing his cock over and over. Rick arched his back and pressed his hips tight to Lani's as searing pleasure shattered him to the center of his being.

When the sky lightened, Rick awoke again and stroked a strand of hair from Lani's face.

"I've got to get ready for work." He kissed the curve of her smile, breathing in her vibrant scent. "Have breakfast with me."

"Mmmm." She nuzzled his neck. "Too bad you can't play hooky."

"You tempt me." He laughed softly. "I work today and tomorrow, and then I'm off for the next two days. So don't make any plans that don't include me, all right?"

She kissed his ear and whispered, "Okay."

The doorknob rattled, and then a knock interrupted the morning quiet. Lani bolted upright, clutching the sheet to her chest, her eyes wide.

"Lani. Is Dad in there?" Trevor's muffled voice came through the door. "He's not in his room and I can't find him in the house. His bed's already made up, too."

"Ah—" She bit her lip, a panicked look on her face.

Rick caressed her shoulder. "I'll be out in a minute, Trev. Lani and I are talking."

"How come the door's locked?"

"Never mind. Go eat breakfast and I'll be there after I take a shower."

"Okay, Dad."

Lani fell back on her pillow and covered her head with the sheet. "Oh, my god. What were we thinking?"

Rick traced her features through the cloth, and kissed her nose. "It's okay. As far as Trevor knows, we're just talking. He's only nine." He peeled the sheet away from her face and kissed her lips. "Come on and get up."

"What about Sadie and Chuck?" She looked so worried that Rick had to struggle to hold back a smile.

"We're two consenting adults. Besides, Mom and Chuck like you."

Lani groaned. "I can't believe I did this. In their home."

Rick kissed her soundly. "It's my home, too. Don't regret what we shared last night. It was too special."

She smiled, the warmth coming back into her chocolate eyes. "You're right. It was wonderful. Incredible."

"Good." He sprinkled kisses over her face, eyes and nose. "Now get up. I've gotta take a quick shower."

He grabbed his robe from where it had landed the night before, and slipped into it. After he made sure the hallway was clear of nine-year-olds, he dodged into the bathroom.

Just thinking about Lani and her passionate lovemaking made Rick's cock hard all over again. With a curse, he switched the water from warm to cold.

When he finished showering, he ducked into his room and pulled on jeans, his bulletproof vest, a T-shirt, and then a denim shirt over that. As he headed to the kitchen, Lani came out of her room, wearing shorts and a blouse, her hair back in a French braid.

"Ready to face the cavalry?" he asked.

She attempted a smile, but the corner of her mouth trembled with nervousness, he was certain. "I think so," she murmured.

He kissed her then followed her into the dining room, letting her get there a little ahead of him. He didn't care if

Chuck and Sadie knew he and Lani were together, but he knew that she needed to get adjusted to it.

Lani slipped into a chair and scooted up to the table. "Looks like a gorgeous day out."

"Well don't you look fine," Chuck said as he put orange marmalade on a biscuit.

"Thanks." Lani smiled as she reached for a biscuit and started to butter it.

Sadie speared a sausage. "Did you get a good night's rest in spite of Trevor being sick?"

Lani nodded, her eyes avoiding Rick's.

"'Morning." Rick ruffled his son's hair, then slid into the chair next to Lani and pressed his knee close to hers. "Feeling better, Trev?"

"Yeah. I could eat ten eggs." Trevor smiled at his dad. "Hey, how come you were in Lani's room this morning? Did you sleep in there? What were you guys talking about?"

Lani dropped the butter knife, and it clattered on her plate. She blushed a deep pink and Rick had to hold back a grin.

"We were just talking." He turned to Sadie. "Please pass the sausage links, Mom."

Sadie raised her brows and glanced from Rick to Lani, who was intent on ladling scrambled eggs onto her plate. Sadie passed the platter of sausages to Rick, and he could see that she was trying to hide a smile.

"Well then." Chuck reached for the gravy. "Let's have us some breakfast."

Lani was mortified. Her palms tingled and her face flushed so hot she felt like her cheeks were sunburned. As wonderful as the scrambled eggs, sausages and biscuits smelled, the food tasted like rubber and sawdust.

She couldn't believe she'd made love to Rick in the same home as his son and parents. What was wrong with her?

But was it ever wonderful. She blushed again at the turn of her thoughts, and avoided looking at anyone.

Trevor's chatter rolled over her like the sound of a June bug buzzing on a summer day. He jabbered on like he'd never been sick, telling anyone who'd listen about his plans for taming the new calf in the barn and starting a rock collection.

Rick squeezed Lani's knee beneath the table, and she almost jumped out of her skin. A slow burn invaded her belly when she looked at him. He was so sexy. And she had seen every charming inch of him. The thought of their passion sent another wave of heat over her skin.

He leaned close and whispered in her ear, "Don't be embarrassed, and don't regret anything. You're too special. We're too special together. All right?"

She nodded, unable to speak, feeling like a lump the size of a baseball had lodged in her throat.

"I've got to get to work." He grabbed his plate and headed to the kitchen. "Great breakfast, Mom."

As Rick drove to work, his thoughts remained on last night and making love to Lani. It was better than he'd imagined. The woman was so warm and sensual. He wasn't sure he would be able to get his mind off her and onto his job.

When he arrived at the Border Patrol station, he forced himself to get a grip on his thoughts and get them back on the problems at hand. He had to track down Gordo and *El Torero* and he needed his usual single-minded focus to accomplish it.

Rick walked into the station and found a message from the Herald reporter, David Connor, waiting for him.

Maybe the worm had a conscience after all.

Rick dialed the number.

"Connor," a voice answered.

"This is McAllister."

A pause. "Thank you for returning my call, Agent

McAllister. Can you meet me at Mario's at noon?"

"I'll be there."

The line went dead. Real sociable guy. Probably killed Connor to make the decision to talk to him.

Rick arrived at Mario's early to make sure he could snag a good booth and grab a bite to eat. The lunchtime boozer crowd was there, the air so thick with cigarette smoke it was like walking into a giant ashtray. The corner booth was open where he'd met with Jorge Juarez, and Rick eased into it, facing the door, and waited for Connor.

His skin crawled at his nape, and he knew someone watched him from the back room. He glanced over his shoulder and saw Mari, the waitress. Her full lips were painted in shimmering red. The color matched her low cut dress that looked like she'd been poured into it then tossed in a dryer for good measure.

She slunk up to Rick on spiked heels that must've been a good four inches high. "Have you come back to see me?" She leaned forward and her hair swept across his arm, her breasts almost spilling from her dress.

He forced a tight smile. "I'll have a plate of *nachos supremos*, and iced tea."

"Is that all?" She traced her red-tipped fingernail along his bicep.

"That'll do it."

Mari gave a seductive pout and walked away with swaying hips.

Rick had little patience for women like Mari, but in his line of work, she could eventually make a good contact. That is if a man didn't have to sleep with her to get information.

Within a few minutes, Mari brought Rick the *nachos* and tea. She slipped her arm around his shoulders, her gold bangles scraping his neck, and probably would've slid onto his lap if the bartender hadn't called her away. Cheap perfume hung in the air along with the smell of sour beer. Wood-bladed fans spun overhead, but about all the good that did was re-circulate the stench of sweat and smoke.

The *nachos* were tasty, and Rick had munched down half the platter by the time Connor walked through the front door. The reporter strode to the bar and ordered, then looked around like a man checking to see if there was anyone he knew. He nodded to a couple of guys then spotted Rick. With a beer in one hand, Connor sauntered to Rick's table.

"McAllister."

"Connor. What's up?"

Mari brushed by Connor, and he said loud enough for her to hear. "If you ever want to spill your guts, give me a call." He flipped a business card on the table and walked back to the bar. Rick heard Connor order another beer and ask the bartender to turn on the Arizona Diamondbacks' game.

The side of the card facing up had Connor's name and office information. Rick didn't bother to turn it over. He left the card where the reporter had dropped it, and finished eating his lunch. Out of the corner of his eye, he saw Mari serving a patron on the other side of the bar, her gold bracelets glinting in the artificial light. When Rick stood, he dropped a ten on the table, slipped Connor's card into his pocket, and walked out the front door.

The sky was hazy bright, like the morning after a good rain, but clouds were building over the mountains. They'd be getting a good storm that night, no doubt. He slid into the driver's seat and started his truck, then pulled Connor's card out of his pocket, and flipped it over. Pedro Rios, 123 "A" Street was written in sharp black letters.

Rick radioed the station on a secure channel and informed them that he had a lead, and gave the name and location. Then he put the truck into gear and drove to the address Connor had given him.

Weeds and refuse choked the front yard of the small house. The blue paint—vivid at one time—was now bleached ghostly pale and crackled like a parched riverbed. Like most homes in the border town, iron scrollwork barred the windows.

The rusted gate creaked as Rick swung it open. As he walked up the concrete steps, he saw the door standing open about an inch. His gut clenched. He glanced up and down the street and pulled out his gun, shielding it. No cars were parked in front of the house or the houses next door. The street was empty of people.

As soon as Rick crept up to the door, he smelled it. The heavy miasma of decomposing flesh. Bile rose. He leaned back, his head against the house, fighting to keep his stomach from heaving up the *nachos.*

A rhythmic whoosh-whoosh-whoosh echoed from inside the house. With his gun in his right hand, Rick eased the door open with his left.

No sign of anyone inside.

He knocked. "Border Patrol."

No answer. Not that he expected any.

Rick pushed the door wider with his boot, but remained out of sight. When nothing moved and he heard no sound but the whooshing noise, he held his gun in front of him and rounded the corner.

The overwhelming stench slammed into him, enough to damn near drive him to his knees. His eyes and throat burned, and he struggled to swallow. He pulled a handkerchief out of his pocket and covered his nose.

The body hung on a rope. A rope tied to a meat hook. A man. His swollen head tilted at a bizarre angle, and his tongue...Rick closed his eyes for a moment, then made himself look again. That thick, engorged tongue—and the face, hideous purple-blue like the hands. His hands looked like surgical gloves blown up and painted black.

A ceiling fan churned next to the corpse, the blades skimming the top of his black hair and striking the rope, causing the whoosh-whoosh-whoosh noise. The room was trashed. Chairs smashed, garbage littering the floor, the couch on end.

Damn.

Rick listened for sounds inside the house and heard none. He headed back outside and jogged down the stairs, filling his lungs with clean air.

From the looks of the man, not to mention the smell, he'd been dead for a while, and Rick doubted if anyone had hung around to see what happened next. He kept his gun drawn and went back to his truck to radio the BP headquarters and the police.

While he waited for the cops to arrive, he checked out the front room again. He didn't recognize the man, but the face was too bloated to be sure. The cadaver's feet were at least two feet off the floor. No chair, or anything else he could've stood on, was close enough to the man for it to be a suicide. Plaster had chipped away from around the meat hook, exposing the beam it was screwed into.

Sirens screamed in the background as he glanced at the garbage around the room. Fast food wrappers, a sock with a hole, a toothpick, a matchbook cover, and sunflower seed shells were scattered among the trash.

Rick noticed a torn piece of paper. He couldn't quite make out the word, but he thought *Toro* was scrawled across the top of the scrap.

Was it related to *El Torero*, meaning the matador? Or *toro*, meaning bull?

Two hours later Rick headed home, after giving his statement to the police about how he'd come across the body, and why he was there. He'd hung around to gain information during the police investigation. Identification in the corpse's pockets said the man was indeed Pedro Rios. After examining the scene and the body, the homicide detective said he suspected Rios had been murdered.

David Connor would be in for a nasty surprise when he got hauled down to the police station for questioning. Protecting sources was one thing. Murder was another.

* * * * *

After she returned from her interview with another rancher, Lani headed out to relax beside Sadie's pond. She sank into the swing's cushions, slowly rocking back and forth in time with the sound of toads croaking by the pond. The waterfall's gentle babble soothed her nerves, and a late afternoon breeze stirred to caress her face. The air smelled of rain, the sky dark with pregnant storm clouds.

Pregnant. What would it be like to be pregnant with Rick's child? To have his baby? Lani stretched out on the swing and covered her face with her hands. How could she think of such a thing, when she'd known the man for such a short time? He probably wanted nothing more than a little fun in the sack. Well, he was certainly all that.

What an incredible night they had, not to mention the hours before dawn. She never knew it could be like that. So fulfilling. So incredibly good.

That's what Theresa and Calinda had been talking about.

Rick was right. No matter what happened next, she couldn't regret what they shared last night.

She relaxed, imagining all the tension in her body seeping through the cushion of the swing, swirling into the ground, deeper and deeper, until everything around her faded and she slid into a deep sleep.

The sun warmed Lani's face, caressing her lips, her eyelids, her brow. A heady sense of pleasure enveloped her and she sighed, content to bask in the gentle, loving heat.

"Lani," the sun called to her in a throaty whisper.

"Mmmm," she murmured, then opened her eyes to see that it was dark outside and Rick was bent over her. "Rick."

He balanced on the edge of the swing, his arms propped on either side of her hips. He shifted and ran his finger down her nose. "Wake up, sleepyhead."

She smiled. "I dreamed the sun was kissing me."

"Not the sun." He bent and brushed his lips over hers. "Me. I kissed you here." Her lips. "And here." Her nose. "And here...and here." Her eyelids. "And I want to kiss you in places the sun can't reach. In places that only I can touch you."

Lani flushed and wrapped her arms around his neck. "I want to kiss every inch of you."

Rick gave her his sexy grin that made her stomach flutter. "I'll consider that a promise."

She noticed his hair was wet and he smelled of apple shampoo. "You've taken your shower."

He ran his hand down her neck and over the curve of her breast, and she gasped, her nipples tightening at the sensual touch.

"It was one of those days," he murmured. "I knew if I came near you first, I couldn't control myself." He nuzzled her ear, then kissed it. "See? I can't even keep my hands or my mouth off you."

"Mmmm. Let me sit up."

"Why?" Rick nipped at her chin and then her lips. "I like you where you are. Beneath me. But if you want to be on top..."

Lani smiled. "All right."

He helped her up, then drew her onto his lap. Lani tried to protest, but the strength of his arms made her feel safe and secure, and wanted, something she hadn't felt since her parents and sister had died.

"Are you ready to tell me what your ex did to you?" he murmured, surprising her with the directness of his question.

She slipped one arm behind him and the other across his hard stomach. The scent of Sadie's roses mingled with the smell of impending rain. A chorus of crickets filled the night and in the distance a *coyote* howled. The only light came from the windows of the house, and stars had begun to appear through patches of clouds in the evening sky.

Lani gave a deep shuddering sigh as Rick caressed her shoulder, down her arm and back again. "Do we have to talk about him?"

"I think it'll be good to realize that he was just a bastard who didn't deserve you." Rick gently massaged the nape of her neck. "How did someone as sweet as you ever hook up with a sonofabitch like that?"

She tensed at the thought of her ex-husband's courtship. "We started dating when I was in college. James was charming, attentive, and handsome. And I was young and naïve."

A raindrop landed on Lani's ankle and soft splatters hit the canopy above. When she started talking again, her voice was flat. "After the accident he was always around. A few months after I lost my family he stopped by my apartment and found me crying. He fixed me a glass of wine and said it would relax me. Next thing I knew it was morning, and we were in bed, naked."

Rick made a sound like a low growl. Rain pattered harder, but Lani continued, knowing she needed to tell him everything. "I couldn't remember a thing. I freaked out, but James said I drank the entire bottle of wine on my own, then pleaded with him to stay."

Memories twisted in her gut like a serrated blade. "He insisted that I begged him for sex, and told him I didn't want to be a virgin any longer. He said we should get married because he loved me, and in case I was pregnant.

"I thought I was in love with him. I trusted him." She curled her fist. "I was so stupid. I really thought he loved me."

Rick caught her chin in his hand and made her look at him. "Stop beating yourself up over the guy. You were young and innocent, and the bastard took advantage of you."

She reached up and kissed him. "You're so good to me."

"You're so good for me." He brushed his lips over hers and she shuddered, every nerve in her body raw with desire. "Think anyone would notice..."

"Out here?" She gave him a horrified look.

"I'm just teasing you." He kissed her again. "Though I find the idea appetizing."

Rain began pouring down and a barrage of lightning split the sky. Thunder rumbled, an unearthly sound that made her heart pound.

"We'd better get inside." Rick scooted her off his lap. "We're sitting on a metal swing, and that's not a smart thing in a thunderstorm."

He grabbed her hand and they raced in the rain to the house. They reached the porch just as lightning flashed again, the crash of thunder immediately following. They were still laughing, still holding hands, when they walked into the house.

When she saw Trevor, Chuck and Sadie, she tried to pull away, but Rick wouldn't let go.

"How come you're holding Lani's hand, Dad?" Trevor's face twisted as if in thought. "Is she your girlfriend?"

Lani blushed, but Rick nodded, his face solemn. "Yes, she's my girlfriend."

Trevor bounced up and down. "Cool. Can I have a little brother or sister?"

Chuck and Sadie burst out laughing, and Lani wanted to hide.

Rick smiled and looked at her. "One step at a time, Trev. One step at a time."

Chapter Thirteen

🔊

"Damn straight I'm upset about what those illegals did." John Stevens scowled around his toothpick in response to Lani's question.

They were sitting in the office of the former sheriff's sprawling ranch home. After asking the rancher's permission, Lani had set out her small recorder, and she checked her list of questions as they talked.

"Exactly what happened?" Lani kept her expression professional, but her pulse beat a little faster at the heat in Steven's words.

He narrowed his hazel eyes, his scowl deepening. "A group of 'em passed through the east pasture. Instead of climbing through the barbed wire fence, they cut it with wire cutters. Hundreds of my cattle got out." Stevens clenched his fists and his face reddened. "My herd got into some bad feed and it killed 'em all. We're talking thousands of dollars gone to hell."

Before Lani could reply, a phone rang. Stevens withdrew a cell phone from the breast pocket of his denim shirt and checked the display.

"'Scuse me, ma'am." He shifted in his seat and glanced toward the doorway. "I've got to take this call."

"I'll wait in the hall until you're done." Lani stood and wandered out of the ranch office as she heard Stevens answer the phone, speaking in fluent Spanish.

As she waited for him, she studied framed photographs and newspaper articles on the man's walls. Apparently the rancher was active in local politics. He and Mayor Montaño shook hands in one shot. In other clippings, Stevens had posed with other men and women that were local politicians and businessmen according to the various captions.

A few minutes later, Stevens came out to the hall to let her know he was done with his phone conversation, but he'd have to cut their interview short. Lani followed him into the office, sat down and hurried through the remainder of her questions. In some ways she was glad for the earlier interruption. The rancher seemed more relaxed, even jovial after the phone call, like he'd received good news.

When she finished the interview, Lani gathered her recorder and notebook, and thanked the rancher. The phone rang again as she was leaving, and she told Stevens she'd see herself out.

As she drove the SUV along the dirt road leading from the ranch, she passed a vanload of people heading toward Sweetwater. The van was traveling so fast that a cloud of dust rose around it, and the driver almost swerved into Lani's vehicle. She bit her lip as she gripped the steering wheel.

The man driving the van barely spared Lani a glance, even though he'd almost run her off the road. She clenched her teeth. Some people shouldn't be allowed to have a license.

In the Turner's study, Lani sat before her notebook computer and typed in John Steven's responses to her questions as she transcribed the recorded conversation. When she came to the part where she'd left the room and the rancher began to speak in Spanish, she reached for the fast forward button. She hadn't even thought about the fact she'd left the recorder on when he took the call. She paused when she recognized one word.

Not a word—a name. Gordo. The same name Dee MacLeod Reynolds had mentioned.

Was Stevens speaking to or about someone named Gordo? Or was he talking about something else altogether?

Sadie breezed into the study, interrupting Lani's train of

thought when she handed her the cordless. "It's your editor."

As Sadie walked out of the den, Lani put the phone to her ear. "Hey, Theresa."

"How's my favorite reporter and shopping bud?" Theresa's pleasant voice flowed over Lani, making her homesick for her friend.

"Wonderful." Lani smiled and sighed. "Couldn't be better."

"Mmmm—hmm. You sound awfully satisfied. Does that mean you've found yourself a decent man?"

Warmth crept up Lani's neck, and she tried to keep her voice from betraying her. "What in the world makes you say that?"

Theresa snickered. "You can't fool me."

No use trying to keep anything from Theresa — talk about an investigative reporter. She'd been one of the best. The woman definitely could scent anything out of the ordinary.

Lani settled in the office chair and eyed the door of the den. "His name is Rick and he's the most incredible man I've ever met."

"Way to go." Lani could picture Theresa's devilish grin. "So, how's he in bed?"

A wave of embarrassment swept over Lani. "Theresa!"

"I want details. Come on, give it up."

"Well." Lani glanced at the door again and lowered her voice. "The man is amazing."

Theresa's throaty laugh was so loud that Lani had to pull the phone away from her ear. "'Bout time you found a real man. You deserve better than that loser you were married to."

Lani picked at a loose thread on the hem of her blouse. "I'm sure this is a fling for Rick, nothing more. Besides, I'll only be here a short time more."

"You're having fun, aren't you?"

Smiling, Lani said, "He makes me feel beautiful."

"You are beautiful. I've been telling you that for ages. You should never have listened to a damn word the jerk ever said."

"Yeah, yeah. So how's Calinda? Keeping you company since I'm not there?"

"We're having lunch tomorrow, as a matter-of-fact."

"Tell her hello for me." Lani spun around in the chair. "Did you call just to chat?"

Paper rattled, and Lani imagined Theresa was shifting one of the many piles on her desk. "Yeah, and thought I'd check to see how your feature is coming along."

"Good." Lani rattled off a summary of what she'd learned so far.

"Great job." Theresa's voice held approval. "I've got one more question."

"What's that, dare I ask?"

"After meeting and bedding this hunk named Rick, are you still coming home on the eighteenth?"

Lani shook her head and giggled. "What do you think I'm going to do? Park myself here permanently just because I met a man who's incredible in bed?"

"I think that's as good a reason as any."

Letting out an exaggerated sigh, Lani said, "You're incorrigible."

Theresa gave a wicked laugh. "Just come up for air every now and then, okay?"

After Lani said goodbye, she punched off the cordless, set it aside, and wandered into the kitchen. She was still smiling when she saw Rick's mother.

"Need help with anything, Sadie?"

Sadie grabbed her gardening gloves off the counter. "If you'd like, you can help me with dinner, but I won't be starting it for at least an hour. I'm off to gather a few squash, tomatoes and onions out of the garden."

Trevor tore into the room and almost smacked into Lani. "Hey, Lani! Wanna come outside and play with me in my hideout?"

Lani looked from Trevor to Sadie. "Sure, if your grandmother doesn't need me in the garden."

"You two go ahead." Sadie picked up a wicker basket from the table. "It'll give my ears some rest."

Trevor took Lani by the hand and practically dragged her through the orchard to where his hideout was hidden in the windbreak. His hand felt small and warm in hers.

Through the trees, Lani could see the dirt landing strip where Rick kept his plane, and she shivered. Beyond that, stubby mesquite bushes seemed to go on endlessly to the foot of the mountains. One thing she'd noticed about this part of Arizona was how she could see for miles and miles in the valley. No trees or hills blocked the view, other than those planted around the ranch house.

When they reached the playhouse, she scooted in after Trevor and sat cross-legged on the floor.

"Wanna play chess or checkers?" Trevor snatched a game board from a pile beside the toy box. "Dad and Grandpa taught me how to play both of those games and I'm really good."

Lani laughed. "You'd probably destroy me at chess, so how about checkers?"

Trevor set up the board in record time, and proved to be a great checkers player. She was amazed at the mature strategy he used to beat her.

When it became too dark to play anymore, they packed up the game and went back to the house. As soon as they walked in the door Lani saw Rick, his hair wet from his shower. Her pulse picked up and butterflies filled her belly.

"Dad!" Trevor ran up to Rick and hugged him. "I beat Lani three times at checkers and she only won two times, but then it got too dark and we had to come back into the house."

Rick ruffled his son's hair. "You'll have to challenge her to chess, next."

"I did but she said I'd destroy her, so we played checkers." Trevor whirled and headed for the kitchen. "I'm so hungry I could eat ten peanut butter and jelly sandwiches. I'm gonna ask Grandma what's for dinner."

When Trevor raced around the corner, Rick grasped Lani's waist and kissed her long and hard. "I've been wanting to do that all day long," he murmured.

"I've missed you." She settled her head against his chest, her hands resting on his shoulders, allowing herself to feel wanted in his embrace. "How was your day?"

"Great, now that I'm home, and you're in my arms."

When the house was quiet, and when he was sure Trevor was asleep, Rick went to Lani. Rain fell from the eves outside her bedroom window in soft patters.

She was waiting in one of his denim shirts, the snaps undone to where he could see the curve of her breasts. After he locked the door, he turned to her and she slid her arms around his waist.

"About time." She tilted her head up to smile at him. "I've been dying to get my hands on you."

He kissed her hard, letting her feel all the passion built up inside him. When he pulled away, his breathing was already ragged from desire. "I almost said to hell with waiting."

Lani led him to the bed. "Yesterday I promised to kiss you all over, but we were a little, ah, rushed last night," she said, remembering how they could hardly wait to tear each other's clothes off once everyone went to bed. This time she wanted it slow, wanted to pleasure him in the ways that he had pleasured her.

Rick helped her pull his T-shirt over his head and his lips

quirked into a grin. "You were a quite the little wild thing. Not sure I can wait, though."

She ran her fingers through the hair on his chest and smiled at the teasing note in his voice. "Well you're just going to sit back because it's my turn," she said as she lightly ran her fingernails over his flat nipples.

Lani skated her fingers down his rock-hard abs to the waistband of his jeans. She unbuttoned them, her knuckles brushing his cock with every movement. His erection seemed to grow harder and longer and she smiled when she saw Rick grit his teeth and clench his hands at his sides. She took her own sweet time as she pushed the jeans to the floor and then he stepped out of them. Before she pulled down his briefs, she ran her hand over the length of his erection, tracing the outline with her fingertips, teasing and taunting him.

"I can't get over how big you are," she murmured.

Flames roared in Rick's gut at her every touch, her every word. The feminine approval in her eyes was obvious as she gazed at his naked body and especially his cock that jutted toward her.

She pulled his briefs slowly down to his feet. "I plan to kiss you everywhere."

"Everywhere, huh?" He kicked off the briefs then sat on the bed. In a fluid motion he settled on his back, his hands behind his head. "I'm all yours, darlin'."

"That's what I want." Lani eased onto the bed and straddled him, and he almost roared when he felt her bare pussy against his thighs. "All of you." His denim shirt looked so damn good on her, and he could see the dark circle of her nipples through the opening.

He groaned, wanting to roll her onto her back and thrust into her hard and fast. To hell with it. He wanted to take her now. "You're gonna torture me, aren't you, woman?"

"Yeah." She trailed her fingers through the hair on his chest to his waist and back, but avoided his cock. "I love your body."

A rumble rose within his chest and he ached to stroke her. He slid his hands under the denim shirt and felt nothing but the satin skin of her hips. Blood pooled in his groin, almost to the point of explosive pain.

Honey-gold hair fell across his face as she brushed her mouth against his. She ran the tip of her tongue over his lips, then slipped into his mouth. She tasted of mint from her toothpaste, along with her own unique flavor. He clenched her hips in his hands as he drank her honeysuckle scent.

Her lips met his nose in a kiss as light and fleeting as a butterfly. Slowly she moved her lips to each eyelid, softly kissing each one. When she trailed her tongue to his ear, she murmured, "I love how you sound like a purring mountain lion when we're together."

He reached under the shirt and captured her breasts, then traced her nipples with his thumbs. With a small gasp she arched her back, pressing her hips closer to his, her pussy damp against his cock. She pulled at the snaps of the shirt until it was completely undone, and then let it slide from her shoulders.

Rain continued to pound on the rooftop in time with the beating of his heart. In the low lighting of the Victorian lamp, Rick could clearly see every curve, the way Lani's breasts rose firm and high and the way her nipples jutted toward him. She was silk and satin, heat and fire, and he wanted her in ways he'd never imagined wanting any woman.

Lani lowered her head and scooted further down his body. She flicked her tongue over his Adam's apple then kissed the hollow at the base of his throat. With slow deliberate strokes of her tongue, she worked her way over his collarbone and down to his pecs. She bit softly at one of his nipples before licking her way across his muscular chest to his other nipple. Lower and lower she moved, licking, biting and kissing until she reached the curling hair between his thighs.

His breath hissed out. "You're about to make me lose my mind, woman."

"Good." She looked up at him, a wicked glint in her eyes. "That's what you do to me."

The corner of his mouth curved into a sensual smile. "Witch."

She gave a soft laugh. "I want to taste you again, like you've tasted me." He groaned as she licked his cock like an ice cream cone, swirling her tongue over the head. Then slid him into her mouth, raking him softly with her teeth. He grabbed her head between his palms and clenched his hands in her silken hair.

Her head bobbed up and down as she slid her mouth along his erection and Rick guided her. He raised his hips to meet her, enjoying the sight of his cock thrusting in and out of her hot mouth.

When Rick couldn't take any more without climaxing, he grabbed a foil package from the top of the nightstand. "I can't hold off much longer and right now I want to fuck you, honey."

Lani smiled and took the condom from him. She eased it onto his cock, her tongue leading the way, like fire licking at his soul. After the protection covered him, she moved up to straddle his hips. She grasped his cock with one hand and placed it at the entrance to her core. She slid down on him, taking him deep, as deep as it could reach, until it hit her G-spot.

"Yes, there." She moaned as he filled her, as he thrust up to meet her. She wriggled her body and rode his cock, her breasts swaying as she rocked her hips. "I want all of you, Rick. Deeper. Harder."

He grasped her hips, raising her up and down the length of his cock.

Keeping their bodies joined, he rolled over and brought her under him so that she was pinned beneath him. He plunged into her as she started to close her eyes.

"Look at me." His voice was a demanding growl.

He wanted to see her passion, wanted to see her release. The rapture in her eyes nearly sent him over, but he held back, watching her as he rocked his hips against hers.

She gasped and her eyes rolled to the ceiling and he could see her losing herself to the sensations. Her body jerked hard beneath him and she bit her lip to hold back her cries. She trembled, her body quaking with the force of her orgasm.

Rick pounded into her, harder and harder yet. He loved to watch her, to see her face flushed with desire for him. He braced his hands to either side of her and held off as long as he could, wanting to draw out her orgasm as long as possible.

But his own orgasm wouldn't wait any longer and he had to bite back a shout. Just as a powerful climax stormed his body and his cock released his seed, he felt the condom tear.

Shit.

His muscles clenched as his body pulsated. He held himself still, unable to withdraw from Lani's body. It was too late.

He closed his eyes and relaxed between Lani's thighs, still joined, not wanting to separate from her.

What was done was done. It was too important to be with her.

Lani could get pregnant.

The idea of Lani carrying his child gave him a heady feeling. But he wasn't sure how she would take it.

"Mmmm," she said, easing her hands into his hair. "This could be addicting."

"I'm already addicted to you." Rick propped his head on one hand and ran his other over her silky skin, drawing circles around her nipples. "What if I told you the condom tore?" he asked, not taking his gaze from her face.

Lani's eyes widened and her body tensed beneath him.

She dropped her hands to his shoulders. "Did it?"

"I'm almost positive."

"Oh. My. God." She closed her eyes, and he wished he knew what she was thinking.

Rick trailed his finger down the tip of her nose to her lips. "We could get married."

Her eyes flew open. "No—I—no. Oh, god. We barely know each other. I can't marry you just because I might be pregnant." Her voice trembled like she was about to cry.

"We know each other pretty well." Rick rained kisses on her face, hoping to calm her fears.

She remained silent, not meeting his eyes.

And then it occurred to him how eerily familiar the situation was, and he cursed himself for his stupidity. Lani's SOB ex had convinced her to marry him in case she became pregnant after he raped her. And that's what Rick thought of it. Rape. She hadn't given herself to the man with her consent. The bastard had taken her virginity and used her.

Time. She needed time.

Rick eased out of Lani, and sure enough, the condom hadn't made it. He disposed of it and pulled her into his arms. "Don't worry. Everything'll be fine."

"How can you say that?" She covered her face with her hands. "It never occurred to me the condom could tear." Her voice was muffled behind her palms. "What if it happens again?"

"The odds are you won't get pregnant from one time. And the odds are definitely against a condom breaking a second time." He pulled her hands away from her face and kissed her. She stiffened then gradually melted against him as he deepened the kiss.

She sighed and slid her hands around his waist. "You shouldn't be here when Trevor wakes."

"I'll be back in my own bed when the sun rises," he

promised, kissing her forehead. "And when my son rises."

Lani smiled faintly and snuggled into the curve of his arm. Rain pattered on the roof as he held her. It felt so good holding her. Like he'd just come home from a long journey to find her there, waiting for him.

Rick waited until her breathing was soft and even, and she'd completely relaxed. He finally fell into a light sleep, dreaming of babies with sun-kissed hair and chocolate-brown eyes.

Lani woke alone, the bed cold and empty without Rick. As she stretched, she thought about their lovemaking last night and smiled.

Then she remembered. The condom had torn. Her smile vanished as she slid her hand to her belly. What if she was pregnant?

The thought heated her, a slow flush of pleasure that eased over her body like warm rain on a summer day.

A baby. Their baby.

Lani curled into a ball and hugged herself. Last night Rick had mentioned marriage—probably wanting to do "the honorable thing." But she'd never marry him because he felt he had to.

A knock jarred Lani from her thoughts. She pulled the sheet up to her neck. "Yes?"

Rick slipped in the door and locked it behind him. He was dressed in jeans and a blue denim shirt that intensified the color of his eyes. The bed sank under his weight when he sat beside her and gave her a light kiss. His lips were warm and firm, and she couldn't help but remember how it felt having those lips all over her body.

He nuzzled her ear. "Are you planning to sleep all morning?"

Smiling, she slid her arms around his neck. "I missed

waking up with you next to me."

"I'd like nothing more than to wake up with you every single day." He smiled and gave a lock of her hair a light tug. "Now get up, before I decide to pull off my clothes and join you."

She lowered her lashes and gave him a coy look. "Best idea you've had yet."

He started to pull back the sheet when they heard Trevor's frenetic chatter in the hallway. He sighed and kissed her forehead. "I'll head off Taz. You get dressed."

She threw the pillow at his back. "Slave driver."

After he closed the door, Lani put on his robe, grabbed her clothing and then dodged into the bathroom for a quick shower. For some reason she felt utterly feminine that morning, and instead of dressing in jeans, she wore a silk blouse and a short skirt that flattered her curves.

When she walked into the living room, Rick's low whistle caused a thrill in Lani's belly. She thought he was going to kiss her in front of his family, so she dodged away, not ready for that kind of demonstrative affection in front of everyone.

"Your calendar clear?" he asked after breakfast, when they were alone in the kitchen. Sadie and Trevor were gardening and Chuck was feeding the calves.

Lani slipped her arms around Rick's waist and hugged him. "I'm all yours."

"I have something I want to show you." He slid his knuckles across her cheek. "Then I'd like to take you to dinner afterwards."

She smiled and brushed his lips with hers. "Take me away, cowboy."

Late in the afternoon, they left in Rick's truck and drove a few miles, past fields of cotton, corn, and alfalfa, past rangeland dotted with red cattle, to empty acreage that butted up to the low mountain range. After crossing a cattle guard, they traveled down a dirt road that was little more than a pair of tracks through grass and mesquite bushes. At the end of the road, they parked and climbed out of the vehicle. Rick took her hand and brought her around to the front of the truck.

"What do you think?" he asked, watching her expression.

Lani took in the rugged mountain that hugged the edge of the property and the high desert terrain. Mesquite bushes were green from summer rains, the earth dark brown from last night's storm. A family of quail skittered into the bushes, their nervous calls a gentle sound in the desert quiet. The air smelled clean and fresh. The sky was a brilliant blue, but outlined by clouds building up over the mountain tops.

"It's wonderful," she said, and meant every word.

"This is my land." Rick released her hand and went back to his side of the truck. He reached in and pulled out a brown tube from behind the seat then came back to where Lani was waiting for him. He withdrew a set of blueprints, unrolled and spread them on the hood of his vehicle. "These are the prints for the house I'm having built here."

He put his arm around her as she leaned closer to get a better look. "I bet it'll be incredible." She traced a line with her fingertip.

"A split-level house." Rick pointed to the blueprint with his free hand. "Here, on the bottom floor, is where the kitchen will be, the living room, study, library, guest room, and family room." He moved the top page aside and showed her the one under it. "This is upstairs. Trevor's room will be here, a couple more bedrooms here and here, and this is the master bedroom. The master has a covered balcony that faces the mountain."

"Perfect for enjoying summer rainstorms." She smiled up at him.

He trailed his finger down her nose to her lips, and held her gaze with his intense blue eyes. "Perfect for raising a family."

Chapter Fourteen

∽

Lani stopped breathing. The way he looked at her. The way he mentioned raising a family. Like he was asking a question with his eyes. Nervousness rose within her like a flock of panicked birds.

"The builder's scheduled to break ground in August." He took his arm from her shoulders and focused his attention on rolling the blueprints and shoving them into the tube.

She took a deep breath and tried to calm the tremors in her hands. No, he wasn't asking her anything. He was just sharing his plans. She knew better than to start thinking that way.

"What does Trevor think of it?" she asked.

Rick shrugged. "I haven't told him yet. He'll miss living with his grandparents, but he's old enough now, and they don't need him underfoot all the time. Mom wants to continue watching him when I'm at work. They love that kid."

"He's a wonderful little guy."

"Yeah, he is." He put the tube into the truck. "You ready for dinner?"

"Absolutely. Where are we headed?" she asked as they climbed into the vehicle.

Rick started his truck and the powerful engine roared. "There's a popular place in Douglas that serves excellent Mexican food."

Lani smiled. "My favorite. Anytime. Anyplace."

He raised an eyebrow. "With anyone?"

She laughed and buckled her seatbelt. "Especially blue-eyed cowboys."

When they arrived at the restaurant, it was almost dark. Most of the parking was taken, but they managed to find a space not too far away. The restaurant was located in one of the older buildings in downtown Douglas. "Downtown" consisted of a single street lined with ancient two-story buildings and a historic hotel.

"*Los Dos Hermanos* means 'the two brothers' in Spanish," Rick explained as they walked to the door, his large hand engulfing Lani's. "The García brothers opened the restaurant twenty years ago, and then sold it to Montaño a few years back."

"Montaño?" That same sense of unease tickled at her belly. She held her purse a little tighter to her chest. "The mayor?"

Rick stopped at the door, his hand resting on the wooden handle. "You've met him?"

She nodded. "I interviewed him a few days ago. I didn't realize he owned this restaurant."

Rick pulled open the door and guided her inside. As they entered the cool interior, smells of Mexican food and sounds of voices, clinking plates and mariachi music swept over Lani.

The interior was dimly lit, but decorated in splashes of vivid colors. *Serapes* and *sombreros* graced the walls, and baskets of colorful gourds were arranged artistically around the room. *Piñatas* in red, green and white hung from big metal hooks anchored into the ceiling's exposed beams. Wood-bladed fans stirred the air, the *piñatas* dancing in the breeze they made.

To the right of the hostess station was a larger than life plaster statue of a matador, the color chipped and peeling. It stared ahead with sightless eyes where the paint had apparently flaked off.

"The man sure likes matadors." She glanced from the statue to Rick. "Has tons of them in his office, too."

Rick frowned. "He does?"

She nodded. "I saw his collection when I interviewed him."

A trio approached them from inside the restaurant, and Lani saw that it was John Stevens, Dee MacLeod, and a good-looking man she didn't recognize.

Seeing Stevens reminded Lani of the interview she hadn't finished transcribing yesterday, and she wondered if she should mention to Rick the phone conversation she'd inadvertently recorded.

"Lani, Rick, it's wonderful to see you both." Dee smiled and gestured toward the handsome man beside her. "Lani this is my husband, Jake."

"My pleasure, Lani" Jake said to Lani and nodded. He turned to Rick, "Haven't seen you around much lately."

Rick nodded. "Been busy as hell."

"McAllister," John Stevens said as he chewed on a toothpick. He tipped his hat at Lani. "Ma'am."

Dee smiled at Lani, her green eyes sparkling. "How's your feature?"

"Terrific." Lani smiled in return. She couldn't help but like the redhead. "The information you provided has been invaluable."

"You just missed Sal," Dee said to Rick. "John was bullshitting with him at the bar when we got here."

After Stevens and the Reynolds said their goodbyes, the hostess arrived. She was beautiful, with high cheekbones, dark hair, and skin like flawless beige silk. Her nametag read *Isabel.*

As they followed the hostess through an archway to a nearby booth, Lani wondered if Rick noticed the woman's beauty and how slender she was. The insecurity that had developed during the five years of James'ss emotional abuse crawled up her throat, threatening to surface. Threatening to suffocate her. Why couldn't she let those old feelings go?

When they reached the booth, Rick slid next to Lani on the padded bench. Isabel left them with two menus. "*Buenos noches,*" she said in a lilting Hispanic accent.

Lani watched the hostess leave. She was so elegant, the gentle sway of her hips probably as natural to her as breathing. *She's gorgeous,* Lani thought, and then realized she'd spoken the words aloud.

"Who?" Rick glanced up from his menu.

"The hostess." She picked up her own menu and chanced a look at him.

He gave her that slow sexy smile that made her knees tremble. "You're the most beautiful woman here, and I bet you don't even realize it."

Warmth eased through her, but she shook her head. "You're a good liar, cowboy. But I think I'll keep you around."

He took the menu from her and captured her hands in a movement so fast she caught her breath in surprise. "Lani, I've never lied to you and I never will. That's one thing you can count on." The intensity of his gaze trapped her, and she didn't know how to reply. He brushed his lips over hers, and then released her hands. "Don't ever forget that."

"Okay," she whispered.

They decided what they wanted, and then Rick ordered in Spanish from Dora, their waitress, who wore a flowing red skirt and a white peasant blouse with colored ribbons woven around the neckline and sleeves.

Dora left, then returned minutes later with their iced tea and a basket of tortilla chips that were so hot they burned Lani's fingers when she put a few on her plate. This time she didn't make the mistake of dipping one into salsa before asking for the mild version.

When the platters of food arrived, they were heaped with beef tacos, cheese enchiladas, Mexican rice, refried beans, guacamole and sour cream. Rick's food vanished, while Lani managed to eat less than half the contents of her plate.

"No, I'm stuffed," she complained when Rick said she needed to eat more. "If you're still hungry, you finish it."

She grabbed her purse and excused herself to go to the ladies room. Her sandals clicked on the tile as she walked through the archway, past the matador at the front entrance, and through a door marked *Baños*.

The hallway was dark, and she blinked to adjust to the dimness. There were three more doors, and she went into the one labeled *Señoritas*. After using the facilities, she washed her hands and touched up her pink lipstick.

When she finished she stared at her reflection in the mirror. Her brown eyes were warm and expressive, her honey-blonde hair flowing in soft waves to her shoulders. Maybe Rick was right, she was pretty. She'd let James'ss verbal assaults eat at her for far too long, and it was time she let them go.

Live for now, Lani. Enjoy your time with this wonderful man and then move on.

When she returned to the table, Rick had paid the bill and was ready to head out into the night.

With his arm around Lani, Rick opened the front door and led her out of the restaurant. As soon as they stepped into the warm night, she stopped and wound her arms around his waist. Her fingers brushed the gun at his back and she froze.

"Why do you have your gun?" she asked, her voice muffled against his shirt.

"Just my line of work, honey. I always carry it."

"Oh." She gave him a worried look. "I keep forgetting what a dangerous job you have."

"Don't worry so much." He rubbed her shoulders and all he could think about was getting her alone. "What do you think about heading up to Bisbee? There's a nice bed-and-breakfast we can stay at. A good friend of mine, Nicole, owns it."

"Yes." She looked up and smiled. "I'd love to."

On the way to Bisbee, Rick used his cell phone to call Nicole to see if she had an available room. Fortunately she did have one left, and said it was all theirs.

He also called Sadie and let her know that he and Lani wouldn't be back until the following night. He could hear the smile in his mom's voice when she told him to have a good time. Sadie was delighted with Rick's interest in Lani, and if he knew his mom she was probably working hard to finish that wedding ring quilt. More and more, Rick was finding he hoped she would need to.

"We're fortunate Nicole had an available room," Rick said as they walked into the bed-and-breakfast. "Couldn't get into this place normally. We're in historic Old Bisbee. A real tourist magnet. Tomorrow, I can show you the sights—all two of 'em."

He signed the old-fashioned guest register with the plumed pen provided by a man who looked like he came straight from the sixties. He wore a faded tie-dye T-shirt and frayed jeans, had a flowing beard, and long blonde hair held back with a leather strap.

"All we have is the honeymoon suite." The clerk handed them a set of brass keys, rather than a modern key card.

"Where's Nicole?" Rick asked. "I'd like to introduce her to Lani."

The clerk shrugged. "She's out with her cousins Lily and Sabrina."

"Maybe we'll catch her in the morning," Rick said as he took Lani's hand and led her up the stairs.

A paisley carpet runner covered the polished wooden staircase, and every step creaked. Old-fashioned gas lamps lit the stairwell and hallways, and the walls were painted a deep mulberry. At the top of the staircase, their room was the first to the left.

When he opened the door, Rick thought it was a nice

room, as far as rooms went. But Lani seemed enchanted.

"Oh, look! All the furniture is at least 1800's, and this pitcher and wash basin are fabulous." Lani tossed her purse on the bed and then dodged into the bathroom. "This is so wonderful. And the tub is enormous."

She peeked around the corner and gave him a sexy smile that made him hard in a rush. "Big enough for two." She went back into the bathroom. "Oooh, and champagne bubble bath, too." He heard the pop of a cork and then running water.

"Right behind you." After he pulled a foil package out of his wallet, Rick tossed the wallet into the top drawer of the dresser, slid his gun next to it, then peeled off his clothes. An ice bucket with a chilled bottle of champagne sat on the vanity, along with two crystal glasses and a note that read *Compliments of the staff for your honeymoon.*

Rick smiled at what he was sure was Nicole's mischievousness. He had dated her a couple of times, but they'd decided they enjoyed being friends more than they liked dating one another.

He opened the bottle, poured two glasses full and managed to carry both and the bottle to the bathroom. By the time he joined her, Lani was chest-deep in bubbles. She was leaning back in the tub with her eyes closed and total relaxation on her face. He set the champagne bottle on the vanity beside the tub before he climbed in.

Water and bubbles rose and splashed over the side as he settled next to Lani, his naked body sliding along hers. He pressed one of the chilled glasses against her left nipple and her eyes flew open.

"That's cold," she murmured as the nub grew taut and he brushed the glass across the other nipple, making sure it had equal attention. "You naughty boy."

He winked and handed her the glass. "How about a toast?"

"Mmmm, champagne." She took the crystal stem and

held it up. "To what?"

"To us." Rick brushed his lips over hers. "And to first times."

"First times?" Her breath was warm on his mouth.

He took his glass and slid it to the sensitive spot between her breasts. "First time making love in bubbles."

"Oh, my." Lani gasped and shivered at the feel of the crystal sliding over her skin. "I'll toast to that."

Rick clinked his glass to hers, the sound like the sweet chime of a bell. Feeling utterly content, Lani took a single swallow of the golden fluid, the bubbles tickling her nose and her throat.

He drained his glass and set it on the vanity beside the tub. "Drink up, sweetheart," he said with a glint in his blue eyes. "I want to take as much advantage of you as I possibly can."

Lani couldn't help a giggle. "All right." She raised her glass. "Here's to being taken advantage of by the hottest cowboy in the west."

The corner of Rick's mouth quirked as he watched her sip from the champagne. "Come on now, down it, honey."

She took the challenge and tilted her head back and swallowed the rest in one long draught. When she handed him the glass, she was already feeling a bit woozy from the champagne.

He set her glass on the vanity with his then grabbed the bottle of champagne. When he brought it towards Lani, she raised her eyebrow. "What are you going to do with that?"

"I like dessert with my champagne." Rick tipped the bottle and Lani gasped as he poured some of the sparkling fluid over one of her nipples, washing away the soap bubbles from the hard pink nub and her breast. He lowered his head and licked the champagne with long strokes of his tongue.

With a moan Lani arched up to him, reveling in the

contrast of the cold champagne and now his hot mouth licking and sucking her nipple. He poured more of the bubbly over her other breast and proceeded to lick it all away, too.

Lani could only feel, could only give herself up to the sensations. The champagne was affecting her senses and she felt so relaxed yet so hot for Rick.

"Hold on, honey," he said as he set the champagne bottle aside again.

Rick settled on his haunches between her thighs. He positioned Lani so that her back rested against the side of the tub and her ass was in his lap, against his cock. She slid down a bit in the bubbles, but braced her hands to either side of her. Her head was still above water as he hooked her legs above his shoulders, raising her ass up in his palms so that her mons was wide and exposed to him. Somehow he managed to hold onto her and grab the champagne bottle, and then poured more of the fluid over the soft curls on her mons and onto her folds.

Lani cried out at the incredible feel of champagne bubbling over her mons. And when he set the bottle aside, he raised her up while lowering his head and began licking and sucking her from the sensitive spot between her folds and her ass, all the way up to her mound.

The tipsy feeling from the champagne, combined with the feel of Rick's warm mouth on her mons was almost more than she could bear. Her arms trembled as heat rushed over her, expanding to every pore in her body. It was like fire, fire licking her from her toes to her thighs, her belly on up over her breasts and her cheeks to the roots of her hair. She gave a choked cry and almost slipped under the bubbles as her climax hit her.

Rick released her long enough to catch her to him and pull her up out of the water and onto his lap, facing him so that her legs straddled his and his cock was hard against her folds. His jaw was tense, his eyes sparking with blue fire as he cupped her head and brought her roughly to him and kissed her. With her dazed senses she could swear he tasted of fire as well as champagne and her juices.

"I've got to fuck you." His expression was fierce as he pulled away. "Now."

Lani was burning up as he grabbed a foil packet that he'd apparently left on the vanity. He tore into it and in no time he tossed aside the wrapper and sheathed his enormous erection.

"I want to fill you up," he said. "I want to take you rough and hard. Is that how you want me to fuck you?"

"Yes." Lani nodded, wanting this wildness, this freeness that she'd never before experienced. "Please, Rick."

She gripped his powerful shoulders as he raised her up and brought her down on his cock, deep and fast. God, how he stretched her wide and filled her so, so deep. She let herself go and rode him hard, raising herself up and down his length. Her breasts bounced and her nipples ached as she gripped his shoulders.

He had a tight hold on her ass and he moved her even faster. "That's it sweetheart. Fuck me just like that."

Lani watched his face, his intent expression, the fire in his blue eyes, and the way he gritted his teeth as if holding back with everything he had. She pressed her hands on his shoulders and rose up and down on his shaft and slamming down on his cock so that it reached her G-spot again and again. Water splashed and blood roared in her head as he *fucked* her like they never had before.

All the sensations were too much. Rick's tongue flicking against her nipples, his cock deep within her, water sliding over her body. Lani came in a rush, her body so hot that this time she thought she'd burn into cinders. Her channel contracted around his cock, gripping and releasing him in wild flares as her body continued to tremble. Several more thrusts and Rick's growl told her he'd climaxed. He gripped her hips tight and she collapsed against him, their bodies melding together completely.

* * * * *

Sunlight spilled through sheer curtains at the bay window and onto their bed, caressing Lani's face with its gentle warmth. Rick had molded his body to her back, his arm snug around her waist, and she could feel his cock hard against her ass. She smiled, loving the feel of him against her, not wanting the moment to end.

His breath tickled her neck, and she shivered. He moved his hand to her shoulder and traced a pattern on her back with his finger.

"What are you doing?" Her voice was husky with sleep.

"Playing connect-the-dots," he murmured. "You have the cutest freckles across your shoulders."

She rolled over in Rick's arms to face him. "Oh, yeah?"

"Mm-hmm." He ran his finger along her collarbone, then down to the swell of her breasts. "More freckles here. And here. And here."

Lani stroked his cheek with her palm, his stubble coarse to her touch, yet somehow erotic, inflaming her desire for him. He slid his thigh between her legs and she felt his erection hard against her stomach.

She wiggled so that his thigh was higher, pressing against her mons. "We'll be late for breakfast, cowboy."

"It's a bed-and-breakfast. Bed comes first, then breakfast." He lowered his mouth to hers, his kiss waking every nerve in her body. "Or breakfast in bed, which is what I'm interested in."

With a teasing grin she slid her palm down his muscled chest, his tight abs and down to his cock. "Can I have seconds?"

His mouth quirked into that drop-dead sexy grin of his. "And thirds."

Lani kissed his chest, flicking her tongue and tasting the salt of his skin and breathing in his masculine scent. She didn't care if they ever got out of bed. She couldn't imagine a more perfect moment than this.

A rumble rose up in Rick's chest and he worked hard at regaining his self-control. He intended to make love to Lani this morning, not fuck hard and fast like they had last night. But the way she was kissing and touching him, he was finding it harder and harder to hold back, but he was a man with a mission.

A mission to make her his…forever.

He loved her slow and easy, taking his time to taste and touch every inch of her. And when he finally slid his cock into her silky heat, it was like everything around them slowed to that one point in time. He rocked his hips against hers, feeling a sense of satisfaction welling up inside him in tune with his building climax. This was *his* woman, and there was no way on Earth she was getting away from him.

Chapter Fifteen

ॐ

They barely made it to breakfast in time. Lani let out a sigh of contentment as the desk clerk escorted them to a garden courtyard with a fountain splashing in the midst, a sheer rock wall hugging one side of the patio.

Sunlight filtered through leaves of oak and mulberry trees, their shadows dappling the white patio furniture. A hodgepodge of geraniums and roses in brilliant hues of reds and pinks crowded the tables. Because she and Rick had arrived during the night, Lani hadn't realized that the B & B was nestled against a mountain.

A breeze caressed her skin, as soft as a newborn's breath, the perfume of roses light in the air. Lani wore her hair in a French braid, but felt grungy wearing the same clothes she had the day before. Rick promised to take her shopping after they ate, but once Lani got a look at the casual clothing of the hotel staff, she didn't feel a bit out of place.

Rick introduced Lani to his friend Nicole who owned the B & B.

"You've got a real cutie here," Nicole said to Rick with a good-natured grin as she ushered them to a table for two and set out a menu for each of them.

Heat reddened Lani's cheeks, but Rick said, "Don't I know it."

Once they had ordered, the vivacious Nicole stayed and chatted for a few moments, then went to greet more guests.

In no time at all, the waiter brought plates heaped with toast, scrambled eggs, sausages and Danish pastries, then poured glasses of fresh-squeezed orange juice. Lani looked at the mounds of food and her appetite vanished.

Wild Borders

"Is that all you're going to eat?" Rick asked as she finished a piece of buttered toast and pushed her plate away.

She gave him a smile. "I'm full."

Rick's vivid blue eyes bored into her. "Sure you're okay?"

"You worry too much." Smiling, she reached down to squeeze his knee under the table. "When I'm with you, everything's all right.

"So, tell me about this town," Lani said, changing the subject before the moment got too serious.

Rick shrugged and reached for a cheese Danish. "Bisbee does have a pretty interesting history. Back in the late 1800's until the mid 1970's, it was a major copper mining community. It was called 'Queen of the Copper Camps.'" He took a bite of his Danish.

Lani smiled, enjoying watching him. "Bisbee is an unusual name."

He nodded and finished chewing. "It was named for a guy that never even set foot in this town. DeWitt Bisbee, a judge and investor from San Francisco." Rick drank his orange juice then set the empty glass next to his plate. "When I was a kid, I'd wonder how a guy could never bother to go see a town named after him."

"Hey, he was from San Francisco. Can't beat the snobs in my home city." Her smile faded as she thought of James, the epitome of a successful elitist.

After breakfast, they strolled onto Main, a narrow street that snaked its way down Tombstone Canyon. Homes and trees clung to the steep sides of red canyon walls.

"Reminds me a little of home," Lani said. "Though in San Francisco you don't usually see houses that look like they're going to slide off the side of a mountain at any moment."

"A lot of people compare it to Frisco," Rick replied. "But the weather here beats the hell out of your hometown. When I was in San Francisco a couple of weeks ago, I like to have frozen my ass off, and it's the middle of the summer."

Lani nodded and laughed. "My favorite quote about the city is one by Mark Twain. I think it goes, 'The coldest winter I ever spent was a summer in San Francisco.'"

Rick chuckled. "Twain also said that in Arizona the temperature 'remains a constant 120 degrees in the shade, except when it varies and goes higher.'"

She leaned against his arm, feeling relaxed. And wanted. Something she hadn't felt since her parents and sister had died. She didn't care to think about how limited their time together was. Too soon the magic would end. Only in fairy tales could anyone be as happy as Rick made her. It couldn't last. But today she would pretend that it would last forever.

Hand-in-hand they walked down the sloping sidewalk, from Castle Rock to the century-old masonry buildings along Main Street. Art galleries, potters and antique stores filled the buildings that Rick said used to house department stores, jewelers and banks when he was a kid.

They found an eclectic clothing store where Lani bought a filmy skirt and blouse that had been hand-dyed a soft rose. The skirt swirled around her ankles, just above her silver sandals, and the peasant blouse rested off her shoulders. And she wasn't wearing a bra or panties, which made her feel both sexy and naughty.

Rick smiled when she came out of the changing room wearing the new outfit. "Beautiful."

Lani blushed at his approval, and they paid for the purchase, the clerk giving Lani a bag to carry her other clothes in.

They spent the morning exploring shops along Main. At a pottery store, she fell in love with handmade dinnerware in an unusual pattern of soft mauve, sea green, and butter yellow.

"Think this would go good in the kitchen when our new home is built?" Rick asked as she ran her hand over one of the glazed plates.

For a second her heart stopped when he said *our home*.

Stop it. He meant his and Trevor's.

She collected herself and replied, "Absolutely." Lani pointed to the price tag. "It costs a small fortune, though."

He nuzzled the top of her head. "I like it. Let's get it."

Their conversation with the potter was an experience. Half the time Lani thought the woman was in another discussion altogether. The potter wore a clay-streaked T-shirt and jeans, her long black hair tied back with yarn away from her thin face, and her hazel eyes seemed vague, like she was thinking about something else the entire time. Rick ordered the entire dinnerware collection and arranged to have it shipped to Sadie and Chuck's home.

Rick glanced at his watch when they left the shop. "It's after twelve. Ready for lunch?"

"Sure." Lani hadn't regained her appetite, but didn't want him worrying.

They chose a small sidewalk café where she was able to look out the picture window as they ate, and observe shoppers and tourists. A sense of contentment filled her and she sighed.

"What?" Rick asked as he looked up from his menu.

She smiled and shook her head. "This day is too perfect."

Her stomach flip-flopped as he gave her his slow, sexy grin. "If you could travel anywhere in the world, where would you go?"

"I'm happy right here." She tilted her head. "But I've always wanted to go to Kauai. It seems so wild and beautiful from all the pictures I've seen."

"Not as beautiful as you." He took her hand in his and studied her fingers, then placed his palm against hers. "Your hand is so small."

"Next to yours, maybe. But for a woman they're not small."

"Oh they're small all right. Your ring finger is only the size of my pinkie." He turned her hand over and placed his lips to her palm. "And your skin is much softer than mine."

Lani gasped at the sensual contact, the feel of his lips against her skin. Her eyes locked with his and she couldn't move. Couldn't think.

She only knew that she was truly lost.

When they finished eating, Rick and Lani walked outside the café, and ran into Sal Valenzuela.

The Border Patrol agent slapped Rick on the back. "*Buenos tardes, amigo.*" He turned to Lani and held out his hand. "Hello, Lani. You look beautiful. Rick's a lucky man."

She blushed and returned Sal's friendly smile. "Get out of here."

"So, Rick." Sal slid his hands into his pockets. "Coming to CP tomorrow night?"

Rick shook his head.

"What's CP?" Lani asked.

"Uh—choir practice." Sal's mustache twitched and mischief sparked in his dark eyes.

Lani folded her arms and looked from one smirking man to the next. "Uh-huh."

Rick ran his hand over his head. "Well, it's CP if we're referring to our Check Points, like the one where you met Sal."

Sal laughed. "But it's also the term for an after shift party to relieve stress—usually involving beer."

Lani raised her brows.

Rick slipped his arm around Lani's shoulders. "The guys refer to it as a Choir Practice to give the tongue-in-cheek illusion to our spouses and significant others that we are not drinking, not smoking and not swearing."

Sal wiggled his eyebrows. "And not talking about past sexual conquests."

Lani's eyes widened and Rick just chuckled. "You can get lost now, Sal."

"See you at work tomorrow," Rick said, then steered Lani down the sidewalk.

"Past sexual conquests, huh?" she said as they walked.

He hugged her closer. "Sal's full of shit, so don't listen to him."

It was mid-afternoon when he took her to the Bisbee Mining and Historical Museum.

"The brochure says this museum was the first rural Smithsonian affiliate in the country," Lani said, just as the guide started speaking.

Their tour guide was a middle-aged woman who spoke with a soft lilt, the movement of her hands like butterflies floating in the wind. She wore a velvet patchwork skirt that reminded Lani of a crazy quilt, and heavy silver and turquoise jewelry blossomed at her neck and wrists.

"In the early 1900's, Bisbee sported a population of around twenty thousand, and it was the largest city between St. Louis and San Francisco," the guide said. "The town burned down three times, survived outbreaks of typhoid, annual floods, labor strikes, and the closing of most of the mining operations in the mid 1970's. Our population hovers right around six thousand now, and the town has reinvented itself as an artists' colony and retirement community. Travelers come from all over the world to drink in the history and enjoy the culture.

"You may want to visit our Romanesque style Copper Queen Hotel," she continued, waving her hand toward one window, in the direction of the hotel. "It was once considered one of the grandest in the west. Even Teddy Roosevelt stayed there."

The guide waved her hand again in another direction. "Just around the corner from the Copper Queen is Brewery Gulch, an infamous part of our history, which was home to almost fifty saloons and bordellos around the turn of the century."

Her butterfly hands fluttered in a different direction. "Another of our attractions is the Lavender Pit Mine. It's three quarters of a mile wide, nearly a thousand feet deep, and one of the largest surface mines in the world."

"Amazing," Lani said as they left the museum. "Fifty saloons on one street?"

"Don't forget the bordellos." Rick kissed the top of her head. "The history of this town has never been so interesting to me before coming here with you."

The sun was low over the mountains and the streetlights flickered on. Lani sighed, wishing they could stay forever in this perfect time, this perfect place. Of course, they couldn't. Fairy tales only came true for children, not grown women with too many scars and mileage.

Hand in hand, they strolled toward the bed-and-breakfast, toward Rick's truck, and toward a reality Lani wished she could escape for another day. Even another hour. She knew that was impossible, but the dream felt pleasant even as they drew closer to the truck.

She leaned against his shoulder, feeling tired but content. And happy. She'd never felt so happy in all her life, even though she knew she only had a short time longer with Rick. "Thanks for a wonderful day."

He eased his arm around Lani and squeezed her to him. "Darlin', every day that I'm with you is wonderful."

Lani had nodded off on the drive home, her head resting against the window. She looked pale, and Rick was concerned that she wasn't feeling well. But when they arrived at the ranch and he woke her, she insisted she was all right.

"Dad! You're home!" Trevor bounded into Rick's arms when they walked in the door and gave his father a hug and a sticky kiss on his cheek. The boy wriggled free and then wrapped his arms around Lani's waist and hugged her. "I'm glad you're back."

To Rick's surprise, she gave Trevor a kiss on his dirty cheek, and the boy gave her a big smack in return.

"You're just in time for dinner," Sadie said as they entered the kitchen. "I made a big batch of spaghetti and a tossed salad. And a fresh pitcher of iced tea."

Rick sniffed the air and his stomach grumbled in appreciation.

"Breadsticks with garlic and butter, too." Trevor pointed to a basket on the counter covered with a gingham cloth. "Can I have one now?"

"You hold on 'til we all sit down to dinner." Sadie playfully slapped at Trevor's hand as he lifted up the edge of the cloth. "Go on and wash up."

"All right, Grandma," he grumbled and ran off toward the bathroom.

"I bet the spaghetti is wonderful," Lani told Sadie. "But I'm not hungry and I'm tired. I think I'll lie down."

Sadie patted Lani's hand. "You go rest up, and if you get hungry there'll be plenty of leftovers in the fridge."

Rick walked Lani down the hall and into her room. "You okay?"

She nodded and smiled. "Just tired."

He drew her close and she sighed, leaning against him and sliding her arms around his waist. For several minutes they stood in each other's embrace, until he thought she'd fallen asleep standing up. With more than a little reluctance, he parted from her and she opened her eyes. Her lids drooped like she could hardly keep them open.

"I think I plum wore you out." He ran his finger down her nose to the tip.

"Feel free to wear me out anytime," she murmured.

He kissed her then closed the door behind him when he left her room.

Lani had only intended to take a nap when they returned home from Bisbee, but she didn't wake until just before dawn. Apparently, Rick had slipped into bed without disturbing her and held her all night.

Her head was tucked under his chin and she was facing him, his arms tight around her. He smelled so wonderful, felt so great in her arms...and he was good and naked, his early morning erection pressing against her belly. She wished she was as bare as he was but she was still wearing the skirt and peasant blouse they'd bought yesterday, and no underwear.

Lani sighed. *A girl could get used to this.*

Fascinated by the hair curling on his chest, the powerful muscles of his arms, the scent of him, the taste of him—she slid her hands across his skin and kissed his warm flesh until he stirred and woke.

Rick gave her a sleepy grin. "Now this is one hell of a way to wake up."

"Mmmm-hmmm." Lani's tongue circled his nipple and the tiny nub tightened. She smiled and moved her mouth to his other nipple and she teased it just as slow and deliberate.

He rolled her onto her back in a swift movement that took her breath away. He braced himself above her, his hands to either side of her breasts. For a moment she just stared up at him, his sleep tousled hair and morning stubble making him even sexier.

"You're so beautiful." His face was intent as his gaze raked over her. "Waking up with you is the best thing I can imagine."

Before Lani could respond, he pulled down the rumpled peasant blouse and dipped his head to lick first one nipple and then the other. She gave a little moan as she reached for his cock, needing to feel its rigid warmth in her hand. *In her.*

Still bracing himself on one arm, Rick reached for her skirt and she released his cock to move her hands to his shoulders. He pulled up her skirt around her waist and his eyebrows rose when he saw she wasn't wearing any underwear. "If I'd known you were naked beneath your skirt, I'd have taken advantage of you yesterday."

Lani gave a soft laugh. "Well take advantage of me now, cowboy."

In moments he had sheathed his cock with a condom from the nightstand.

"Spread your legs wider for me, honey." Rick held his cock, ready to penetrate her, as she opened her legs as wide as possible.

In a single thrust he buried himself deep within her. Lani groaned and slipped her hands beneath his arms to hold onto his back. As he moved in and out of her, she dug her nails into his back and it seemed to spur him on. Harder. Faster.

Her senses whirled and everything blurred around her. Warmth pooled in her abdomen and grew, larger and larger until her orgasm exploded within her. Rick continued pumping in and out of her and then he came with a low rumble that sent aftershocks through her.

With a sigh of contentment, he rolled onto his side, still locked with Lani, her leg hooked over his thigh.

"A guy could get used to this," he murmured as he kissed her forehead. "Real quick."

Later, after Rick got up to get ready for work, Lani dressed and joined him and his family at breakfast. As she was picking at her slice of French toast, Lani's thoughts turned toward her feature, and to her interview with John Stevens.

Should she mention the recording to Rick? Or was it nothing?

Maybe he'd think she was overreacting, but her gut told her differently. She trusted her instincts—at least when it came to reporting.

When he carried his empty plate to the kitchen, she

followed.

She slipped her own plate into the dishwasher beside his. "Have a second?"

Smiling, he tweaked a strand of her hair. "Always for you, darlin'."

"I interviewed John Stevens at his ranch a couple of days ago."

Rick wrapped the strand of her hair around his finger. "I'll bet Bull had something to say. He lost a big chunk of cash due to illegal immigrants."

Lani explained how she'd left the room when Stevens took a call, but she'd left her recorder on, and how she'd transcribed her notes afterward. "His conversation was in Spanish, but I understood a name. At least I think it was a name."

As Rick raised one eyebrow, she continued, "I'm sure he was talking to someone named Gordo."

She winced as his finger tugged a bit too hard on her hair. "Sorry," he murmured and caressed her scalp. But he looked distracted, like wheels were churning in his mind.

He moved his hand from her hair and settled it on her shoulder. "Where's the tape?"

Lani led him to the office and gave him the cassette. While he listened to the one-sided conversation, she chewed the inside of her cheek, wishing she'd taken Spanish instead of French in high school.

"Mind if I take this?" he asked when he clicked off the recorder and popped out the cassette.

She nodded her agreement. By the look in his eyes, she didn't think it would have mattered if she'd refused. He was taking it regardless.

He slid the tape into his shirt pocket. "See anything or anyone out of the ordinary while you were there?"

"No." Lani started to shake her head then paused.

"Wait—when I was leaving, this guy was driving a van loaded with people up to the ranch and he almost ran me off the road."

Rick narrowed his gaze. "What did he look like?"

"Early forties, Hispanic, handle bar mustache. Big guy." The man's image came easily to her. "I remember because he swerved so close and I was angry that he almost hit me."

"Fits," Rick muttered. "On the tape Bull was talking to someone on a cell phone who was on his way to the ranch." He gave Lani a quick kiss and headed out the door. "Don't mention this to anyone, all right?"

"Okay." But he was already gone.

When Rick made it to the Border Patrol station, he found Miguel Martinez at the water cooler. "Hey, Mikey. Got a minute?"

Miguel waved Rick to his office, then shut the door behind them. The Special Operations Supervisor was below average in height and had a slim build, but he had a presence that filled a room and commanded respect. "What's on your mind?"

Rick paced around the cramped office. "As you know, a couple of names keep popping up. One is Gordo, the other *El Torero*. From the information I've gathered, Gordo is head *coyote*, but Torero runs the show."

Miguel scrubbed a hand over the stubble on his chin. "Just got in some surveillance today. We think we've made Gordo—a guy named José Hernandez."

Miguel gave Rick the description and Rick whistled through his teeth. "Good news and matches what I came across."

"As far as *Torero* …" Miguel shrugged. "Nothing solid."

"I think I have a line on *Torero*." Rick dragged his hand over his face and through his hair. "I need surveillance set up on John Stevens."

"The cattle baron and former sheriff?" Miguel dropped into his chair and looked at Rick like he'd lost a cog. "He's funding the campaign for Eduardo Montaño, the man most likely to win the election for U.S. Congress. And Montaño's running heavily on his immigrant platform."

"I've got proof." Rick sat heavily in the seat across from Miguel.

Miguel frowned.

Rick ran over the recorded conversation. "The tape only has his side of the conversation, but it was enough to convince me that Gordo was on his way across Sweetwater. And when Lani Stanton was leaving the property, she saw a man who meets the description you just gave me."

With a sigh, Miguel said, "Doesn't make sense. Stevens hates smugglers for what they've done to his herd."

"He's been pretty bitter about it. Maybe he's found a way to recoup some of that cash."

Miguel shook his head. "What else have you got?"

Rick rattled off the rest of the information he'd gathered, including the scrap of paper with *Toro* written across it and the toothpick amongst the garbage he'd noticed when he found the dead informant. "Stevens's nickname is Bull, so *Toro* could refer to him. And the man's always chewing on a toothpick." He paused. "I've got a gut feeling about this, Mikey."

Miguel stared at the ceiling before returning his gaze to Rick. "I trust your instincts—they've never failed you before. But we'll need to keep this quiet. If it gets out that the mayor's being backed by a smuggler, all hell will break loose." He pushed a frog paperweight along the edge of his desk. "Montaño's probably the most popular man in this town. Hell, one of the most popular men in the whole damn state. Loads of connections. Running for Congress."

"Yeah, I know." Rick stood and hooked his thumb in his belt loop. "But if Stevens is our man, we need to put him away."

Nodding, Miguel shoved the paperweight to the back of his desk. "You bet."

Rick turned on his heel, walked out of the office, and almost ran into Sal.

"What's up, *compadre*?" Sal asked, falling into step beside Rick. "You don't look like a guy who just spent the weekend with one gorgeous woman."

Pushing open the front door of the station, Rick stepped into the hot July sunshine. "I think I've made *El Torero*."

"Yeah?" Sal nudged the brim of his hat up and scratched his head. "Who?"

"John Stevens."

Sal narrowed his gaze. "You gotta be kidding."

"Nope."

"Well, if that don't beat all." Sal checked his watch. "You up for some dinner?"

Rick shook his head. "Thanks, but I've got something I need to take care of."

Chapter Sixteen

ဆ

After he visited a jeweler in Douglas, Rick headed home, smiling as he thought about Lani. He'd found the perfect ring to give her, and had left it at the jeweler's to be sized. Now he just had to find the right time to propose.

Lani was still gone on an interview when he arrived at the ranch. Rick took a quick shower, then went in search of Trevor and found his son in the windbreak. The boy was digging in the rich soil beside the playhouse.

"Dad!" Trevor jumped up and hugged Rick with his dirt covered arms before going back to his Tonka trucks and a giant mound of earth. "I'm building a city around a mountain made of gold, and digging a swimming pool with the backhoe behind this stick house that's really made of gold, too. Wanna help?"

Rick crouched beside his son. "What do you want me to do?"

Trevor pushed a bright yellow truck over to his dad. "You run the dump truck and I'll fill it full of dirt with the backhoe."

Memories of his own childhood came back in waves as he spent time with his son. When he was a kid, he would dig in the dirt, build forts in the mesquite bushes, or ride his bike. His biological father had never taken the time to play with him, and by the time Rick was Trevor's age, his dad was long gone.

The day Rick had learned Lorraine was pregnant, he vowed he would be there for his child. As often as possible, he would be at Trevor's Little League games, school recitals, 4-H competitions and birthdays. He would take him to the county fair, play catch and play in the dirt. He'd hoped to have more children, brothers and sisters for Trevor, but he'd never found a woman he wanted to spend the rest of his life with.

Until Lani.

"Say, Trev. What do you think of Lani?" Rick asked as he guided the truck to the mountain of dirt and dumped its load.

"She's cool and lots of fun." Trevor used the little backhoe to dig more earth and lifted it into the back of the dump truck when Rick had pushed it in place. "When you're not here, sometimes she plays games with me and I show her all kinds of stuff." He looked up at Rick and squinted. "Can we keep her?"

Rick chuckled. "That's a great idea. But I think that'll be up to Lani."

Trevor jumped up and brushed his dirty hands on his even dirtier jeans. "Let's ask her."

"Now hold on." Rick grabbed the boy's arms. "Don't say anything to Lani, okay?"

"Why not?" Trevor frowned. "I want her to stay here, with us."

Rick paused, trying to think of a way to explain it to his son. "She lives where Aunt Callie does, which is far away."

Trevor scrunched his eyebrows as he thought about that. "In Sanfrisco?"

"Yes, San Francisco. That's Lani's home, and she may want to go back there when she's finished with her job here."

"We could ask her to stay with us."

"But what if she misses where she lives?" Rick asked. "She might not like living here, so far from her home."

"Oh." Trevor eased off his dad's lap and stood. "What should we do?"

"Leave that up to me." Rick patted Trevor's shoulder. "Lani's supposed to be here another week, so for now, promise that you won't say anything about keeping her, yet. Okay?"

His son had a dejected look. "If she leaves I'm gonna

really, really, really miss her."

Rick stood and hugged his son. "Yeah. Same here."

* * * * *

With the aid of Marnie Torres as interpreter, Lani spent the afternoon interviewing two illegal migrant farm workers. The men explained how poor their families in Mexico were and how the money they earned in the U.S. helped to keep their relatives from starvation.

Lani learned from their point of view how badly the smugglers treated them, yet the men were willing to accept it as a means to sneak into the U.S. and better their families' lives.

When she finished the interview, Lani thanked the men and Marnie, and headed back to the ranch in the waning light. The sun was setting low behind the mountains, crimson and tangerine streaking across the western sky. Her customary energy had vanished and she felt so tired that all she wanted to do was crawl into bed and sleep. Hugging Rick.

While she drove, gentle warmth filled her as she recalled waking up in Rick's arms that morning. She couldn't get enough of the man.

That was going to make it all the harder when it was time to go back to San Francisco.

Lani sighed and tried not to think about leaving him, but it was impossible. Less than a week now. Just days until her flight was scheduled to depart from Tucson. Originally, she'd considered changing her flight to stay and interview for a position with the Tucson magazine. But now she wasn't sure she could be that close to Rick, and not be with him.

One day at a time. She would cherish whatever time she had with him, and then get on with her life, no matter how lonely that life would be without him. It took some effort, but she reminded herself again that she wasn't ready for a permanent relationship. Her heart and soul had been so badly bruised by her ex-husband and her hard-hearted father that she couldn't help but think that Rick was too good to be true.

It was dark when she drove up to the ranch. Her pulse picked up when she saw Rick's truck parked in the driveway. She couldn't help but feel like she was home. And that these people were family. The thought surprised her. No place had truly felt like home since her family was taken from her.

Thinking that way was only going to make things harder when she left.

Roxie bounded up and greeted Lani when she climbed out of the SUV, and she scratched the dog behind her ears. Roxie proceeded to slobber all over Lani's shoes and jeans as she returned the greeting. There was just enough light from the porch that she could make her way to the house.

Lani caught her breath as a shadowy figure stepped out from behind the vehicle. When she realized it was Rick, her muscles went limp with relief.

"Rick," she murmured, hand to her pounding heart.

"I missed you," he said as he drew her close. His arms felt so good around her, she never wanted to leave his embrace.

"You scared me," she said against his chest, her heart still pounding. She poked him in the ribs with one finger. "Don't do that."

Chuckling against her hair, he said, "I came outside so that I'd be able to kiss you without an audience."

"I'm glad you did." Lani reached up and brushed her lips over Rick's. "Just don't sneak up on me again. Got that, cowboy?"

"Uh-huh." He grinned against her mouth. "What do you say to a little walk in the dark?"

She cocked an eyebrow. "Oh, and what do you have in mind, mister?"

With a roguish grin, Rick took her hand. "I want to take advantage of you."

A low thrill skipped within her belly as he led her into the dark windbreak and past Trevor's playhouse.

Lani's panties grew damp and excitement flowed in her veins at just the thought of what Rick had in mind. But before she realized it, they were approaching his plane. She tried to stop, fear overwhelming her and replacing her arousal. "I can't." She shook her head. "Not in there."

Rick gently pulled her toward the plane. "We're not going to fly anywhere, honey. I just want someplace where I can have you all to myself."

Taking a deep breath, Lani forced herself to go forward, telling herself it was all right since they were going to remain on the ground. Just the warmth of Rick's big hand covering hers helped to calm the fear churning in her belly.

When they got to the plane, Lani's heart was pounding like mad, but she let Rick help her into the back and she settled herself on the edge of the seat like she might bolt at any moment. It was a little four-seater, not a six like—

No. Don't think about it, Lani.

When Rick climbed in he shut the door behind him. He sat in one of the back seats and pulled Lani onto his lap. For a long time he held her, just kissing her hair and hugging her close. She smelled that peculiar odor that small planes had along with dust, night air and Rick's comforting smell.

Gradually the fear eased and Lani relaxed. Instead she focused on Rick's erection pressed against her rear. He felt solid and real against her and he smelled so good, like testosterone and his own elemental scent. The fact that they were in a small plane didn't seem to matter any longer as she focused on the man who held her so tightly against his chest. She felt safe and secure and she knew that he would never let anything happen to her.

Rick felt Lani's body relax, and he squeezed her tighter to him.

She turned her face to his and lightly kissed his mouth.

"I'm all right now," she murmured as her lips brushed his cheek. "And I want you. Right here and now, I want you."

He trailed his thumb across her lower lip and smiled. "Let's get you out of those jeans.

After she kicked off her shoes, Lani sat on the floor and Rick helped her shimmy out of her jeans and underwear. She tugged off her blouse and tossed her bra aside. In the dim light from the half-moon he could see her voluptuous shape and he couldn't wait to get inside her.

Rick unzipped his jeans, releasing his erection. He was still sitting on his seat and Lani rose up, sliding between his thighs and grasping his cock in her small hand. She lowered her head and gave a little sigh as she slipped her lips over the head of his cock. She clenched one hand in his jeans while using the other to stroke his erection while she applied light suction with her mouth.

A groan rose up from Rick as he slid his hands into her silky hair. "You go down on me so good."

Lani merely replied with, "Mmmmm."

Rick groaned again and clenched his hands tighter in her hair. "Your mouth feels so hot and wet on my cock. And what you do with that tongue of yours...*damn*."

When he was so close to coming that he almost lost control. He held her head still as he pulled a condom out of his pocket. "I've got to fuck you now," he rumbled and pulled her away from him. In the dim light pouring into the plane, he could see her satisfied smile. The little vixen enjoyed getting him off, but he liked to fuck her even more.

He sheathed his cock and grabbed her around the waist, pulling her up and over his erection. She sank down on him, his cock sliding into her hot silken core.

"You feel incredible." Lani couldn't believe how she just couldn't get enough of this man. She braced her hands on his shoulders as he gripped her hips and moved her up and down. "I love it when you're wearing all your clothes—your jeans and cowboy hat—and I'm naked and you're—you're…"

"Fucking you?" Rick said with a teasing sound to his voice.

Heat rose to her cheeks and she nodded. "Yeah."

"What about making love to you?" he murmured, and more heat flushed over her.

She didn't know how to respond, so she just rode him harder. Her breasts bounced and Rick licked her nipples and gripped her ass, guiding her along even faster.

Everything around Lani blurred until she felt as though she was flying—that the airplane was gliding and she was riding it out in a storm. But she wasn't afraid, she was safe with Rick.

Higher and higher she soared until she came with a shuddering cry that echoed in the small plane. Rick continued to raise her up and down on his cock and she held onto his shoulders for support, too boneless to guide her own moments.

Several more thrusts and Rick groaned and climaxed, his cock throbbing in her channel. He held her still for a few moments, riding out his orgasm until he was spent.

With a soul-deep sigh, Lani relaxed against his chest, her naked breasts pressed against his shirt, his cock still deep within her. "Ready for another round?" she murmured, and Rick laughed.

"Anytime, sweetheart." He kissed the top of her head. "Any place."

* * * * *

A couple of days later, Lani drove back to the Turner Ranch. She felt exhausted after her interview with Kev Grand, although he certainly wasn't the reason she was feeling so poorly. The rancher was sexy in a hard and dangerous kind of way. No doubt it would take a hell of a woman to tame that man.

Chickens scattered in front of the SUV as Lani pulled up to the ranch, and thoughts of Rick washed over her. How did she manage to fall so completely for his charm? To fall so completely…

No. She wasn't even going there. She pushed the thought to the back of her mind as she noticed Chuck's truck was gone, and that Rick wasn't home yet.

Late afternoon shadows stretched across the driveway, and when Lani checked the dashboard clock, she saw it was after three. Rick could be home soon, or might come in as late as seven at night, depending on how his day went. She parked, grabbed her belongings, and headed for the front door.

Roxie gave Lani her normal greeting, slobbering all over Lani's pants. She'd come to love the Rottweiler as much as every person in the family.

The house was locked, and she opened the door with the key the Turners had loaned her. A note on the fridge said that Sadie, Chuck and Trevor were at the Torres home for a surprise birthday party for Bobby and would be gone through dinner, and that Lani was invited.

After tossing her purse and laptop onto her bed, Lani changed into shorts and a T-shirt, and wandered into the kitchen, barefoot. The house was eerily quiet, save for the tick of the kitchen clock. She missed Trevor's chatter, Chuck's dry wit and Sadie's musical laughter.

And Rick. His presence that filled the room. His touch. His teasing grin.

Lani couldn't hold back a smile, thinking about the time they'd spent together last night in his plane. She now had at least one positive thing to think about when it came to small planes.

A sound like a car door slamming came from outside, interrupting her thoughts.

Rick. Lani hurried to the bathroom, ran a brush through

her hair, and touched up her lipstick. She smelled Rick's apple shampoo from the shower, the scent reminding her of him, the feel of his hair under her fingers. She ached to touch him.

The front door opened and shut, the sound reverberating through the house. She couldn't help but smile as she walked back to the living room.

He was kicking off his boots and when he saw her he gave her a weary smile. "Damn but it's good to see you when I get home."

Lani's heart skipped a beat. "I'll bet. You just want some good hard sex."

Rick's lips quirked into a grin. "I'd have to say that's an added bonus."

She laughed and went to him but he held her off with an upraised hand. "Gotta take my shower, sweetheart. Been one of those days."

"How about I lather you up real good, cowboy?"

Rick raised an eyebrow. "I could live with that."

After he threw his clothes into the washing machine and he grabbed a condom, they slipped into the bathroom. Lani stripped out of her clothes while Rick climbed in under the spray. She followed him and took the bar of soap he was holding.

She began lathering his whole body, starting with his muscled chest and shoulders and working her way on down. The soap had a clean outdoorsy scent that she identified with Rick. Water streamed over her as she soaped his thighs and ignored his erection that was so big it damn near poked out her eye.

"Turn around," she ordered him after she soaped him all the way down to his feet. He looked a little disappointed that she'd ignored his package, but he faced the spray so that his back was to her.

Still on her knees, Lani was now staring at his tight butt cheeks. She sighed. *Yeah, an ass you could just bite.*

A bit of mischievousness rose up inside her and she leaned forward so that her lips were against his wet skin. And then she bit.

"Hey." Rick turned his upper torso and lightly pulled on her hair so that she was looking up at him. He had an eyebrow cocked and a spark in his eyes. "Who said you could bite my ass?"

She grinned. "I did. Now turn around and let me finish the job."

"Ass-biting wench," Rick grumbled in a teasing tone.

"Now brace your hands on the wall while I take care of you, mister."

He obliged and she proceeded to soap the back of his body, up his legs to that fine ass that she was tempted to bite again. She continued on up to the broad expanse of his back and his shoulders. Soap and water streamed down his back and shoulders and water pelted her face and hair.

"Face me," she demanded, doing her best to sound forceful.

Rick turned with his hands up and a stern look, like he was being arrested.

Lani laughed and started soaping the fine curls around his cock and he lowered his hands, closed his eyes and tipped his head back in the spray. She sighed at the sight of her wonderful man, his power, his masculine beauty.

Her man.

Lani shook away the thought and washed his cock then let the water rinse away the soap. She set the bar aside in the soap dish. "I want you to stroke yourself now. I want to see how you pleasure yourself."

"You mean jack-off?" he said, opening his eyes and raising his eyebrows.

She narrowed her gaze. "Do it, cowboy."

An amused expression crossed his face and he gripped

his cock in his big hand. Lani watched in fascination as he worked his staff from his balls to the head, his thumb rubbing over the tiny hole at the top before sliding back down his staff. He studied her while he did it, and she wondered where her sudden confidence had come from, in ordering him to do things she'd fantasized about. It occurred to her that she felt so comfortable with him now, like she knew him better than anyone she'd every known.

Could he feel the same way?

Again she dismissed that line of thinking and instead lowered her head to lick the top of his cock. Rick released his erection and moved his hands into her wet hair as she slid her mouth over him, taking him deep.

She loved the way he felt in her mouth, the way he felt in her hand as she licked and sucked his cock. She loved the way he gripped his hands in her hair and guided her up and down.

Just as she thought he was about to come, he commanded her, "Stop." When she looked up at him, he said, "It's my turn now."

Lani let his wet cock slide out of her mouth. "Oh?"

"Yeah." He took her by her shoulders and raised her, then grabbed the condom he'd left open on the edge of the tub and rolled it over his cock.

"Put your arms around my neck," he said as he brought her flush against him. Her mons ached and excitement skittered throughout her when Rick gripped her ass and said, "Hold on."

She squealed in surprise as he lifted her up and impaled her on his cock. Lani clenched her legs around his hips and hung on tight as he raised her up and down, thrusting in and out of her. Water from the shower poured over her head and face, and it was so like her fantasy that it made her all the more excited.

The power in his arms, his muscles flexing and the concentration in his expression undid her. She came so fast it made her head spin. Rick came moments later and hugged her tight to him as his cock continued to throb within her.

Chapter Seventeen

ജ

The following morning, when Rick reached the station, Miguel waylaid him in the hallway. "McAllister."

Rick ran a hand over his stubbled cheeks. "What's up, Mikey?"

"I've got something you'll want to hear," Miguel said as he motioned to his office and Rick followed his supervisor.

After Miguel shut his office door behind them, he motioned to a chair and Rick seated himself. Miguel eased back in his own chair and said, "Thought you might be interested in hearing about the surveillance we set up on Stevens."

"Yeah?" Rick leaned forward.

"I put a couple of undercover agents on Stevens's tail last night." Miguel spun the frog paperweight on his desk. "He had an interesting visitor drop by his ranch, around midnight."

"Who?"

"Gordo, aka José Hernandez."

Satisfaction gripped Rick and he hit his thigh with his fist. "I knew it."

Miguel held up his hand. "Of course that's not enough, but it's a start. We've got a helluva lot of work to do."

"Damn straight," Rick said, feeling a thread of satisfaction. "We'll nail that SOB."

He got to his feet and took his leave from Miguel. *Gordo.* Yes, that bastard was the key to everything. Thoughts of Lani knocked at the back of his mind, but he shoved them aside as Daryl Jones, the admin assistant, waylaid him in the reception area.

"Got a call for you, Rick."

Rick took the phone. "McAllister here."

"This is Juarez." The informant's voice shook. "Meet me at Mario's at one."

"*Sí, amigo*," Rick replied and hung up.

Lani would be at the station to interview Miguel at ten. Rick was tempted to hang around, but he had work to do.

He spent the morning tracking down surveillance info on Gordo and Stevens, and worked over a couple of other leads.

One o'clock sharp Rick arrived at Mario's Cantina. As soon as he slipped into his customary booth, Juarez appeared and slid onto the seat across from him. The informant smelled of sweat, like he hadn't taken a bath in days. Something in the man's eyes made Rick's gut tighten.

Glancing around the bar, Juarez licked his lips. "Your life is in danger, *amigo*."

Rick's muscles tensed and he leaned forward. "What do you mean?"

Juarez's eyes shifted from Rick to the bar and back. "*El Torero* wants you dead. He suspects you are closing in on him. He will do anything—take anything from you he can. Kill you. Kill your whole family. Back off, *amigo*. Hear me. Back off."

A chill crept over Rick's skin. Before he could ask Juarez for more information, the informant slid out of the booth and vanished out the front door.

* * * * *

When it was time for her to leave for her interview, Lani dressed in navy slacks, low heels and a pink silk blouse, her press badge attached to her belt loop. She smiled and waved goodbye to Sadie and Trevor who were working in the garden, and headed for Douglas.

Due to the increase in the number of Border Patrol

Agents, the agency had recently built an enormous facility on the outskirts of the Douglas city limits. Rick had explained that the old station, near the county fairgrounds, was originally designed for a staff of only fifty agents.

The new station was sleek, modern and efficient in appearance and smelled of paint and new carpet. A man with red hair, freckles, and a million-dollar grin, manned the front desk. His nameplate read *Daryl Jones, Administrative Assistant*, and he had an ID badge attached to his belt. He reminded Lani of a kid she'd had a crush on in the third grade, and she smiled.

"Hello, Mr. Jones." Lani's voice was smooth and professional as she switched into journalist mode. "My name is Lane Stanton, and I'm a reporter with *City by the Bay* Magazine. I have an appointment with Miguel Martinez."

"Hold on a sec." Daryl dialed the phone. A moment later he said, "He'll be right up."

As Lani waited for Miguel Martinez, her gaze wandered around the busy station. A picture of the President of the United States graced one wall, next to the American flag. Dirt and scuffs marred the polished linoleum floor, attesting to the volume of human traffic in the building.

Men and women agents walked in and out of the reception area, some clothed in spruce green 'rough duty' uniforms, and others wearing jumpsuits of the same color. She noticed agents in shirts and jeans, not unlike Rick. At the thought of him, a nervous tingle spread in her midsection, and she wondered if he was somewhere near.

A man in full uniform approached Lani. He was her height, clean-shaven and smelled faintly of aftershave. He had dark brown hair, green eyes and a deep cleft in his chin. "I'm Miguel Martinez. You must be Ms. Stanton."

"Agent Martinez." She extended her hand and smiled. He had a strong grip, and his pleasant, comfortable manner set her at ease.

"Let's sit in my office," he said as he turned to walk down the hall. Lani followed him through the station, noticing the constant flow of traffic, the hum of conversation.

He closed the door and motioned to a chair, then sat down, his manner relaxed and confident. As she took her seat, she pulled out her laptop and turned it on. "My questions are all on here. May I record you as well?"

He agreed, and as always when she interviewed, the outside world slipped away. "What is your title and responsibilities?" she asked.

Miguel leaned back in his chair and steepled his hands. "I'm a Special Operations Supervisor, abbreviated SOS. I'm in charge of several specialty teams, such as bike, horse and ATV patrol, training, Intelligence, and assorted other duties."

"I understand you have over five hundred agents permanently assigned along this stretch of the U.S. — Mexico border."

"Yes." He nodded. "Usually about one hundred agents work each shift, with three shifts in a twenty-four hour period. The agents are scheduled to work eight hours, but are expected to work ten to ensure that we have constant coverage. And if they're tracking UDAs they're expected to stay on duty until they find the UDAs or lose the trail."

Her fingers flew over the keyboard as she typed notes and scrolled through her questions. "How are these numbers of agents distributed?"

"Most are stationed along the border. Others are in intelligence."

"What about agents patrolling from the air?" She glanced up from her laptop.

Miguel pushed a frog paperweight along the edge of his desk. "Those agents are based out of Tucson, and stay in the west desert during the heat of the summer where the danger to the UDAs is the greatest from heat and lack of water."

"Can you tell me a little about the agents who patrol by

ATVs?"

"ATVs can get into places that vehicles can't, and can be a real deterrent just by the sound they make. The UDAs know they can't outrun them."

"I see." She paused, the thought of Rick flashing through her mind at her next question. "What are the responsibilities of those who work in Intelligence?"

"Intelligence agents gather information to help uniformed officers do their jobs." Miguel ran a hand over the stubble on his cheeks. "A separate intelligence unit operates undercover. These agents infiltrate groups, attempt to get in homes and find out any smuggling information they can."

After he had her sign a waiver form, Miguel took Lani in one of the Border Patrol SUVs and drove several miles along the border. She was amazed at the sheer numbers of vehicles positioned along its length.

Once they completed the drive, the agent gave her a tour of the station, including the areas where the UDAs were detained and processed. When he took her to the control room, he had the agents shut down visuals on cameras where sensors were located. He explained it was standard procedure as no unauthorized individuals were allowed to see the locations of sensors on the remote desert locations.

When Lani concluded the interview with Martinez, he shook her hand and she thanked him then headed out to the parking lot.

A dull pain throbbed behind Lani's eyes when she slid into Sadie's SUV. Her stomach churned and she felt like she would throw up. Lani leaned back in the seat and closed her eyes. She'd been so nauseated since…

Her eyes flew open and a cold chill swept over her. *No. It couldn't be.*

Instead of heading back to the ranch, Lani drove into Douglas, straight to a grocery store.

* * * * *

By the time Rick finished following up on a few leads and made it back to the office, he was burned out and ready to head home. Not to mention concerned by Juarez's statement about danger to his family and himself.

"Hey, McAllister. Take a call before you book on out of here." Daryl Jones held up the phone as Rick started to leave the station.

Rick took the receiver and dragged a hand over his hair. "McAllister here."

"We know where you live," a deep male voice said.

An iron fist clamped Rick's gut. "Who is this?" He barely had the presence of mind to motion to Daryl to have the call traced.

"We know you live with your mother and stepfather. And you have a handsome young son. He is nine, no?"

Rage filled Rick, a wave so powerful that his entire body shook. "Listen, you son of a bitch, you so much as come near my family and you're a dead man."

"Tch—tch. Such anger. Ah, and we must not forget the lovely *señorita* staying with you."

Rick clenched his fist. "What the hell do you want?"

"Turn in your resignation by tomorrow morning and walk away, Agent McAllister."

The line went dead.

* * * * *

"Oh, my god," Lani whispered while she stared at the blue plus sign on the test stick. "I'm pregnant."

Lani's head spun and for a moment darkness closed in on her. The stick clattered into the bathroom sink as she grabbed the rim to steady herself. When the feeling passed, she made sure the toilet lid was down and collapsed onto it.

If Theresa hadn't gone through a pregnancy while Lani worked at the magazine, she would have had no idea that it was possible to get morning sickness so fast. But Theresa had been ill almost from the moment she'd conceived. And thanks to modern day tests, it was possible to detect pregnancies within days.

So many feelings surged through Lani. Intense joy that she'd never known before filled her, and she almost laughed. She felt giddy and lightheaded.

She was going to be a mother. A mother!

It didn't seem real. A life was growing inside her. She did the math, and realized she would be giving birth in April.

Giving birth. A baby.

She was having Rick's baby.

The thought filled Lani with sheer pleasure. Rick's baby. Her baby. Their baby.

If only he loved her…like she loved him.

And there it was. How she'd struggled to deny it.

I love Rick.

What a realization to come to, sitting on the toilet seat in the bathroom, just having found out she was pregnant with his child.

Rick was such a good father. Sadie and Chuck—what would they think about having another grandchild? And Trevor. Would he really like to have a kid brother or sister?

Lani sighed and pulled the clip out of her hair. She couldn't deal with it, not at that moment. She needed time to absorb it all. Even if she was in love with Rick, and even if he did love her, did she want to get married? Hadn't she already learned her lesson?

More doubt crept in, stealing her joy. She didn't have the slightest idea what to do as a parent. How could she be a good mother? And could she make it on her own as a single parent?

After a few moments, she got a grip on her emotions, took

a deep breath and forced herself to stand. She knew she would do whatever it took to give her baby the best home possible.

And maybe it would be with Rick.

* * * * *

As soon as the line went dead, Rick dialed home. "Mom," he said when Sadie answered. "Is everyone okay?"

"Fine," Sadie replied. "Why?"

Rick ran a hand over his head. "I don't have time to explain. Is everyone home now? Lani, too?"

"We're all here."

"Good. Make sure everyone stays inside, and keep the doors locked. Don't open the door for anyone."

Sadie hesitated. "What's wrong?"

"I'll explain when I get there. I'll see if a unit can get to the ranch and sit out front until I make it."

After he hung up with Sadie, Rick asked Daryl to radio for an agent to stay at the ranch, and had a quick conversation with Miguel Martinez.

Before Rick left the station, he asked Daryl to book four seats out of Tucson to San Francisco for late that evening. Rick gave him the passengers' names and his credit card number.

The thirty-minute drive home seemed more like an hour. He pounded the wheel in frustration. Sal radioed in that he'd reached the ranch, and reported that all appeared to be fine.

As Rick drove up to the house, Roxie bounded out to greet him. Sal sat parked in an agency green and white SUV.

Rick climbed out of his truck and walked up to Sal. "See anything?"

"Nada." Sal nodded toward the house. "I called from the car and told them to sit tight."

"Thanks, *compadre*."

"Want me to hang around for awhile?"

"I don't expect anything to come down until tomorrow."

Sal whistled. "I don't have a good feeling about this. Maybe you should do as they said, and resign. For now."

Rick glared at his friend. "No way in hell I'm going to tuck my tail between my legs."

"Sure you don't want me to hang around?"

"I'm going to get my family out of here, and then take care of business tomorrow."

"Gotcha. See you *mañana*."

Rick didn't wait to watch Sal leave. He hurried to the house and Sadie opened the door at once.

He locked the door behind him. "You all need to get packed."

Sadie's face creased with concern. "What are you talking about?"

"I'm sending you to Callie's." Rick raked his hand through his hair. "Daryl booked seats out of Tucson to SFO for eight tonight. That gives you four hours to get packed, drive to Tucson and get to the airport."

Sadie frowned. "You still haven't told me what this is all about."

"Let's get Dad," Rick said and Sadie hurried to find Chuck and returned with him.

After Rick explained the threat, Chuck nodded. "I think a trip to see your sister'll do us some good."

"Where's Lani?" Rick asked.

"She went into the bathroom right before you called," Sadie replied. "I just heard the shower start up. I haven't had a chance to tell her anything."

Rick kicked off his boots. "I'm gonna take a quick shower in your bathroom, while you're packing. And then I'll tell Lani she needs to get her things together."

246

* * * * *

Thinking about her pregnancy, Lani continued to vacillate between joy and sheer terror as she showered. She wasn't ready to be around anyone, and a shower was as good an excuse as any to have some time to herself. It had the added benefit of relaxing her and helping bring everything into focus.

All she could think of was the baby. Every other thought had dissipated. Would it be a boy or a girl? Should she find out beforehand, or let it be a surprise? Where should she shop for baby clothes and furniture?

She had the overwhelming urge to share her news. To shout it from the rooftops.

No. Calm down.

After she climbed out of the shower and dried off, she realized she hadn't thought to grab any clean clothes. She wrapped the towel around her, and cracked open the bathroom door.

From the front room she heard Sadie say, "Come on, Trevor. You can help Grandma and Grandpa get things together in our room." The boy chattered something about visiting his Aunt Callie, and then Lani couldn't hear them anymore.

Otherwise the coast was clear, so she slipped across the hallway into her room.

Just as she was about to drop the towel to pull on a T-shirt, there was a light knock at the door, and Rick opened it. For a moment he stood in the doorway, drinking her in with his azure eyes. An almost pained expression crossed his face, his desire and need as clear as if he'd told her in words.

She straightened and dropped the T-shirt, her pulse hammering in her throat. "Rick."

Warmth flushed over her from head to toe, and she couldn't take her gaze from his.

Easing into the room, he shut the door, never taking his

eyes from hers. The lock clicked, and in one long stride he stood inches from her.

He caressed her cheek with his finger, his touch sending shivers throughout her. "Darlin'. What you do to me."

Then his arms enveloped her. She forgot about the towel and it dropped to her feet as she wrapped her arms around his neck. She couldn't help herself. He held her tight, his denim shirt and jeans rough against her breasts and thighs, his buckle scraping the delicate skin of her belly. They kissed, his need matching hers with such intensity that she was wild with it.

Hard. Fierce. Demanding.

To hell with everything. She needed him.

"My god," he whispered against her mouth. His hands cupped her naked hips and he pressed her close to the thrust against his jeans. "You burn me up."

She brushed her lips over his cheek, softly kissing his stubbled face, leading to his ear. Like hers, his hair was wet and he smelled of soap. He lowered his head and captured her nipple in his mouth. Her knees weakened and she moaned as she melted against him.

"I need you so much." He moved his tongue to her other nipple and she could barely control the cries building up in her throat. "Tell me you need me like I need you."

"Yes, Rick. Now."

She helped him peel off his clothes, running his hands over his bare chest, his hard thighs. They were unrestrained in their haste, and sank to the rose rug. He grabbed a condom, and it was all she could do not to tell him it wasn't needed.

Not yet. Wait for the right moment.

He slid into her and she knew he filled her so completely, in every way. Her body, her heart, her soul.

And when she came, it was like it all fused together, and every part of her became one with Rick.

I love him I love him I love him!

When their lovemaking ended, they were both breathing hard, a sheen of perspiration coating their skin. Even then, he didn't stop kissing her. It was like he couldn't get enough. He kissed her lips, her cheeks, her ears her eyebrows, her throat.

"We need to get dressed," he finally said with obvious reluctance. "Though I would give anything to stay right here with you."

"Mmmm." She nuzzled his neck, drinking in his scent. At that moment she knew that even if he didn't share her love, she would take whatever part of him that he gave her, for however long it would last. "Let's stay like this. No one would miss us, would they?"

"Temptress." He rolled away, eased to his feet, and started putting on his underwear. He looked so good to her, that she could barely take her eyes off him.

She stood while she fastened her bra and then stepped into clean panties. "Who seduced whom, might I ask?"

With a laugh, Rick pulled on his jeans, watching her dress. "You were naked."

"I was not." She sniffed and slid into a pair of shorts. "I was wearing a respectable towel. And you barged in."

His voice was muffled as he yanked a T-shirt over his head. "You left the door unlocked." He pulled on his denim shirt over the T-shirt.

Shaking her head, Lani buttoned up her blouse. "I didn't expect a lecher like you to just waltz in here and seduce me."

"Lecher, huh?" With a grin he brought Lani close and kissed her so long and passionately that her limbs turned to gelatin.

"Wow," she whispered as she clung to him. It was a few seconds before her legs would hold her up.

Just as she was about to tell Rick that she wanted to go somewhere special to talk with him, he said, "I'm going to miss you." He stroked damp hair from her face, his features suddenly serious. "I can't stand to be away from you."

"Are you—" Hair at her nape prickled as a chill crept over her. "Are you talking about when I leave for San Francisco?"

"Yes and no." He brushed his lips over hers. "I came in here to tell you—and then lost my head."

Her soul turned to ice and she stepped out of his embrace.

Rick reached for her hand. "You need to fly to San Francisco with my family tonight. I've made reservations, and—"

You *what*?" She shrugged away from him and planted her fists on her hips. "You think you're going to ship me off like a piece of luggage?"

"You don't under—"

"No man is ever going to tell me what to do again." Her voice rose. "We may have had sex, but that does not give you the right to order me around!"

"Damn it, Lani." He clenched his jaw, his face hard. "I got a call today. A man threatened my family."

A frigid wave of fear crashed over her, chasing away her anger. "Oh, my god."

Rick ran a hand through his hair. "The sonofabitch said if I didn't turn in my resignation, he would come after my family. He named everyone." Rick grabbed Lani by her shoulders. "Including you."

"Me?" She shook her head. "That doesn't make sense."

"Somehow they know that you're my woman." He motioned to the door. "Now let's go. There's not much time. Chuck's driving you all to Tucson and flying you out to San Francisco to stay with my sister Callie, where you'll be safe."

My woman. *He called me his woman.*

She closed her eyes and took a deep breath. When she opened them again, she said. "I'm staying."

Rick clenched and unclenched his hands as Lani stood there, her brown eyes flashing defiance. He all but wanted to shake some sense into her. "This is serious. These bastards threatened you, too. I need you somewhere safe while I hunt them down."

Lani shook her head. "I have two more interviews to do and I am not going to let anyone run me off."

"This is serious. It's not a joke."

"I'm not joking. I'm more than capable of taking care of myself."

"Don't you understand? I couldn't bear it if anything happened to you."

Rick's words poured into Lani's heart. Half of her wanted to give in, to let herself be shuttled off safely away from the bad guys. But the other half of her knew she had a job to do. And the thought of being too far from Rick while he faced danger—no. Not happening.

"I'll be fine."

"You can't stay here."

She tilted her chin. "Are you telling me I'm not welcome in your home?"

He grabbed his socks and boots and started pulling them on. "You know that's not what I meant. They could come after you here."

"I'm not going back to San Francisco until next weekend."

Rick took a deep breath and counted to ten as he finished putting on his boots. "Then we need to take you to a hotel."

Lani seized a pair of sandals out of the closet. "Are you going?"

"No. I'm staying here."

She pursed her lips. "Fine. I'll check into a hotel on my own."

"Tonight."

"Tomorrow." She spun on her bare heel and marched out, carrying her sandals.

"*Well, hell,*" he muttered as he followed her from the room.

Chuck, Sadie and Trevor were packed and waiting when Lani and Rick stalked into the living room.

"Ready, Lani?" Chuck asked.

"I'm not going," she said as she gave him a hug. "I'm checking into a hotel tomorrow."

Rick stood behind her with his arms folded, his brows furrowed and jaw set.

Sadie glanced at Rick, then hugged Lani. "You sure you don't want to come with us? I bet you'd be an excellent tour guide."

Lani smiled. "One of these days I would love to show you around the Bay Area. But I have a couple more interviews and a deadline to meet."

Sadie patted Lani's shoulder. "You go ahead and use my vehicle while we're gone."

"Thanks." Lani squatted down in front of Trevor. "Hey, Taz. Take care of your grandparents and I'll see you soon."

The boy threw his arms around Lani. "You promise you'll still be here when we get back? 'Cause I'm really, really, really going to miss you!"

"I'll try." She pulled back. "I'm going to miss you, too." She ruffled Trevor's hair. "Can you do something for me while you're on the plane?"

"What?"

"Draw a picture for me, okay?"

"Sure!" Trevor nodded, and brushed hair out of his eyes. "I've got my crayons and coloring pencils and paper packed in my backpack. Wanna see?" He started to unzip his pack, but Rick grabbed him by the waist and swung him high. Trevor squealed with laughter.

"Slow down, Pardner." Rick hugged him tight. "You need to get to the airport so you can catch that plane and go see your cousins and Aunt Callie."

Rick set Trevor down, hugged his mom, then helped carry their luggage out to Chuck's truck. Sadie promised to keep the cell phone on, and to call Rick once they hit the freeway, and again in Tucson and in San Francisco. Callie and the kids would be meeting them at the airport.

He breathed a sigh of relief as the red taillights disappeared into the night.

But Lani. He turned to her and frowned. How could he keep her safe?

Chapter Eighteen

๛

The following morning was muggy and overcast, and Rick was sure it would rain later. After feeding the livestock for Chuck, Rick cleaned mud off his boots before he entered the house. His footsteps echoed as he walked to his bedroom.

Last night it had seemed that she had something to tell him, but instead they made love again and again until they were too exhausted to move.

He stopped at the doorway to his bedroom and found Lani still sound asleep. This time they'd slept in his bed. Where he wanted her always. She made him feel so good, just by being there. In a couple of strides he reached the bed, leaned down and whispered, "Rise and shine."

"Mmmm." Her lashes were dark against her pale skin, and her chest rose and fell.

Bedsprings creaked as Rick sat and shook Lani's shoulder. "Get up, sleepyhead."

"Leavemealone." she mumbled and turned her head away.

"Gotta get you out of here." Rick tried pulling the covers off, but she snatched them back.

"Go away."

"Nope. Out of bed."

"A little longer," she moaned.

He leaned over and kissed her ear. "I know how to wake you."

A sleepy smile teased the corners of her mouth as he nipped her lobe. She grabbed a pillow and covered her head with it, swatting his face in the process.

Rick couldn't help but smile as he pulled on his bulletproof vest, T-shirt and overshirt. When he finished dressing, he lifted the pillow and nuzzled Lani's neck. She smelled so good, her skin warm against his nose. "Get up, honey. I've got to get going."

Another groan. "I will. Gimme a minute."

"Only one." He tossed the pillow aside and brushed his lips over hers. "Call me at work and let me know when you make it to the hotel."

"All right." She wrapped her arms around his neck and kissed him back.

As she settled against the pillow, he wanted to tell her then. Wanted to tell her how much he loved her. Was she ready?

"You need to go to work." She captured his hand and brought it to her lips.

"And you need to get your pretty ass out of bed."

"Okay."

She looked beautiful and innocent, her hair splayed across the pillow, her lips soft and swollen. He didn't want to leave. Wasn't sure he should. Or could.

Last night they'd waited up until Sadie called to let them know that she, Chuck and Trevor had arrived in San Francisco and were safe and sound at Callie's. He was relieved they were out of danger. Why did Lani have to be so stubborn? Why couldn't she have gone to San Francisco where she would be safe?

Fear settled in his chest, a hard lump that wouldn't go away. "I'll call in. Tell Mikey I'll be late until we get you settled into the hotel."

Frowning, Lani shook her head. "Absolutely not. I'll call you when I get to Nicole's B & B."

He knew he would only make her angry if he pushed the issue. It was enough that she would at least be away from the house. She would be safe in Bisbee.

"I expect to hear from you by noon," he said. "If you don't catch me on my cell phone and I'm not in the office, leave a message with Daryl."

She smiled. "Gotcha, cowboy."

Lani had fully intended to get up when Rick left. But it felt wonderful lying there, thinking about him, her lips still tingling from his kiss. He had smelled delicious when he came in from feeding the cattle. Of sweet oats and the promise of rain on a morning breeze. She thought about the feel of his hand in hers, the texture of his calloused fingers against her lips, the soft hair on the back of his wrist.

She moved her hand to her belly. He'd given her the world, and she hoped he'd be as happy as she was when she told him. Last night she had wanted to, but she wasn't sure what his reaction would be and she just wanted to enjoy the time they had.

While lying there, thinking about the reason he wanted her to go stay in Bisbee, she realized what Rick's Achilles heel was, and her smile faded.

His love for his family. His concern for others. Whatever it was he felt for her.

The bastards knew exactly how to hurt Rick—by threatening his family. But Rick wasn't one to back down.

He would die fighting to protect those he loves. And to protect those who love him.

The thought chilled her.

She held a fist to her aching heart. She couldn't bear anything happening to Rick. Couldn't bear losing another person that she loved so intensely. How could she walk away and hide in a hotel while he risked his life? Shouldn't she remain at his side? But if she stayed, would that only put him in more danger?

The past few days weighed her down, and she closed her eyes against the relentless images. James. The threat to Rick's family. Acknowledging her love for Rick. The pregnancy.

So tired. Her thoughts moved to the only close friend she had that had gone through a pregnancy. She remembered how exhausted Theresa Cortez had been in her first trimester. The woman could hardly keep her head up or food down for three months, practically from the day she'd gotten pregnant.

Thunder rumbled outside as Lani snuggled into the pillow and drank in Rick's earthy scent that clung to the sheets. She needed to keep her promise to him and get to the B & B so he wouldn't worry. She would just rest a minute longer. The heaviness in her limbs dragged her further down, deeper and deeper, until darkness enveloped her.

* * * * *

When Rick arrived at the station, he headed straight to Miguel Martinez's office.

"Everything okay?" Miguel asked, his green eyes narrowed. He sat at his desk, resting his chin on his steepled fingers.

"Got my family off to Frisco." With a frustrated sigh, Rick ran his hand over his head. "Lani refused to go because she wants to finish her damn feature. But she agreed to stay at a hotel in Bisbee."

Miguel frowned. "A man matching Gordo's description was seen in the vicinity of the phone booth the call was placed from yesterday. I put Sal and Don on him, but they've come up empty."

Fury simmered in Rick's gut. "What about Bull Stevens?"

"Everything's been quiet at his ranch." Rubbing a palm over his stubbled cheeks, Miguel added, "But we tapped an interesting phone call yesterday that might connect him to the threat."

Rick clenched the back of a chair, his knuckles white

against the dark upholstery. Before he could respond, Daryl Jones paged him over the intercom.

"Phone call on line six for Agent McAllister."

Miguel pointed to the telephone. "Take it here."

Rick grabbed the receiver. "McAllister."

"This is Juarez," the informant said in Spanish. His voice trembled. "I have information concerning those who wish to do your family harm."

Clenching the phone in his hand, Rick said, "What do you know?"

"Mario's at noon. Come alone."

The line went dead.

"I think another agent should go in with you," Miguel said again when it was time for Rick to head to Mario's. "We can put someone in undercover."

"It's only an informant," Rick replied. "It's a public place."

"But it's the first time he's insisted you come alone, correct?"

"Juarez isn't a concern."

Miguel picked up his frog paperweight and ran his thumb over the smooth glass. "Nonetheless, I'll have a couple of vehicles keep an eye out as they drive by."

Rick nodded and headed out of the building, then strode through the rain to his truck. The drive took less than five minutes, and right at noon, he took his regular booth at Mario's Cantina. He shook rain from his hair and combed it back with his fingers. Mari didn't appear to be working, and another waitress took his order.

Fifteen minutes later, Rick checked his watch. Juarez was late, which wasn't like him. He studied the regulars, several of whom were already bombed off their asses, and it was barely after noon.

Outside the open door, relentless monsoon rains pounded the sidewalk. A breeze swirled in, the scent of rain mingling with the cantina's odors of cigarettes and alcohol.

Another ten minutes passed and unease twisted in Rick's gut. Something wasn't right. He stood to leave and dropped a five on the table, then caught the smell of cheap perfume.

"*Señor.*" Mari came up to him and laid her hand on his arm, her dark eyes wide and lips trembling. "A man. You were here with him before. He is in the kitchen and asked that you come at once."

Hair rose at Rick's nape. "His name?"

"Juarez." Her gaze darted to the back room and then to Rick again. "He said that he cannot risk being seen out here."

Keeping his right hand close to the gun at his back, Rick followed Mari through the doorway. The kitchen floor was littered with scraps and smelled of sour beer and stale grease. He glanced behind him as they turned a corner, then back to Mari.

She stopped in front of a dingy room. Rick caught a glimpse of papers piled on a desk and an empty chair.

Her eyes darted toward the office. "He's in here, *Señor.*"

As he eased up to the office, an enormous man rounded the doorway. Before Rick had a chance to react, he saw the flash of metal. Blinding pain splintered his head as the man slammed the butt of an automatic onto the side of his skull.

* * * * *

The crack of thunder jarred Lani awake and she bolted upright. "Rick!" she cried, holding her hand to her pounding heart.

Panic clawed its way up her throat.

She glanced at the digital clock on the bureau. Twelve thirty? How had she slept so late? She took a deep breath, then exhaled. Nothing was wrong. It was just the time making her nervous. She'd promised Rick she would go to Bisbee and she should have been gone already.

A flash of lighting and another rumble sent shockwaves through her. Thunderclouds darkened the sky and rain poured from the heavens.

She needed to call Rick. Let him know she was running late.

Still naked, Lani scrambled out of bed and grabbed his robe. His scent enveloped her as she tied the belt and hurried to the phone in the study. She flipped through the card file and called his cell phone. No answer. She dialed his work number and tapped her fingers as she waited for an answer.

"Border Patrol. Daryl Jones here."

"This is Lane Stanton. Is Rick McAllister available?"

"I'm sorry. He's out of the station right now. May I take a message?"

She closed her eyes. "Yes. Please tell him I'm running late and probably won't be leaving the ranch until after one. I'll call him again later."

After Daryl repeated the message, she hung up and took another deep breath. Rick was fine. She just needed to get to Bisbee so he wouldn't worry.

She hurried to take a shower and then packed enough clothes for four days. She French-braided her hair to keep it out of her face, then pulled on loose jeans, a baggy T-shirt and tennis shoes.

When she was ready, she grabbed her laptop bag, purse and suitcase, locked the front door and headed through the rain to Sadie's SUV, the Rottweiler trailing after her. She tossed everything onto the floorboard of the passenger side and slammed the door shut.

She rounded the vehicle and grabbed the handle to open the driver's side door when Roxie's bark caused her to jump. The dog bounded into the driveway and growled. The sound grew more ominous and threatening as Roxie stared down the road that led to the ranch.

Lani's heart thudded as the dog's deep-throated bark pierced the rain. Then she saw it. A car she didn't recognize tearing up the dirt road, about a quarter mile away.

Oh, my god. What if it was the men who had threatened Rick?

She thought about jumping into the SUV, but knew the car could cut her off before she made it to the main road. With only stunted *palo verde* and mesquite bushes surrounding the property, there would be no place to hide a vehicle, and they would see her before she had a chance to get far.

Lani spun and ran onto the lawn, toward the front door. No. Not the house. If those were the men after Rick's family, the house would be the first place they would look, and she wouldn't have time to call anyone. The ranch was so far from town that no one would have a chance to get there before anything happened.

She dodged around the house and eyed the barn. No, she was likely to sneeze so much they would hear her.

Trevor's hideout.

Wet leaves and branches slapped her face as she raced through the orchard and into the windbreak. Her foot slid on the wet grass and she tumbled to the ground. Without pause, she scrambled to her feet and hurried on until she reached the playhouse. She scurried through the door and collapsed onto the floor. Trembling, she struggled to catch her breath.

"Calm down, Lani," she murmured as she wiped rain and mud from her face onto her sleeve. "It's probably neighbors coming to visit Chuck and Sadie. You're overreacting."

But even as she said the words, her gut told her different. The same instinct that told her Rick was in trouble.

In the distance she heard a car's engine and squeaking brakes. Roxie continued to bark, more ferocious than Lani had ever heard her. A sound like a gunshot echoed across the yard and the dog yelped.

Silence.

Lani clapped her hand to her mouth. *No!*

Her entire body shook and she wanted to curl up in a ball and hide. But she needed to see who was out there. Needed to figure out what to do. As she scooted closer to the window, she remembered Trevor's binoculars. Fortunately, she didn't have to dig far into the toy box to find them. Sitting on her knees, she brought the binoculars to her eyes and pushed open the shutters, just far enough to allow her to see.

At first Lani saw nothing, but as she adjusted the lenses, the image of an enormous man swam into view. The man who'd almost run her off the road on John Stevens's ranch. The name Gordo popped into her mind — it had to be the man Stevens had been talking to on his cell phone.

Beside Gordo was a man who's face reminded her of a lizard. Lizard was waving a gun and pointing to the house. Gordo shook his head and walked to Sadie's SUV. He yanked open the door, searched the vehicle, then slammed the door shut again. Lizard gestured to the muddy ground. Gordo nodded and they both started across the lawn toward the house.

The two men reached the front door and jiggled the handle. Lani heard the faint sound of glass shattering as Lizard used the butt of his gun to break a glass pane in the door. He reached through the broken glass, unlocked it and walked into the house.

Anger churned in her stomach. How dare they violate Rick's home? She kept the binoculars trained on the house, occasionally catching glimpses of the men through the windows. Searching for her, or one of Rick's family members.

Lani set the binoculars down and pressed her palms to her temples. What should she do?

Rain beat on the roof of the playhouse and lightning struck so close that for a moment Lani was deafened from its thunder. A rain-drenched breeze swirled around her and chills crawled up her spine.

How was she going to get out of this alive?

* * * * *

The searing odor of ammonia assaulted Rick's nostrils and his eyes snapped open. Blinding light caused him to shut them again, but not before he caught the image of a hand waving smelling salts under his nose. His temples throbbed as he struggled to remember where he was and what had happened, and he had a strange feeling in his head. Like he was underwater.

"Wake up, *amigo*." Sal's voice.

Rick brought his hand to his forehead and blinked until he was able to focus. He was sprawled on the floor of the Cantina's office, Sal crouched beside him. In the background he heard the hum of voices, and vaguely made out an agent questioning someone in Spanish. It sounded like Don Mitchell.

"How many fingers am I holding up?" Sal asked.

"Three, to go along with your three goddamn eyes," Rick mumbled.

Sal grinned and pressed a cloth to Rick's forehead. "Your pupils are dilated. You've got one hell of a lump and a bruise, but you might get lucky and walk straight in a few hours."

Rick took the cloth from Sal and groaned as he eased himself up to sit with his back against the desk.

"Did you get a look at the guy who hit you?" Sal asked.

Pain slammed into Rick's head when he tried to nod. "Damn," he muttered. "I only got a glimpse, but the guy looked like those surveillance photos of Gordo. Big belly, handle bar mustache, enormous gold buckle."

"Miguel had Don and me drive by to keep an eye out for you. About twelve thirty I headed in to take a look. When I saw you weren't in the bar, I called Don for backup and we found you back here." He motioned to a pile of ropes beside

Rick. "The SOB's started to bind you, but I must've spooked them. They managed to escape out the back door."

"It was my own damn fault—I walked right into it." Rick scrubbed his hand over his head and winced when his fingers brushed the bump growing at his temple. "What's the time?"

Sal checked his watch. "Twelve forty."

Rick's shoulders knotted as he thought of Lani. She'd probably arrived at the bed-and-breakfast, so he shouldn't be worried. He reached into his back pocket for his cell phone, but it wasn't there. Probably left it in the truck.

"They pulled this off you, but left it on the desk." Sal handed Rick his firearm. "Must've been in a hurry to get out of here."

Rick tucked the gun at his back as he got to his feet. He grabbed the phone on the desk and called the station. When he asked Daryl if there were any messages for him, Daryl said, "Yeah. Got one from a Lane Stanton. Said she was running late and probably wouldn't get away from the ranch until after one."

"What?" Rick shouted, the sound of his own voice splitting his head. "Never mind." His hand shook as he hung up and dialed the ranch. He let the phone ring at least twenty times.

No answer.

"Don called the paramedics," Sal said when Rick slammed the receiver down. "They should be here any minute."

"No time." Rick headed toward the door. "I'm going to the ranch. I think Lani's still there and I've got to make sure these bastards aren't after her. Call the Sheriff's Department and call for backup."

He didn't wait for Sal's reply as he ran into the thunderstorm. Sirens approached as he jumped over water flowing in the gutter and stumbled into his truck. Gritting his teeth against the throbbing pain in his head, he started the vehicle and swung into traffic. His reflexes were off, causing him to drive erratically, and horns blared as he weaved on the road.

Cursing the distance to the ranch, he fought to maintain focus and control of the vehicle. He discovered his cell phone wasn't in the truck, and he had no way to call Lani to see if she was still at the house. Even the pouring rain mocked him, the washes already running with water from the downpour, forcing him to slow down as he crossed them so he wouldn't flood his engine.

When he finally arrived at the ranch, he took a back road and parked behind a clump of mesquite bushes, hoping the dark truck blended in well enough and couldn't be seen in the rain. He grabbed his field glasses out of the glove compartment, pulled out his gun and hurried out of the truck, careful not to slam the door.

Rain poured and thunder rumbled as he waded through floodwaters and crawled to the top of the muddy dam. He prayed that he was wrong. That Lani wasn't in danger.

But as soon as he looked through the binoculars, he saw the unfamiliar car in the driveway. And Sadie's SUV still parked there. He swung the glasses to the house and glimpsed a man through a window.

Rage seared him and he had to force himself to think calmly. Then two men stepped outside the house, and he recognized the man who's knocked him cold. The bastard gestured to the yard.

Lani must be hiding somewhere. Where would she hide? Not the barn. Her sneezes would bring attention to her immediately. Possibly the garden, but not enough cover. Certainly not the plane. She was terrified of it. If it was Trevor, he would know to go to the playhouse.

The playhouse. It dawned on Rick that Trevor had told Lani about his dad's instructions. Would she remember?

Gordo started searching around the outside of the house

and the other man headed to the barn. Rick scrambled over the dam, slipping in the mud and sliding to the bottom of the incline. He fought another wave of nausea, then crouched low and ran to the windbreak. The playhouse came into view. He raced toward it, then paused at the door. If Lani was in there, she might scream, thinking him one of the men hunting for her.

Lightning struck, close enough that the clap of thunder was unbearably loud to his pounding head. He pushed open the playhouse door and saw Lani on her knees, her back to him, her face in her hands. He eased into the doorway, and as she raised her head he clapped his hand over her mouth, and pulled her close to him.

Terror ripped through Lani and she struggled against the hands that held her.

"It's me," Rick said and released her.

Her limbs went slack with relief. She turned and threw her arms around him, pressing herself against his wet and muddy body. "I'm so glad you're okay. Thank god you're here."

He kissed her forehead, but when he pulled away, his face was grim. "You were supposed to be in Bisbee by now."

"I'm so sorry. I overslept." She gasped when she noticed the wound on his head. "What happened? You're hurt!"

Rick eased by her, mud covering the floor of the playhouse behind him. He picked up the binoculars and looked out the window. "Damn. They've spotted my truck." He dropped the glasses and took her hand. "Keep low." He pulled her through the doorway of the playhouse and into the storm.

While she crawled out, Lani wiped rain from her eyes and started to ask Rick how they would escape, but her heart stopped as a figure stepped in front of them. She signed with relief when she saw that it was Sal.

"Sal." Rick put his arm out to block Lani from walking

forward. "What the hell are you doing?"

It was then that she saw the gun.

Chapter Nineteen

&

Lani's heart pounded as her gaze snapped from the weapon to Sal's face, his expression ruthless in the pouring rain.

"You couldn't leave well enough alone, could you, *compadre*?" the man said, water dripping from the brim of his hat. "I convinced them to give you a warning. A chance to walk away." He spit onto the dirt, but kept his eyes on Rick.

Rick pushed Lani partially behind him. "Leave her out of this." His voice was as hard and cold as steel. "You and I can talk."

"Too late. The man wants the both of you taken to him." Sal pulled Rick's cell phone out of his back pocket. "You're going to visit *El Torero* now."

Lani's gaze darted from Sal to Rick and back, her heart pounding. What could she do to help Rick? To help them both?

"Hands up, palms facing me." Sal stepped closer. Pushed his gun into Rick's belly. "Don't move while I make this call, or you're dead." His cold gaze cut to Lani. "You run off and I'll shoot him."

Rick raised his hands, his movements slow and easy. Raw terror filled Lani while Sal punched buttons on the weatherproof phone, the electronic sound surreal in the pouring rain. In the distance, somewhere behind them, men shouted in Spanish.

She struggled to calm the fear raging within. How were they going to get out of this? If only Rick had his gun.

His gun.

Slowly Lani raised her left hand that was hidden behind Rick's back. He stiffened as her hand moved under his over shirt. She kept her eyes focused on Sal. The man spoke rapid-fire Spanish into the phone, but so low and unintelligible that she wasn't sure Rick could even make out the words.

Her fingers eased over the rough texture of his denim jeans and then met cold metal above the waistband. She withdrew the weapon, afraid that Sal would hear the sound of the gun moving across cloth. She eased the gun under her baggy T-shirt and into her left front pocket where Sal couldn't see, praying her shirt was loose enough that Sal wouldn't notice the bulge.

The front of her shirt dropped down just as Sal punched off the phone. "Let's go. But first give me your weapon."

Lani froze.

"I don't have it," Rick replied evenly. "I lost it in the dam when I was coming after Lani."

"Bullshit." Sal gestured for Rick to turn around. "Keep your hands up. I won't hesitate to shoot the woman if you try anything."

"You can see I'm covered in mud from when I fell." Rick turned in a slow movement.

As Sal patted him down, Rick stared at Lani, asking her with his eyes what she'd done with his gun. She glanced at her pocket and he gave her a grim smile.

"All right." Sal nodded. "My truck's by yours. I'll follow you."

"Tell me why you're doing this." Rick turned and lowered his hands.

Sal shrugged. "Money. I'll never get rich working for the government. I've already made more cash in the past few months than I could in an entire year as an agent."

"You've been tipping off the bastards," Rick said. "You gave them the names of my contacts. My family. Lani."

Sal's dark eyes flashed and he nodded toward the dam. "Let's go."

"I never thought you'd turn." Rick worked his jaw as he stepped forward.

"That's your biggest weakness." Sal grinned. "You're too damn trusting."

Before Lani could even grasp what was happening, Rick swung his right leg around and kicked the gun out of Sal's grasp. The man howled and cradled his hand. Rick caught his balance on his left foot and then shot his right foot toward Sal, plowing his boot square into the man's midsection.

Air whooshed from Sal's lungs. He doubled over and dropped to his knees. Rick swung his foot again, connecting with Sal's head. The man fell to his side and lay still.

Lani dove for Sal's gun where it had landed on a patch of wet grass. Her hands shook as she scooped it up and handed it to Rick.

Men's voices were approaching.

"Damn," Rick muttered. "There's only one way we can get out of here now." Holding Sal's gun in one hand, Rick grabbed Lani's with his other and pulled her through the windbreak.

"How?" But even as she asked, horror slammed into Lani and she started to shake. She tried to stop running, but Rick pulled her forward until they burst through the trees, straight toward his plane.

"There's no way. I can't." Every part of her quivered as Rick yanked open the cockpit door. Flashes of flames and her sister's dead face filled her head.

Shouts erupted from behind them. She didn't have a choice.

It took everything she had to force herself to climb into the plane, knowing that this time they would be flying.

Rick helped her up and then dropped Sal's gun between

the seats. "Everything'll be okay."

Somehow she managed to get into the co-pilot's seat and buckled in. She shook so hard her teeth chattered. Clenching her eyes shut, she tried to fight the horrific images in her mind.

The engine roared to life, and she felt the movement of the plane as Rick guided it down the muddy runway.

OhGodohGodohGodohGod. Naya's voice rang in Lani's mind and she gripped the armrests so tight her hands ached. Flashes of the plane crash erupted in her mind, and she could barely keep from screaming her terror.

"Keep your head low." Rick's voice was tight. "They're at the end of the runway."

She forced herself to open her eyes and saw his clenched jaw, his hands taut on the steering column. His normally tan skin was pale, the wound to his forehead vivid red. Mud and water dripped from his clothing, onto his seat and the floor.

Lani looked out the window and choked back a cry as the men came into view and the plane began to lift from the ground. Both men aimed guns at the cockpit.

Glass cracked as a bullet hit the windshield. She screamed as another zinged by her ear. She heard the ping of more bullets against metal as the plane rose higher. Then nothing but the sound of the engine and blood roaring in her ears.

"We're okay." Rick reached over and patted her hand. He glanced at the gauges and cursed. "Damn. It looks like they hit the gas tank."

"What?" Lani croaked.

He gave her a sharp look. "We'll be fine. It just means that we need to head to the closest airport. Rather than chance going over the mountains to Bisbee, we'll land at the airport outside of Douglas, by the prison."

Rivulets of water streamed down Lani's face and her wet clothes clung to her body. His gun dug into her hip, but she couldn't pry her fingers from the armrests to take it out of her pocket. He radioed ahead and she berated herself for putting him in such danger by not getting away from the ranch like she'd promised.

When he approached the field, an air traffic controller informed him that for security reasons they wouldn't be allowed to land and would have to go to the airport in Douglas. Rick argued that it was an emergency, but the controller insisted Rick take the plane to the next airport and that it would be prepared for the landing.

"What the hell?" he muttered. He cut a look to Lani and managed a small smile. "We're losing fuel. But it's a slow leak. We'll make it."

She tore her gaze from Rick's and closed her eyes.

And prayed.

Lightning flashed and the plane bounced with the turbulence. Lani gasped and Rick looked at her again. Her eyes were squeezed shut, her face ashen. He thought about the day he'd met her. And now he wanted to spend the rest of his life with her.

He could only hope that would be longer than it took to get the plane landed.

"It's all right," he said. "We'll be there in just a few minutes."

She didn't answer, and he wished he could take her in his arms and hold her tight.

Head pounding, he struggled to concentrate and control his clumsy hands. That bang on the head—must have banged up his coordination, too. He forced himself to focus on the air traffic controller's voice and the approaching landing strip. The blue runway lights blurred in the rain.

"We're about to land. It might be a bit bumpy." Rick tried to keep his voice calm and soothing. "I've got a concussion, so my hands are a little shaky, but we'll be fine."

"I trust you," she whispered, but when he glanced at her, he saw that her eyes were still closed.

Steady. Steady. Rick gritted his teeth and eased the plane down.

The nose dipped in the wind, and the plane pitched. Lani's gasp was audible.

He swore under his breath, fighting the wheel more than he should have. Five hundred feet. Four hundred. Rain made visual impossible. He was flying on instruments, and on his gut instinct. Hopefully concussions didn't affect instinct as much as hands.

Two hundred feet.

One hundred.

The plane dropped hard, skittering. Lani screamed and grabbed her knees. He dragged hard on the brakes, his breath catching with each shimmy and bump until they rolled to a stop in front of the hanger.

He leaned back in his seat, his muscles slack with relief. He looked at Lani's pale face.

"Did — did we land?" she asked, eyes squeezed closed, lips trembling.

"We're safe."

She opened her eyes. Her breasts rose and fell as she took a deep breath. "I'm so sorry I put you through this. I should have listened to you and should have gone straight to Bisbee."

"Hey, it's okay." Rick hooked his finger under her chin. "I'm just glad we made it. Now let's get out of here." He grabbed Sal's gun from where it lay between the seats and tucked it into his waistband at his back.

Damn Sal. How could he have been so blind to such deception?

After he helped Lani climb out of the plane, she flung her arms around his neck and hugged him tight. Rain poured down as he squeezed her to him and kissed her wet hair.

"*Señor,*" a man said behind them.

Rick released Lani and spun around, his hand close to the

gun.

"We have been expecting you," the man continued. "Please come in out of the rain." The man was dressed in coveralls with the airport insignia.

Rick nodded, his head swimming with pain from his injury.

They followed the wiry man into the hanger, which was so dim he could barely see. Only a black truck was parked inside the building. Rick's skin crawled.

Even as he reached for Sal's gun and tried to push Lani outside, something struck him in the small of his back. His breath knocked from him, he pitched forward and hit the floor.

"Rick!" Lani screamed.

A boot pressed into his back.

"Don't move or I'll shoot the little lady," a familiar voice said as the man in coveralls frisked Rick, then took his gun. The door of the hanger slammed shut, the only light coming from a single bulb hanging from the ceiling.

Rick's vision swam. He turned his head to the side—his blood ran cold as he saw Stevens holding Lani by one arm, the barrel of an automatic to her temple.

"Get up," Stevens ordered, a toothpick hanging from the corner of his mouth. "Hands where I can see them. Dominguez has got a gun pointed at your head. Let's don't leave a mess, McAllister."

Heart pounding, he eased to his feet and faced Stevens. Dominguez stood about a foot away.

Rick's eyes met Lani's and he tried to tell her everything he wanted to say with that one look. Her lips parted and he could see her trembling. He tried to keep his face calm, but inside he was dying. One wrong move and Stevens could kill her.

Rick fixed his gaze on Stevens. "How'd you track us?"

The rancher's face was impassive. "Valenzuela let me

know you'd gotten away. I called in a few favors and had you routed here, everything kept quiet. I pump a lot of money into this town."

"What—" Rick fought for focus, his injury making it difficult to think clearly or even speak. "What do you want with us?"

The rancher pressed the gun tighter to Lani's head and she gasped. "Sorry, Rick," Bull said, "but you should've turned in your resignation."

Stevens cocked his head toward Lani. "She'll come with me. For now."

Rage filled Rick. His vision became sharper. He had to keep Stevens talking. Find some way out of the mess they were in. "What kind of man smuggles people across the border and leaves them to die?"

Stevens's tone was calm. "Payback for all the damage done to my property. Payback for the thousands of dollars I've lost. Might as well see some of the cash if they're gonna be crossing my land."

"You killed Pedro Rios, didn't you?"

Stevens rolled his shoulders. "Rios revealed too much to the reporter. He might've spilled his guts to the wrong folks."

Fighting back a wave of nausea from his injury, Rick said, "Don't add another murder to your charges."

A smile tugged at the rancher's mouth. "I've been doing this for years, and with you gone nothing'll change."

Rick shook his head. "You've been under surveillance. Gordo, a known *coyote*, has been seen going to and from your ranch. Your phone has been tapped, conversations recorded. It's over."

The smile faded from Stevens's face, and Rick's heart dropped when the gun against Lani's temple trembled. The man worked the toothpick between his teeth as if chewing on what Rick had just said.

Slowly, Rick lowered his hands. He glanced at Dominguez out of the corner of his eye and saw the man's attention was on Stevens.

"With a name like Bull, it wasn't too sharp, allowing yourself to be called *El Torero*. A matador," Rick said. "And you left one of your toothpicks at the crime scene with Rios. A DNA test on the saliva on the pick'll prove you were there."

Stevens spit out his toothpick and turned the automatic on Rick. "You'd better be shittin' me."

It was what Rick had been waiting for — to get Stevens's gun off Lani.

Rick charged Dominguez, driving him back, back toward Stevens and the gun.

Stevens fired.

Pain exploded in Rick's arm.

Dominguez slammed to the ground, striking his head. Hard.

Lani screamed.

A hot knife split Rick's chest. He felt the bullet before he heard that second shot, and then — darkness.

"No!" Lani's mind whirled.

Rage swept over her, fast and furious. She spun around. "You bastard!" With all the strength she possessed, Lani rammed her knee into Stevens's groin.

Total shock crossed his features. The gun toppled out of his hand and he dropped to his knees.

"Son of a bitch!" Lani reared back, and as Stevens tried to straighten, she kicked him in the balls again as hard as she could.

The man gasped and collapsed onto his side, curling into a fetal position and whimpering.

Lani kicked Stevens's gun to the back of the hanger, well beyond his reach. She pulled Rick's gun from her front pocket and trained it on the rancher as she checked on the other man and saw that he was completely still. She didn't have the slightest idea how to use the gun, but Stevens wouldn't know that. She hoped.

Sirens approached as she ran to Rick. "Oh, god!" she sobbed when she saw blood pooling across his shirt and mixing with the mud covering his clothing. "Don't leave me. Please don't die. I love you, Rick. I love you so much."

His eyelids fluttered and his hand clenched hers. "I know, honey." A weak smile, then his face went slack and he passed out.

She caressed his stubbled cheeks, her lips trembling, hot tears spilling down her face. His skin was clammy. "Damn it, Rick. Don't you dare die on me!"

Dominguez moaned beside Rick. Lani scrambled to her feet and kicked the man's gun to the back of the hanger, near Stevens's weapon. She turned and saw that the rancher still writhed in pain on the floor. She held Rick's gun with both hands, keeping it pointed toward Stevens.

Lani heard the sirens and the screech of brakes outside the hanger. She checked to see that both Stevens and Dominguez were still down, then threw Rick's gun to the back of the hanger near the others. She ran to the door and yanked it open and saw police cars and an ambulance crowding the runway.

"Help, please!" she cried to the first officer that approached her. "John Stevens shot Rick McAllister. And there's another man that held a gun on him. Rick knocked him out, but he's coming around."

Officers poured into the building and in moments had cuffed Stevens and Dominguez. When the building was secure, paramedics rushed in and started attending Rick.

Lani turned to follow when Don Mitchell took her by the arm.

"How is he?" Don asked.

She blinked, for a second unable to process his question,

then told him what had happened.

She started to shake. "There's so much blood. He can't die. He just can't!"

Don patted Lani's arm awkwardly, then pulled her to him and she sobbed against his shirt.

"Rick's one tough *hombre*." Don rubbed her back like an affectionate father. "He'll come through."

Unconsciously Lani clenched the fabric of his shirt—and felt something hard beneath it.

"His vest!" she turned and ran into the hanger.

Rick was lying on the stretcher, his shirt and vest gaping open, the paramedics working on him. An enormous bruise covered the left side of his chest, below his heart.

"He had on his vest." Her voice quavered and she was dizzy with relief.

Don walked up behind her as one of the police officers came to Lani's side. "Sure enough did." The officer nodded toward Rick. "Saved his life."

"But the blood." Her knees weakened and she grabbed Don's arm to keep from falling. "So much blood."

"From the flesh wound to his arm," the officer replied as Don pulled Lani against him and held her up. "He's got a bunch of bruises and he's lost blood, but other than that, the paramedics think he'll be fine."

Lani's stomach roiled. She tore away from Don, ran outside and vomited. Even after there was nothing left, dry heaves continued to wrack her body.

Lani sprawled in a chair in the hospital's waiting room, her hair drying but her clothing still damp from rain. She was cold and exhausted, but all she could think about was Rick. She drew the blanket around her shoulders that a nurse had provided earlier, seeking warmth even though nothing would take away the chill of her fear for Rick.

"You need to let a doctor examine you," Don said as he watched her.

I'm fine." Her stomach churned again as she inhaled the horrid antiseptic smells, but she was sure there was nothing left in her belly to throw up.

"You're in shock." Don stood and started pacing, reminding her of his wife Kitty. "That's why you're vomiting and still shaking."

Lani pulled the blanket tighter around her. She wasn't about to tell Don the real reason she was throwing up. Maybe shock had something to do with it, but she was pretty sure it had a lot more to do with her pregnancy. Not to mention the hospital's pea-green walls. They were ugly enough to make anyone puke.

"How did you know where we were?" Lani asked, trying to draw Don's attention away from her and how she was feeling at the moment.

Don shrugged. "When Rick tore home after you, Sal followed. I've had a strange feeling about him lately, so I checked in with Miguel and found out that Sal never called for backup like he said he did. So Miguel called the Sheriff's Department and also sent out the closest Border Patrol units. They arrived just as Rick's plane took off."

Lani shuddered at the mention of the plane, but only nodded.

"Sal had just put down the cell phone when the agents and deputies surrounded him and the other two men. They were all arrested." Don stared at a framed print of yellow gladiolas. "There was some confusion as to where Rick was landing, or we would've arrived sooner. We were misdirected to the wrong airport while you were told to land in Douglas."

Don sat in a chair across from Lani. "When's Rick's family getting home?"

"Late tonight." Lani said. "They have seats on the last flight out of San Francisco to Tucson."

A silver-haired woman in a white lab coat came through the double doors into the waiting room and Lani sat up in her chair. "I'm Dr. Taylor," the woman said. "Are either one of you a family member of Richard McAllister?"

Before Lani could speak, Don said, "This is his fiancé, Lani Stanton. The rest of Rick's family is out of town."

Lani blushed as the doctor shook her hand with a firm grip, but didn't contradict Don. "How's Rick?"

Dr. Taylor smiled. "He'll be fine. He lost a lot of blood so we're going to keep him here a couple of days and then he'll be able to go home."

Lani's head spun and her stomach cramped. She was so relieved that she barely heard the doctor's explanation of the extent of Rick's injuries.

"May I see him?" she asked when the doctor finished.

Dr. Taylor nodded and indicated to Lani to follow her. "Only for a few minutes. He needs his rest to help him recover more quickly."

A humming noise filled her head as the doctor led her into Rick's room. Her chest tightened when she saw how pale he was. Bandages were wrapped around his upper arm. Bruises covered one side of his face and his eyes were closed.

Her hand trembled as she caressed Rick's cheek, his stubble rough to her fingertips. He opened his eyes and gave her a weak smile.

"Lani," he said, his voice hoarse.

"Shhh." she touched his lips with her finger. "Get some rest, cowboy." She kissed him and watched him drift off to sleep.

Chapter Twenty

௭

Lani pulled off her glasses and set them on the desk. She was so tired that the words had begun to blur across the screen. After leaving Rick at the hospital last night, Lani hadn't been able to sleep, too wired after the traumatic experience. Instead, she'd plunged into writing the story of yesterday's fiasco and sent it off to her editor before midnight.

Theresa had sent Lani a quick e-mail, promising to call. She'd raved over the article, apparently ecstatic over Lani's involvement in bringing down a notorious smuggler who just happened to be backing a candidate for U.S. Congress. But she'd also expressed her relief that Lani and Rick were both fine.

Of course Montaño had called a press conference, claiming ignorance to Stevens's activities. But the damage had been done, and it was possible that the mayor's candidacy for Congress was in jeopardy.

Once she had returned from visiting Rick in the hospital that morning, Lani had thrown herself into her work and finished the last of the interviews by telephone. She had a bit more to do, but it could wait until morning when she could think more clearly. It was now late afternoon and Lani was ready for a nap.

"Telephone," Sadie said when she peeked into the study. "Your editor."

"Thanks," Lani replied with a tired smile as Sadie handed her the cordless. She was definitely due for that nap—she hadn't even heard the phone ring.

"Hey, Theresa," she said as she put the receiver to her ear.

"Girlfriend!" Theresa cried. "I wanted to call you first

thing this morning, but I was practically held hostage by the boss woman herself. Do you realize that you're national news? The AP picked up your story and now it's everywhere."

Lani gave a tired sigh. "I've been too busy to think about it."

"Are you okay?" Concern came into Theresa's voice. "I should've called this morning, but I figured you must be all right to have written that article only hours after it happened."

"I'm fine, just tired enough to sleep for a week. Maybe two."

After they hung up, Lani stared out the window without seeing. Should she risk telling Rick again that she loved him, and if by some chance he loved her in return, should she risk a future with him?

* * * * *

"Done," Lani said as she e-mailed the last article to Theresa Cortez. She leaned back against the den chair and relaxed.

It was hard to believe that at this time two days ago Sal had betrayed them, Stevens had held them at gunpoint, and that Rick could have died. Her skin chilled and she shivered. No use thinking about that now. It was over and he would be fine.

The house was eerily silent and Lani was home alone. Chuck had headed to Bisbee to buy a new pane of glass for the front door. Sadie had gone to Douglas to run errands and then to see Rick. Trevor was staying home with Lani since he had a cold and they didn't want to risk Rick catching it.

And if she could work up the courage, Lani planned to tell Rick how she felt when he came home.

Was she making the right choice? Could she do it—could she tell him that she loved him again? And what if he rejected her?

In her heart she knew Rick was the only man she'd ever love. And if there was any chance he loved her, she had to know.

Sighing, she rubbed her belly, trying to imagine what it would look like in a few months. She wouldn't tell him about the baby — yet. She wouldn't be able to handle it if Rick insisted that they get married based on his outmoded cowboy sense of honor and duty. If he didn't want to continue their relationship, she'd wait until after the baby was born. She owed him that much.

Lani wandered around the house that smelled of ham cooking in the crock pot and bread baking in the bread machine. Afternoon sunshine spilled through the windows on the west side of the house, giving everything in the living room a soft glow. To avoid seeing the boarded up pane in the front door, she headed out the back door to the pond.

Monarch butterflies danced over Sadie's irises, zinnias, and roses. The flowers were a bright splash of purples, oranges, and reds in the midst of all the greenery. The bees' hum as they gathered pollen was oddly soothing as a warm breeze caressed her skin. She smelled wet earth and moss from the pond.

Roxie barked and hobbled past her to the driveway. The bandage on the dog's haunch was dusty but bright against her black hair. Lani still couldn't believe that Roxie had only been shot in the leg. Like Rick, the dog was injured, but she'd be okay.

Trevor came out of the house, smiling and chatting. They spent the afternoon together, Lani following wherever the boy led. Even though he'd been sick earlier, he sure had a lot of energy now. She played with him in his hideout, tossed the ducks grain, helped him feed his potbellied pigs, and pitched a game of horseshoes in the windbreak.

It was almost dark when they finally walked back to the house. Trevor slipped his hand into hers. "I told Dad I wanted to keep you."

Lani's heart twisted as she stared down at him. "That was sweet of you."

He sighed and hung his head. "I wasn't supposed to tell you that."

"Oh," she whispered.

Rick had told his son not to tell her that he wanted her to stay.

Her face felt frozen, her heart numb as they entered the house. "Trevor, I'm not feeling well," Lani said. "I'm going to lie down for a while."

"You gonna be okay?" His little face puckered in concern. "You don't look so good."

She forced a smile. "I'm tired and need to rest."

After she kissed his cheek she slipped into the guest room and threw herself onto the bed. She wasn't going to cry. She was finished with crying about anyone.

Lani turned on her back and stared at the ceiling. The back porch light was on, shining through the leaves of the mulberry bush outside her window. Shadows winked and moved in a collage of light and gray above her.

Her head ached from holding back the tears, but her heart ached more. She felt empty. Hollow. Alone.

She placed her hand on her belly and caressed it. No, she had her baby. The precious life growing inside her. The gift Rick had given her.

Lani found the strength to smile. Everything was going to be all right.

* * * * *

The following afternoon, the Turners went to pick up Rick from the hospital. Apparently he'd be checking out today and Lani would have to face him.

She stood at her bedroom mirror and studied her reflection as she brushed her hair. Thoughts of all the things

Rick had said to her over the past couple of weeks flooded her mind. Showing her his property and talking like he was including her in his plans. Picking out the stoneware pattern that she'd fallen in love with.

Calling her *his* woman.

"Damn it, Lani." She thumped the brush down on the dressing table. "You can't blow this chance. Just maybe Rick loves you, too."

The sound of someone clearing his throat caused her heart to drop to her belly. She cut her gaze to the doorway and saw Rick standing there with his good arm hitched up against the doorway.

Heat flushed over her from head to toe. "You heard that."

He gave a slow nod and the corner of his mouth twitched.

Well, he already knew she loved him — she told him that when he was shot — so what did she have to lose?

"I love you, Rick McAllister." She stood a little straighter and faced him. "I need to know how you feel about me."

Rick smiled and in two steps had his good arm wrapped around her shoulders and her body pressed to his. He squeezed her tight to him and kissed the top of her head. "Don't you already know, honey? I've loved you from the beginning. I just had to wait until you figured out you loved me, too."

Lani sagged against him, unable to believe it was true. He *did* love her. "I was so afraid you didn't."

He lightly tugged on her hair so that she was forced to look up at him. "How could you not know? I said it in a thousand different ways."

Emotions swirled within like one of their summer monsoons. Happiness, yet worry over what he'd think about her being pregnant.

Before she had the chance to say another word, he said, "Come on. I want to take you somewhere special." He turned away, heading toward his room, and tossed over his shoulder, "Pack your overnight bag."

Insisting that he could drive just fine with one good arm, Rick drove from the ranch toward Bisbee, but Lani couldn't help worrying about him.

He loves me!

They talked about nothing and everything. About her time with Trevor and how much Rick disliked hospital food. Yet he didn't mention the future.

When they reached Old Bisbee, she smiled as she thought of the day they'd spent there. As Rick drove up the winding Main Street, memories assailed her. She saw the shop where they'd bought the dress. The museum. The café they'd had lunch at. The shop they'd picked out the dinnerware.

The bed-and-breakfast where they'd stayed.

And then Rick parked right in front of it.

Lani turned toward him. "What are we doing here?"

He trapped her in his azure gaze. "I have something to show you."

Rick took her hand after they got out of the truck, and he smiled. Warmth seeped into her and she wanted to melt against him. Instead, she let him lead her into the inn, where he approached the guy at the front desk. The pony-tailed clerk tossed Rick a key without either of them saying a word.

"What's going on?" she asked as Rick led her up the stairs.

"You'll see."

At the top of the staircase, Rick inserted the key into the lock of the same room they'd stayed in before. He opened the door and gently pushed her inside.

Lani stared openmouthed while the door closed behind them. Flowers completely filled the room. Bouquets of red and yellow roses sprinkled with baby's breath covered the vanity.

Vases brimming with white lilies and orchids topped the bureau. Baskets of purple irises, blue bachelor's buttons, and pink carnations lined the walls. The only space left open was the bed and a pathway to it.

She looked up at Rick and saw him watching her, a silly grin on his face. "Do you like it?" he asked, his voice almost shy.

"I've never seen anything as wonderful in my life." It smelled like a florists shop, sweet with the perfume of roses and carnations. "You did this for me?"

"It's only the beginning." He brought her to him and kissed her so thoroughly that her knees gave out and he had to catch her with his good arm. He started nibbling at her ear.

"Your injuries." She gave him a worried look. "Are you sure you're okay?"

"When I'm with you everything's fine." Rick tossed his Stetson on the table.

Lani shivered as he started unbuttoning her blouse. He undid the front clasp of her bra and she gasped as his mouth captured her nipple.

She buried her hands in his hair and moaned. "Oh, god."

"God, huh?" He pushed her blouse off her shoulders. "I've never been called that before."

Before she could stop herself, she giggled, and Rick chuckled. She kissed the wound at his temple and the cuts and bruises on his face. When she helped him unbutton his shirt, she winced at the sight of the bandage around his arm.

In moments they were both naked, and tumbled to the bed. She kissed the bruises on his chest, her heart twisting at the sight of the dark purple and blue flesh.

He pushed her back against the pillow. "Let me," he murmured. His lips took possession of her, loving every inch of her body. He slowly eased down her belly, to the soft hair, to the delicate skin of her thighs.

And when his tongue met that most intimate part of her, he drove her almost to climax, licking and sucking her clit, and then stopped and moved over her. She was burning alive for him, wanting him deep within her. She wrapped her legs around him, but he just braced himself on his good arm and smiled.

"Are you trying to drive me crazy?" She slid her arms around his neck. "Don't stop."

"Say it," he whispered.

"What?" She squirmed under him, begging him without words to take her.

"Tell me you love me," he said "Say it. I want to hear it again."

He lowered his head and captured her nipple in his teeth and she moaned as she murmured, "I love you, Rick."

He kissed her hard as he slid into her, filling her, his strokes slow and purposeful. She clenched his hips and raked her nails over his skin, urging him on.

"Look at me," he said, his voice husky.

She gazed up into his blue eyes, their normal brilliance clouded with passion. Shockwave after shockwave rolled over her as she climaxed. He groaned and his body convulsed as he found his own release.

Lani closed her eyes, feeling completely boneless. Utterly relaxed with his heart beating against hers. She lifted her lids to see him watching her. "You don't play fair."

"I know."

He withdrew from inside of her, but remained on top as he leaned over and opened the nightstand's drawer. Her eyes widened as he pulled out a red velvet box and laid it between her breasts. "Open it, honey."

Her hands trembled as she opened the box and saw an exquisite diamond and sapphire ring. She looked at Rick and saw him smiling at her.

"Marry me, Lani."

Her thoughts spun. "Wow," was all she could think to say. "Really?"

"I bought this the day after our stay here." He stroked her hair behind her ear and his face was suddenly serious. "Like I said before, I fell in love with you the day I met you. I've wanted to tell you so many times, but it never seemed to be the right moment."

Lani bit her lower lip, then said, "There's one thing I have to ask you. Trevor said you told him not to tell me that he wanted me to stay."

Rick smiled. "I asked him to hold off telling you because I wanted to."

Lani sighed with relief. Even though he'd told her he loved her, a part of her had still held back, afraid to give in. "I was worried you didn't want me around."

"How could you think that?" He kissed her nose, her cheeks, her forehead. "Just the thought of you leaving rips me up inside."

The happiness welling up inside her made tears prick at the corners of her eyes.

"Hey, are you okay?" His blue eyes filled with concern as he brushed hair from her face. "If you don't want to live here, we'll move to Tucson and I'll get transferred there. I'd even move to San Francisco if it would make you happy. I just want us to be together for the rest of our lives."

Her eyes widened. "You would do that for me?"

"Absolutely."

"Oh, god."

"There you go again," he teased, and kissed her. "Say yes, Lani."

She put a finger to his lips. "I have to tell you something first. And then if you're as happy as I am, I'll say yes."

He gave her his lazy smile and ran his finger over the tip

of her nose. "Deal."

"Remember when the condom broke?" She took his hand and moved it between them to her belly. "You're going to be a father again, sometime next April."

His jaw dropped, shock crossing his face. "You're pregnant?"

She nodded.

Rick raised himself up to run his hand over her abdomen. "Beautiful Lani. You're going to be a mother. You're going to have my baby. Our baby."

Hope filled her heart. "Are you happy about it?"

"Hell yes, I'm happy. I want us to have at least half a dozen more kids together."

Laughing, she nipped at his chest. "Half a dozen? Why don't we just start with this one and Trevor, and go from there."

He took the ring from the box. The diamond caught the light, sparkling and glittering with brilliant fire. The sapphires surrounding it were as deep as the blue in his eyes. "Will you marry me?"

She nodded, so unbelievably happy. "Yes. I love you so much it hurts."

He slipped the ring on her finger and kissed her long and hard. The gold felt warm and solid, a bond made of love. It felt right.

"I love you, Lani," he said, his gaze fixed on hers. He kissed her hair. "You've made me the happiest man in the world."

Lani breathed in Rick's earthy scent and sighed. "You can't possibly be any happier than I am."

"Darlin', you have the rest of our lives to prove it."

Chapter Twenty One
One year later

ॐ

"Trevor, pick up your toys," Rick said as he reached the landing. "You wouldn't want someone to trip over them and fall down the stairs, now would you?"

"Okay, Dad." Trevor scooped up the action figures, tossed them onto the floor of his room and dashed back. "Mom's feeding the baby on the balcony. When she's done, can we go over to Grandma and Grandpa's? Roxie had her puppies and Grandpa said I could have one if it was okay with you."

"Oh he did, did he?" Rick grabbed his son and tickled him until he squirmed on the floor in fits of laughter.

Trevor squealed. "Yes! And I want to name one Rex. Can I, Dad? Can I?"

Rick tousled the boy's hair. "Okay, kiddo."

"All right!" Trevor scrambled to his feet and ran to the master bedroom. "Mom! Dad said I could have one of Roxie's puppies!"

He followed his son through the bedroom to the balcony. The sun was settling over the Mule Mountains, the sunset blazing across the sky in pink and orange streaks. Lani was reclining in her favorite chair, a soft smile on her face as she held their daughter over her shoulder, patting the baby's back.

"Mom, what do you think of the name Rex for the new puppy?" Trevor asked as he gently stroked his baby sister's arm.

"Sounds wonderful." Lani hugged him, then looked up at Rick and smiled. "How was your day? No shower?"

Rick leaned over and kissed her. "Showered in the locker room." His heart swelled as he looked at their daughter. "Let me hold Naya."

"She's all yours." Lani handed the baby to Rick and he cradled his daughter in the crook of his arm and kissed the top of her head. Her features were so tiny and perfect. She was as beautiful as her mother.

"How's Daddy's girl?" He let Naya grab his finger with her tiny hand. She kicked and smiled, and made strange gurgling noises that filled his heart with intense joy. Her eyes were dark, and he fancied they would be the same chocolate-brown as Lani's.

Trevor ran his hand over the baby's soft blond hair. "Naya's cute for a baby, but she's not much fun. When'll she be old enough to play with?"

"Oh, give her a few months." Lani pulled Trevor into her lap and hugged him. "And then she'll probably be into all your toys."

"Some things I might let her play with, but not my important stuff." Trevor wriggled out of Lani's lap. "Can I call Grandma and Grandpa and tell them we're going over there in a little while to pick out a puppy?"

"Sure," Lani said, her smile ample.

"Did you finish those book reviews?" Rick asked after Trevor dashed out of the room.

She yawned and stretched. "I managed to e-mail the last one to Theresa while Naya napped."

With a smile, he walked through the French doors into their bedroom and laid Naya in her bassinette. Lani followed and slid her arm around his waist as they looked down at their daughter.

"Do you remember when we made wishes at the lake on Trevor's birthday last year?" Lani asked as she leaned against Rick.

"Mmmm," he murmured and kissed the top of her head.

"My wish came true."

She looked up at him and smiled. "I wanted a baby. A child, like Trevor. But before I made that wish, I wanted to wish for you. I just didn't think I could have you."

He grinned. "Darlin', you had me wrapped around your little finger from the day we met."

She turned and eased her arms around his neck. "What did you wish for?"

"You." Rick brushed his lips over Lani's. "What do you say we take a nice long bath in that huge tub of ours, and start practicing making another brother or sister for Naya and Trevor?"

Lani sighed and melted against him. "I'm all yours, cowboy."

Why an electronic book?

We live in the Information Age — an exciting time in the history of human civilization, in which technology rules supreme and continues to progress in leaps and bounds every minute of every day. For a multitude of reasons, more and more avid literary fans are opting to purchase e-books instead of paper books. The question from those not yet initiated into the world of electronic reading is simply: *Why?*

1. *Price.* An electronic title at Ellora's Cave Publishing and Cerridwen Press runs anywhere from 40% to 75% less than the cover price of the exact same title in paperback format. Why? Basic mathematics and cost. It is less expensive to publish an e-book (no paper and printing, no warehousing and shipping) than it is to publish a paperback, so the savings are passed along to the consumer.

2. *Space.* Running out of room in your house for your books? That is one worry you will never have with electronic books. For a low one-time cost, you can purchase a handheld device specifically designed for e-reading. Many e-readers have large, convenient screens for viewing. Better yet, hundreds of titles can be stored within your new library — on a single microchip. There are a variety of e-readers from different manufacturers. You can also read e-books on your PC or laptop computer. (Please note that Ellora's Cave does not endorse any specific brands.

You can check our websites at www.ellorascave.com or www.cerridwenpress.com for information we make available to new consumers.)

3. *Mobility.* Because your new e-library consists of only a microchip within a small, easily transportable e-reader, your entire cache of books can be taken with you wherever you go.

4. ***Personal Viewing Preferences.*** Are the words you are currently reading too small? Too large? Too... ANNOYING? Paperback books cannot be modified according to personal preferences, but e-books can.

5. ***Instant Gratification.*** Is it the middle of the night and all the bookstores near you are closed? Are you tired of waiting days, sometimes weeks, for bookstores to ship the novels you bought? Ellora's Cave Publishing sells instantaneous downloads twenty-four hours a day, seven days a week, every day of the year. Our webstore is never closed. Our e-book delivery system is 100% automated, meaning your order is filled as soon as you pay for it.

Those are a few of the top reasons why electronic books are replacing paperbacks for many avid readers.

As always, Ellora's Cave and Cerridwen Press welcome your questions and comments. We invite you to email us at Comments@ellorascave.com or write to us directly at Ellora's Cave Publishing Inc., 1056 Home Avenue, Akron, OH 44310-3502.

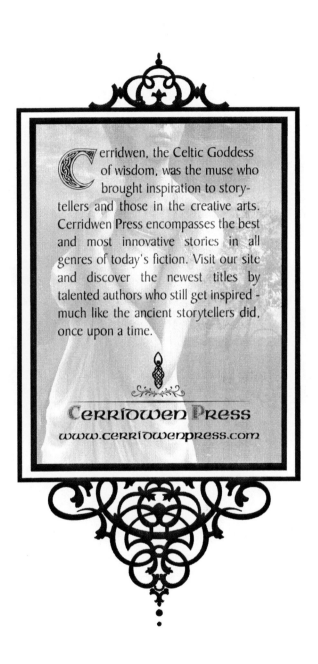

Discover for yourself why readers can't get enough
of the multiple award-winning publisher
Ellora's Cave.

Whether you prefer e-books or paperbacks,

be sure to visit EC on the web at
www.ellorascave.com

for an erotic reading experience that will leave you
breathless.